MURDER AT THE ACADEMY AWARDS®

ALSO BY JOAN RIVERS

Men Are Stupid . . . And They Like Big Boobs

Don't Count the Candles: Just Keep the Fire Lit!

From Mother to Daughter: Thoughts and Advice
on Life, Love, and Marriage

Bouncing Back

Jewelry by Joan Rivers

Still Talking

Enter Talking

The Life and Hard Times of Heidi Abromowitz

Having a Baby Can Be a Scream

ALSO BY JERRILYN FARMER

Desperately Seeking Sushi

The Flaming Luau of Death

Perfect Sax

Mumbo Gumbo

Dim Sum Dead

Killer Wedding

Immaculate Reception

Sympathy for the Devil

MURDER AT THE ACADEMY AWARDS®

A RED CARPET MURDER MYSTERY™

JOAN RIVERS

with Jerrilyn Farmer

**Doubleday Large Print
Home Library Edition**

Pocket Books

New York London Toronto Sydney

This Large Print Edition, prepared especially for Double-day Large Print Home Library, contains the complete, unabridged text of the original Publisher's Edition.

POCKET and colophon are registered trademarks
of Simon & Schuster, Inc.

Manufactured in the United States of America

ISBN-13: 978-1-60751-566-1

**This Large Print Book carries the
Seal of Approval of N.A.V.H.**

MURDER AT THE ACADEMY AWARDS®

1

Best Performance by a Bad Girl

Oscar night. Hollywood. The blaze of klieg lights. The smell of perfume, jasmine, and fear in the air—I love it.

No evening in the year holds greater power. To those who soar or suffer by Hollywood's whims, this annual honor, bestowed by the Academy of Motion Picture Arts and Sciences, is instant and indelible. Tonight, amid the glitter and pageantry, transformations would occur. A thousand well-dressed people would walk into Hollywood's Kodak Theatre, but in three hours' time, only a few dozen of them would walk out holding golden statuettes, branded for the rest of their lives: THE BEST.

And before those worthy names could be called onstage inside the theater, another glittering pageant was well in progress outside. We had a little ritual of our own that also glorified the evening's finest talent but perhaps, in a moment of much-needed balance, punctured a few inflated egos as well—the red carpet preshow coverage. This was where I took my part on the star-spangled battlefield. I, Maxine Taylor, have the privilege of holding a mike and brushing elbows with the great ones—and the battle scars that come with it. While the talent of the stars is luminous, fascinating, unquestionable, their fashion choices may not be. Someone, after all, must play the role of jester at Hollywood's royal court, and that would be me.

The crowd around me, Jack Nicholson bumping into Leonardo DiCaprio, was aswirl. In my earpiece, the voice of my young, hotshot director, Will Beckerman, boomed, "Max, grab Cameron!" And suddenly, as is the nature of the evening, a gorgeous young celebrity dressed in some unfortunate piece of satin was thrust at me by her phalanx of handlers. I let go of Brad Pitt and Angelina Jolie, two solid-gold "gets," allowing them to be pulled off into the onrush of lights and crowds, and I revved up, turning to face my new intervie-wee, pulling her closer beside me into a nice tight two-shot.

"Cameron Diaz is here," I announced to my at-home audience above the noise of the throbbing crowd. I'd snagged another A-lister before any other red carpet re-porter. Everyone kept a scorecard of gets, a list of celebrity interviews one was able to get, and our careers could be instantly over if our ratio of A-list to B-list should suddenly fall. Hundreds of my competi-tors, stretched down a long row beside me, were now quietly seething at my good fortune. I blocked all that out as my cam-era's on-air light glowed red.

Cameron smiled and said, "Max Taylor! It's good to see you." There was the req-uisite hugging and kissing. Then she added, "Be nice."

We both laughed. Like that would hap-pen.

Over broad whitened smiles, Cameron and I eyed each other closely. What she saw was a fairly well-kept faux-blond, thirty-three-year-old woman. (Okay, who was I kidding? Forty . . . *Okay, okay!* Forty . . . nine. But they could put bamboo under my nails, and I'd still deny it.) I was dripping in borrowed estate diamonds and draped in a stunning gold Michael Kors gown. Tasteful . . . yet wow. Cameron's eyes narrowed, recognizing perhaps that I now wore the same borrowed diamond earrings she'd worn two years ago.

I, on the other hand, felt my own eyes grow wide as I gazed at the outfit she'd selected. "Who are you wearing?" I asked, my raspy voice perhaps just a tad raspier, gaping at the monstrous green gown that only a Trappist monk could love.

Cameron mentioned the name of a young designer, then turned 360 degrees so we could absorb the full effect of all those wasted yards of seaweed-hued satin. "Tell the truth, Max," she said like a brave young thing who was ready to take her medicine, "what do you think?"

"It's *something!*" I marveled. "Very few people could wear a dress like that . . ."

Cameron beamed. "You doll."

Then, before I could add, . . . *but you're*

not one of them, she heard her name called from the stands of screaming fans and turned to wave. That's the red carpet. Blink and your interview is O-V-E-R.

I quickly changed gears. As the dewy beauty was whisked away to yet another interview, trailing a long train of poison-green tulle, I turned to my camera. "Cameron Diaz. Someone I love and adore and worship. But I have to tell you—even Winona Ryder wouldn't *shoplift* that dress."

Yes, I said that.

Oh, come on. I'm Max Taylor, and that's my thing. I worked my way up from the cellar comedy clubs in Manhattan by telling the truth and saying what no one else would say. Look, I'll make a promise: if you should discover the cure for cancer, I swear I will not make a joke about what you wear to pick up your Nobel Prize. You, Cancer Curer, are safe with me. Global-Warming Averter, too. But everyone else . . . watch out.

The mad swirl of pre–Academy Award excitement ratcheted up a notch, and I checked my borrowed diamond-encrusted Harry Winston watch: twenty-six minutes until Oscar showtime inside the Kodak

Theatre, if one could trust a $140,000 time-piece to tell good time. Which meant in just twenty-six minutes, our red carpet coverage would end, and I still hadn't nailed an interview to top last year's show. And in the castle where I work, they serve last year's jester as appetizers. Around me, the throng of glittering almost-stars, ministars, megastars, and over-the-hill dino-stars, along with all their nervous star tenders, began pressing forward as they realized it was time to get out of the hot afternoon sun and into their seats.

I, as always, kept right on talking— "Wasn't Julia Roberts gorgeous this year? The government should pay her to stay home and have more babies, you know, like a natural resource"—filling the airtime until my next celebrity was delivered.

Just off-camera was my own crew, the guerrilla commandos who kept me pow-dered and prepped throughout two hours of red carpet combat: hair, makeup, per-sonal assistant, darling pet, all accounted for. Add to this behind-the-scenes cadre my celebrity-wrangler, Cindy Chow, the predatory huntress who even now stalked arriving VIPs, tracking down the most transcendent names for me to interview. Cindy, with her disgustingly thick black hair and tall, slender, pilates-toned body, looked like your typical, everyday fabulous L.A. chick. But don't let the sweet demeanor and those double-C cups fool you. That woman has a vicious streak, which is an excellent trait in a wrangler. She was waving at me to get my attention.

"Ah," I said, spying the man she had in her hot little hands, "here comes a repeat Academy Award nominee, the guy who *Walked the Line,* Joaquin Phoenix." I jabbed my mike in the direction of the tousled, dark, brooding movie star coming up the red carpet. "Joaquin!" I shouted, trying not to spit. It's a hard name to pronounce. Try it.

He slowed down but didn't quite make eye contact.

"Amazing performance, Joaquin," I yelled. Why hadn't Cindy brought him closer? He was just outside mike range. Joaquin, what kind of mother names her son Joaquin? Clearly a mother who doesn't give a damn who spits at her kid all his life.

He took another step toward me, but

then, pulled along by his agent and still several feet from my particular square of red carpet, he came to a complete halt.

My earpiece buzzed alive. "Where the hell is your next interview?" screamed my frazzled director. I was now on the air, live, interviewing nobody. I momentarily envisioned Cindy losing her job in the bloody postmortem of this night's show. It was war, and our side was suddenly at risk of losing.

In the great crush, Deborah Norville stepped off her mark and grabbed Joaquin's arm, snatching him away for herself. I was furious and tried to reach for him myself, but Little Miss Locust Valley Tea Party had a grip on him that could win her a World Wrestling title. Bitch! Of course I kept score. We all do. *"You lost him,"* cried my director into my ear. Like I didn't know that. "We're dying here. Go to Drew," his voice ordered.

"Let's see who Drew is talking to now," I said to the camera, seamlessly moving our live show along, segueing to my daughter, who held an interview position with her own camera crew closer to the door of the Kodak. I checked the video monitor and saw my lovely daughter and cohost standing next to the extraordinarily tall and dreamy Vince Vaughn. Our director, Will, was still yelling something stupid in my ear, but I was at that moment suddenly propelled into mom mode. My daughter is twenty-five years old and single, so why wasn't this naturally endowed girl wearing a "bait" dress with the neckline cut down to her waist? I despaired of her insistence on good taste. Opportunity missed.

"Say hi to Vince for me," I said cheer-fully, handing the show off. Drew laughed her sparkling professional laugh and took it from there, and my own camera light went dark.

It's kindly been noted by the press that with my first red carpet coverage of the Oscars in 1985, I *invented* the red carpet arrival. But now, alas, dozens of entertain-ment news outlets have charged onto the scene: *Entertainment Tonight, Access Hollywood,* along with all the networks and hundreds of magazines, so we are in a glutted market. Drew and I are the featured hosts with cable television's firecracker-style network, Glam-TV, and the suits at Glam expect us to outdo our competitors, star for bloody star. It's cut-throat. With such jackals as Diane Saw-yer, Lisa Rinna, and Charlie Gibson in hot pursuit (I kid, but you don't want to get near an elbow when Charlie is running after Jennifer Lopez), the thing that distin-guishes our trademark red carpet cover-age for Glam boils down to a steady stream of big names, their own unfathomable sense of style, and, frankly, what unre-hearsed and exciting moments Drew and I can coax out of them. Clearly, we are at a disadvantage without some big stars, and standing out on the carpet without a gigantic celeb next to me for more than thirty seconds of wasted time, I was now starting to get cranky.

I looked over at my wrangler, Cindy, my inner temperature rising. Her job was to provide fresh meat. She'd bungled Phoe-nix, and amid this blinged-out courtyard maelstrom of yapping publicists and beefy hangers-on, Cindy appeared not to be giving up without a fight: she was hanging on to the tuxedoed arm of Jamie Foxx as if her career were passing before her eyes. With Phoenix gone, she had been on the lookout for an approaching nominee. She had spotted the superstar's limo as it pulled up to the curb, expertly identifying Foxx through ultradarkened windows; made a beeline up to the rear door, outrunning the wrangler from *Extra,* elbowing aside the wrangler from E!, and tripping the wrangler from the BBC; caught Jamie by the sleeve of his midnight blue Armani jacket just as he stepped out onto the carpet; and herded him, between his stops to wave at the throngs of screaming fans in the bleachers, right down to my portion of the red carpet. On a good day, Cindy was like an Australian shepherd in a beaded Vera Wang. Looked like she was getting back to a good day. Thank God.

Billy Bush, standing down the row of entertainment reporters, called out, "Jamie! Over here!" and almost got his attention. Devon Jones from *Entertainment Tonight* screamed even louder, "Jamie, loverboy!" and at that, Jamie turned his head. But Cindy hung on tight and delivered him to me.

"Here's Jamie Foxx," I said just as my camera's light glared red. Finally. As we chatted about his picks for the Oscars this year, I heard Drew in my earpiece, letting

Will, back in the control booth, know she was ready to go with Naomi Watts.

Drew has been my cohostess on all our Glam-TV *Red Carpet Specials*. While at age fourteen she had shown signs of a mother allergy so severe she had caused me to reconsider with dismay the sixty-one hours of hard labor I'd endured to bring her into this world, Drew had, at age twenty-five, grown up into a friend and wonderful interview partner. We make a good team. All the stars who will no longer talk to me—the bastards—will stop for Drew, who is young and bright and, let's face it, less lethal. Better for our show, she knows and likes all of young Hollywood— she went to school with many of them— and that history works in her favor every time. For our two-woman telecast cover-age, I stand at the head of the line, and she always stands at the last position on the red carpet, ready to catch any celebrities who might manage to float past me on their way into the Kodak.

If I am like the strainer in the sink of Hollywood, Drew is the trap down at the bottom of the drain.

The pace of our preshow was picking

up. Jamie Foxx left. Drew interviewed Naomi. I got a few quick words with Halle Berry, who looked amazing in Prada, and Sigourney Weaver, who didn't. Only twenty minutes until the doors to the Kodak would be closed. A crush of jewel-encrusted attendees choked the courtyard.

As we broke from our nonstop coverage for a quick commercial break, I turned to look at all the splendor and spandex. Between Drew and me was an ever-moving ocean of celebrities: Daniel Day-Lewis, Keira Knightley, and Cate Blanchett, each trailed by cameramen with handhelds grabbing full-length "beauty" shots; film producers checking their cells for text messages, eyed closely by the wives they were most likely cheating on; Denzel Washington escorting his beautiful daughter; young actors and the scantily clad teenagers with whom they were falling in or out of love; the accompanying fleet of agents, public relations mavens, managers, mothers, escorts, flacks, and handlers; closeted gays and their "girlfriends"; out lesbians and *their* girlfriends; and a string of dozens of fixed-camera units focused on entertainment reporters who were feasting on all the glamour like a gang of dolled-up vampires with their fangs in the neck of Hollywood. I shook my head. Poachers!

I looked up to see George Clooney approaching. Now, this was more like it. In my ear, I heard Will's voice barking that we had thirty seconds to air, but with George on the way, I began to relax for just a second. In this business, that is one second too long.

George is always a doll, and the renewed, super-charged-up Cindy had nabbed him, but in the moments we were waiting to get back on the air, *ET*'s Devon Jones circled around Cindy and George, and then begged his publicist, Stan Rosenfield, "Stan, let me have five seconds."

"No!" I shouted over the crowd, glaring at Cindy.

"Three seconds," Devon pleaded, tugging on the publicist, who was holding on to George. "We'll put you on the air, too."

"We're ready right now," I lied. But all could see that my red light was off and Devon's was on.

Meanwhile, Will, watching our lost skirmish from the control booth where he could see us from various angles on many screens, had been in the middle of counting down to my live shot with George. "Five—four—three—" he'd been saying. Then, suddenly, he screamed in my ear, *"Damn it!* You lost another one!"

Cindy, in shock, grabbed hold of the nearest star, Pamela Anderson, who was in midsentence talking to reporter Sam Rubin on live coverage, and spun her around, propelling her in my direction.

". . . two . . . one!" came the disembodied voice of Will in the last of the countdown from my earpiece.

"Hi, Pam," I said brightly, "I see you brought your two most dazzling accessories." Then I immediately launched into an impromptu discussion on her latest marriage and divorce situation, making several bitterly brilliant jokes about failed relationships. This was not the lightest subject for me to joke about these days since Drew's engagement to that idiot Burke Norris had recently been called off. The story goes that she dumped *him.* Technically. But her decision was heavily influenced by his appalling fondness for spending the night at other women's apartments. It made my teeth hurt; I detested him so much, but okay. Drew was moving on. They were simply incompatible. She was a Pisces, and he was an asshole.

"One minute, Mom," Drew sang in my ear as I stood smiling at my live camera, reminiscing off the top of my head about all the brooding leading men I had once known or, frankly, fantasized about.

Meanwhile, Cindy was trying to snatch back our lost star George Clooney, who was now graciously receiving suck-up compliments from Devon Jones as the precious remaining minutes until the Oscar telecast clicked off.

My lineless eyes narrowed. No matter how expensive her borrowed dress, Devon looked, as always, cheap. She had taken thin to an extreme and had yet to find a shade of red that didn't make her look like a hooker long past retirement age, but that was simply no excuse to swipe the A-est of the A-listers from the clutches of my wrangler and keep him for herself. Devon was known to be a talent-challenged reporter, but she had been around the block and had hung on to her job year in and year out by finding ever new ways to stoop lower.

Cindy, at this point, slammed her head in her hands, defeated. Next to her, also off-camera, stood my hearty behind-the-scenes crew. No one in my position can do the job alone, and I do not perform without wonderful backup. Allie, my makeup girl, with her waiting powder brush, and Unja, my hairstylist, with his can of hairspray, shook their heads in sympathy at the lethal Clooney poaching. My stern Samoan driver/bodyguard, Malulu Vai, held my tiny Yorkshire terrier, Killer, and both looked equally miffed.

Pam Anderson said, "And that's why I am planning to take night classes at UCLA." With a wave, she walked on.

Meanwhile, Cindy looked after the one that got away, her eyes frantic. Clooney's publicist was edging George down the runway. Devon's "three seconds" had turned into "a thirty," and she clearly wasn't letting George move on. Noting all this, I still had to keep my head in the game, so I gave my live TV audience a brief review of Pamela Anderson's ensemble. "Chanel. Who could go wrong! She looked amazing from the ankles up, but did you see her shoes? Are you kidding me? The straps. The platforms. The rhinestones. The tassels. Cinderella would rather stay single than put those on."

My support team, off-camera, were all amused. Only *I* really feel the pressure. Only *I* know quite literally how we are doing at every second of the show. This perception of the rhythm of the show fuels my performance but also makes me vibrate on a slightly higher key—all my senses ratcheted up. My support crew, however, never quite gets how seriously we are teetering on the brink of disaster. Even now, Allie was bent over laughing, which drives me crazy. Unja was just happy to be at the Oscars. Even my Yorkie, Killer, had a smile for me. Okay, from Malulu I got nothing, but what else was new?

Then, from out of nowhere, Cindy refished Joaquin Phoenix out of the ocean of stars and pushed him at me.

"Here he is!" I shouted out to all of America. "The guy who so brilliantly played Johnny Cash in *Walk the Line,* a movie, I should point out, that made me realize not *all* country singers pee out the window of their tour buses and wear Roach Motels around their necks. Oh," I assured my audience, "some do. They're animals, believe it. But not *all*! So I learned something. The man you're all waiting to meet. Here's . . ."

Cindy, still out of my camera shot, turned a shade of purple that didn't really go with her peach gown. She had lost Phoenix yet again. This time, he chose to schmooze with the beautiful Scarlett Johansson. Cindy started giving me big, call-it-off hand signals, arms swinging down across her body as if she were waving off a jet from landing on an aircraft carrier in stormy seas.

At this point, time ticking away as it was on live TV, I might have right on-camera broken one of our unspoken rules and glared a bit at Cindy from my upstage eye, but as I had just had that very eye relifted not too long ago, I resisted the urge. Here I was, Maxine Taylor, the Queen of the Red Carpet, with no star to interview.

"Screw him, that bag of no talent," I said to my camera brightly. "Here's an even better star!" Take *that,* Joaquin. And this time, with my famous croak shouting above the crowd noise, I yelled out, "George! George!"

and George Clooney, God love him, waved at me, breaking off from talking to Devon. He came over and spoke to me for a full, undivided minute and gave me the world-wide exclusive on what brand of under-wear he preferred (Calvins). Is there any wonder why women worship this man? It was a glorious red carpet moment!

The next interview was Drew's, and as the red light on my camera went off, my stylists rushed in to powder and straighten and spray.

"You were so funny," giggled Allie as she touched up my lip gloss with a tiny brush. In addition to knowing her Bobbi Brown from her Laura Mercier, Allie was an insistent laugher.

"You don't have to laugh," I told her. "You do makeup. That's enough." She'd been doing my makeup for seventeen years, and we'd had three hundred of these con-versations.

"George Clooney!" moaned Unja, as he rushed up with a hairbrush at the ready. I had recently discovered Unja, my darling new hairstylist, on a visit to London, and for tonight's event I had brought him to the States for his first visit. Surrounded by all this glorious Hollywood manhood, Unja was coming unglued. He'd brought a tiny camcorder and was now documenting every second of the trip. Here, closer to celebrities than he'd ever been in all his twenty-three years, he'd strapped the camcorder to his cap and had it on permanent record mode. Unja fingered my straight blond bangs a quarter inch to the left and said distractedly, "I wish these were longer."

"I can't see."

"Who cares? This is so now," Unja advised.

"I suppose it could help," I added. "I'm blind as a bat, so when I say to somebody, 'I didn't know who you were,' they'll just think it's the hair."

Allie, bringing out her powder brush and swiftly powdering down my shine, giggled.

Unja pushed daintily at the ironed-straight bangs. "I can move them over a smidge."

"Just part it so that the iris shows."

He worked on it. "This style is really hot," he added in his cute British accent. "You look like a Jewish Marilyn Monroe."

"Right. The way she looks *now.*"

With my hair adjusted, I could now see my precious teacup Yorkie, Killer, over on the sidelines. Killer, seven pounds of pure personality and fluff, tilted his little head, and I smiled at the good boy, who was staying so nice and quiet while Mommy worked.

Holding Killer was my Samoan body-guard, Malulu Vai. Tall, swarthy, and devoted to plus-size pantsuits, Malulu had come to me four years ago after a scary fan incident, but I had kept her around long after it turned out that idiot had mis-addressed two hundred passionate love notes meant for *Liz* Taylor. Anyway, I had become fond of Malulu. Okay, she proba-bly wasn't the only graduate of the University of Pago Pago with a BA in philosophy to be employed as a driver, but I appreci-ated her for her other handy skills: she had an instant grasp of every sort of techno-logical gizmo and gadget, was a master of the secret and deadly Samoan martial art, Limalama ("hand of wisdom"), could sew like Betsy Ross, and freely quoted lines from *Twelfth Night* and *Fiddler on the Roof* with a Samoan lilt.

Malulu looked at me, perplexed. "Marilyn Monroe, she was Jewish?" Unfortunately, Malulu has absolutely no sense of humor. Tell me I'm not being punished.

Through the earpiece, I heard Will's squawk: "In fifteen seconds we go to commercial. You can wrap it up, Drew."

I checked the Winston. In just nine minutes we would finish our show and be off the air, but first a long commercial break.

Cindy came rushing up to me. "Joaquin Phoenix. That bastard! I'll make it up to you. I promise. I'm so—"

I waved her apologies away. Like it or not, we are in the major leagues. There is only one Academy Awards night. If one member of the team blows it, we're all out of work on Monday. "Drew," I hissed, "who doesn't even *have* a wrangler, is at this very minute finishing up with Matt Damon!" I let the accusation hang in the air.

"Mom," Drew called, pushing through the crowd. Cindy melted into the background.

I looked up through my bangs, startled. Drew, having completed her interview and thrown to commercial, had rushed over to my camera position to see me.

"Drewie, we only have a few minutes on this break."

"Five," she said. "Mom, we need to talk! I just got the most amazing text message." She held up her BlackBerry, waving it.

"It better not be phone sex from that traitor Joaquin Phoenix, because I'm telling you, I am through with men with scars."

"You won't believe this, Mom. I just got a text from Halsey!"

Oh, no. Not Halsey again. While everyone admired Halsey Hamilton's talent, her life choices were just a shame. Drew had been at private school with Halsey ten years ago, and somehow Drew had appointed herself the rescue ranger for this mixed-up girl, but it was like trying to save a drowning elephant. When it came to screwing up a life, Lindsay and Britney could take lessons from Halsey Hamilton, who was currently the tabloid princess du jour.

I looked at my daughter—beautiful dress, beautiful jewels, beautiful skin she'd inherited from her mother—and worried, yet again, at her commitment to her bent-on-destruction friend. A year of headlines had screamed, "Halsey in Club Raid!" "Halsey

Busted for Pills!" "Halsey in Rehab!" "Halsey in Rehab Again!" "Halsey Fills Out Permanent Change-of-Address Card and Directs Mail to Rehab for Life!" Only in the last few months had the headlines died down. Even after her role in the Best Picture front-runner, *The Bones of War,* brought her a Best Actress nomination, Halsey had kept an amazingly low profile.

"So . . . what? She's in trouble again?" I asked, not surprised. As if that were a question.

"No, no, no," Drew said, smiling. "She's fine. She's great."

"Wonderful," I said, unable to resist pushing my daughter's long, dark hair off her face. Instantly, Unja appeared with a hairbrush, his videocam still attached to his head, and quietly went to work, performing magic on her heavy curls.

Drew knew my feelings regarding her hairstyles and suspected sabotage. "Mom!"

I looked all innocence. "What? Unja thinks you need a little help. Humor him." To distract her, I recalled, "Halsey's in Expectations, isn't she?" I referred to the luxury rehab facility in Malibu that had been the temporary home to many of Holly-wood's young and wasted. It was such a shame about all these girls. But with Halsey it was somehow worse. She'd risen from a celebrated childhood acting for Spielberg and Disney, possessing an adorable mix of innocence and wisdom, and blossomed into that miracle, a child star who still looked good after puberty and could act. But with all the fame and the money came the turmoil. She'd been arrested so many times for drinking and driving, her bail bondsman had given her a by-the-dozen discount.

"She's not at Expectations anymore. She checked out of there in November," Drew said. "She moved to another rehab place called Wonders in Pasadena."

"Thanks for telling me." I looked at Drew accusingly. She and Halsey had been close for several years. Drew, about six years ahead of Halsey at school, had been her "big sister," so you think I would have been told.

"You never listen," Drew replied.

"That's because you never tell me any-thing good."

Mother. Daughter. Does it ever change?

Drew, her hair now completely gorgeous, gently waved Unja away. "Mom, don't be like that. She didn't want anyone to know."

I was impressed. Usually Halsey had her people issue a press release every time she went to the bathroom. Good for her. Maybe this time all the help the poor girl was paying for was actually working.

In our ears, Will's voice snapped, "Two minutes to air. Drew, get back to your place."

"Mom," Drew said, waving her Black-Berry. "Halsey completely disappeared for months. She's been taking care of herself. She's doing the steps. She wanted to stay away from Hollywood until she had four months of sobriety. But . . ."

"But what?"

"Mom," Drew said, abruptly changing the subject. "Tell the truth. How are we doing tonight?"

"We've done better. I counted thirty-two gets."

"Twenty-nine," Drew said.

"Damn you for being better at math than I am."

"We're in trouble, right?"

I could pretend, but what good does that ever do? We were now in a crowded field, and our ratings would only stay high if we delivered the best stars. Twenty-nine gets meant we were down five from last year. That's huge. We'd get the final ratings for our show later, but I knew in my gut we were going down. So, yes, we were in trouble.

Drew knew it too, yet she looked excited. "Mom, Halsey is the answer."

"She's not coming tonight, is she?" It had been rumored and reported for weeks that she would absolutely not jeopardize her shaky sobriety by attending the awards show. Even Perez Hilton, the Web gossip star, assured fans Halsey wasn't coming.

"She's here!" Drew whispered, waving the BlackBerry.

"Can we get her?" This would be phenomenal. Amazing. No one would remember the ones we missed if we got an ungettable star such as Halsey. One Halsey Hamilton was equal to ten other gets. I felt the adrenaline pump. I recalled years past and the many sleepovers at our old Bel-Air house—Halsey hanging out with Drew and her big-girl friends.

From our earpieces we both heard Will's warning: "One minute!"

"Oh, yeah," Drew said, smiling. "She says she'll only do *one* interview, and we have it!"

I smiled back at my adorable, sensible, sober daughter. "I always liked Halsey, Drewie. She's a troubled girl, but good, thank God. She remembers you have always been a very good friend to her."

"No, no, she wants to talk to *you.*"

"What? Why not you?"

"She's wearing an amazing outfit and wants you to do your whole Max Taylor fashion thing. Look, she's pulling up in that white Hummer limo. See?"

I looked off in the direction Drew pointed. God bless Halsey! I would pull this sucker out of the toilet yet. The only red carpet show to get Halsey Hamilton. *On earth.* Exclusive. I could imagine tomorrow's network coverage of the Oscars: wall-to-wall video clips on every channel. The winners. The fashions. And Best Actress Halsey

Hamilton—it could happen—in her shocking return to Hollywood, as seen in her exclusive interview with . . . me. The public would walk over nails to see her. What did Halsey look like after these long months of exile? Had she let her hair grow out? Did she get a few tattoos removed? Had she bought underpants? In an instant, our fortunes had turned.

Drew squeezed my hand, then pushed quickly back to her spot as Will counted down the seconds to airtime in our ears.

My red light blinked on. "Hello, we're back! What a wild night this has been. But get ready. We have lots more show coming. And wait! We have big news. The one nominee who was expected to skip tonight's awards ceremony, the adorable Halsey Hamilton, is on her way here right now."

Quickly, Malulu, always dependable, slipped me an info card on Halsey below camera range as I continued, "It's a night to congratulate Halsey on her magnificent performance in one of the year's best films, and we certainly will, but this one dramatic high point only accentuates many, many lows. Everyone knows the regrettable events. The arrest for indecent exposure on a Singapore Airlines flight to Asia, where charges were eventually dropped. The rush to St. John's hospital after her eighteenth birthday party where her stomach had to be pumped after eating, her publicist later claimed, too many pieces of rum-spiked birthday cake. The fourteen-hour marriage to Thom Denney, the drummer of indie band Whaler, who, it turned out, was still married; and the wedding-night video threesome with the minister— as seen on YouTube. All tragic missteps."

In the background, I could hear an announcement coming from the exterior loudspeakers: "Ladies and gentlemen, doors are closing. Please take your seats. Doors are closing."

I pressed on. "But here's our happy ending. Halsey went away to rehab. She got the help she needed. She straightened herself out. And now the Best Actress nominee for *The Bones of War* is coming here. To the Oscars! Tonight. So stay right with us here on Glam-TV, because I have the one . . . *and only* . . . interview with Halsey Hamilton."

By this point, even I was excited about

what was to come, but scanning the now thinning crowd, I noticed with a weary eye that Halsey had not yet appeared. Damn! I listened to my earpiece and followed Will's on-the-fly advice. "But first," I said brightly to the camera, "Drew has both Colin Farrell *and* Will Ferrell. Take it away, Drew."

The camera light went off and all hell broke loose around me. Danny, my bald lug of a cameraman who was dressed in Teamster chic—a baseball cap and dirty jeans topped by the required formal dinner jacket—was the first to speak. "Hey, Max. No shit. Halsey is talking to us exclusive?"

"Yes. So listen up." My troops—Allie, Unja, Danny, Cindy, and Malulu, holding an alert Killer—gathered. "Look around chickadees. The news has broken." Actually, I myself had just announced Halsey's surprise arrival, but now every news director from here to Uzbekistan had heard me and alerted the media. Damn.

The buzz was working its way around the red carpet. I saw Ryan Seacrest practically drooling and making a run for the open drop-off spot at the curb. MTV's coolest entertainment reporters, those hot young Sullivan brothers, Matt and Kevin, thought nothing of knocking Ryan aside. Mary Hart, Lisa Rinna, Sam Rubin, Devon Jones, and Al Langer were grabbing their portable mikes and heading over. Even Charlie Gibson looked longingly at the curb. Of the thousand other photographers standing by, several hundred were craning their necks to see if Halsey was arriving. We had to get this right.

"Now, look," I said, "Cindy . . ."

My wrangler, tall and gorgeous in her strapless gown, shiny black hair pulled back, looked alert. "I'm on this, Max."

"No excuses, no regrets. Halsey is mine. Understand me? Mine! Do not let this one get away or you'll be floating facedown on the Yangtze River!"

"I'm on this," Cindy repeated, a strained smile on her face. She lifted her beaded gown and ran off. That girl ran like a gazelle.

Allie powdered my forehead, but I shooed her away. "Can you see Cindy? Did she get to Halsey?" The curb was only about fifteen feet away, but even up on my four-inch-high, gold-and-Swarovski-crystal Manolo sandals I couldn't see over the crowd.

"Look," Danny said. At six feet four he had the best view. "Halsey's limo has arrived, but the door hasn't opened. She isn't coming out. Hey, it's a feeding frenzy near that limo."

Despite my Michael Kors and my diamonds, I realized this was not the time for ladylike. I was off-camera, and as long as Drew kept one of her Farrell-Ferrells joking and the other one smoldering—not such an easy task—my mike was not "hot." Stepping up onto a packing crate, which the faithful Malulu miraculously procured, I screamed out, "Cindy! Halsey is ours. Exclusive. Go and get her!"

The circus of reporters and cameramen with handhelds crowding close at Cindy's heels, pressing hard against Halsey's limo, heard me too. For that matter, who, even as far away as Santa Monica, hadn't?

Cindy saluted me, then, shoving the crowd back, she knocked hard on the window of the long, white stretch Hummer. With no apparent response, she opened the rear door and looked inside. Whatever she saw inside Halsey's limo, Cindy threw her hands up to her mouth and didn't make a move.

What? What could Cindy possibly be thinking? Ticktock, ticktock. We were minutes from the end of a live telecast. If Halsey had become momentarily shy of the press—that would be a first, but after four months stashed away at rehab, who could blame her?—Cindy just had to gently urge her along.

On the small television monitor that showed the live feed of our program, I could see the right-this-second live version of our show as it was being broadcast to all of America. Drew was wrapping up her segment, having both laughed at Will Ferrell and drooled at Colin. She was now ready to throw the show back to me.

"Cindy," I yelled to my girl at the curb, just nanoseconds before my mike would go live again. "Just grab her! Bring her! *Get her now!*"

It was a battle. The crowd of reporters and cameramen with handhelds didn't give an inch, but Cindy knew what was at stake. She slivered herself into the open limo door and disappeared.

Minutes seemed to chug by. Hours. Days. Then Cindy's Vera Wang–covered butt backed out into view.

"Are you getting this, Danny?" I called to my cameraman as he worked the lens to focus a close-up on Halsey Hamilton emerging from the Hummer. From my earpiece I heard the end of Drew's ". . . so back to you, Mom. And say hi to Halsey for me!"

"Yes, Drew. I will!" I said into my suddenly hot mike. Just a few feet away at the curb, Cindy, having pulled Halsey onto the red carpet, cautiously kept her hand locked on Halsey's wrist. But Cindy stepped out of the way and allowed the world to welcome this returning princess.

"Oh my God! Oh my God!" whispered Allie with a hushed giggle.

"What is she wearing?" demanded Unja in his stiff British accent, from behind his little personal camcorder, aghast. "Do you like her gown?"

"Dat not funny," added Malulu, holding a well-behaved Killer.

Halsey Hamilton, the nineteen-year-old beauty with the head of shining auburn tresses, was now standing in full view of the screaming fans, amid dozens of flashbulb-popping paparazzi and the entire international press corps.

Did I like her gown?

What gown?

Tall, slender, stunning Halsey was standing on the red carpet.

She'd remembered to do her hair.

She'd remembered to do her makeup.

She'd forgotten to put on her clothes.

2

Best Performance by a Supporting . . . Corpse?

Those long legs. That tiny waist. Those enormous boobs.

"There she is!" I said into my mike. "Halsey Hamilton, wearing nothing more than a black strapless bra and a hot-pink"—what should I call that piece of string and a postage stamp?—"thong."

She stood there, the paparazzi going mad, smiling and waving to the screaming fans.

I kept talking to the camera. "One thing I have to say about the four missing months that Halsey has been away from her public, that girl has been working out.

All-over toned. All-over tanned. All-over fabulous. Hey, when you're nineteen years old and look like that, who needs clothes?" I scanned Halsey's smooth skin and minimal black bra and had to admit—the effect was simple yet elegant. "Mark my words, next season we'll all be showing up at formal parties in nothing but push-up bras and a smile," I joked into the mike. And then I thought, note to self: call Dr. Bob for fashion-necessitated boob lift.

Cindy, gripping Halsey tightly by the upper arm, practically dragged her right up to me. Along the short walk, a dozen reporters crowded around shouting, "Halsey!" and "Where's your dress?" and even, to Cindy, "I'll give you two grand if you bring her here!" Not an easy few yards of red carpet. As Cindy steered Halsey along, the gorgeous young star wobbled on her high heels. I sighed. Post-rehab wobbling was never a good sign. I hoped Drew wouldn't be too disappointed.

"Here's Halsey Hamilton," I was saying to my camera, just as the dark-haired beauty was delivered to my side, "wearing possibly the boldest Academy Awards fashion statement since that girl wore a dress made out of AmEx cards. Halsey, honey. I gotta ask. Who are you wearing— 18 Hour or Cross Your Heart?"

Halsey, smiling a sleepy smile at me and not entirely making eye contact, slurred, "Wha . . . Bajja . . . Hiya, Max!"

Cindy tried to back out of our camera shot, slowly releasing her grip, but Halsey grabbed on to my tall star-wrangler and wouldn't let go.

"Halsey, sweetheart!" I said, sizing up the situation. The girl was drunk. Or stoned. Or both.

"Mama Maxo," Halsey slurred. "I made it. I'm at the Ossars!"

"So we can see." My camera guy, Danny, was focusing closer on Halsey's midsection as I continued, "Every part of you. Viewers have gotta know. Arriving here at the Academy Awards without a dress, are you making a political statement? Is it a stab at global warming—that we don't need clothes? Did Al Gore put you up to this?"

Halsey began to laugh, and my gal Cindy shook free and quickly stepped away. Standing alone in her pink satin thong and jet-black bra, Halsey put both hands on top of her head as she tried to complete one coherent thought, but the effort was too much. She almost swooned.

In my earpiece, I heard Will's tense warning: "Max, get to it already. Get her talking!"

With Hasley in this condition, I knew the viewers would be stunned. This was huge. We should turn this into its own one-hour special!

"Move it," he said urgently.

Live TV is a bitch, but what we had here was the mother of all interviews with a clearly altered nominee, and no one, not even my ridiculously inexperienced director, could miss that.

"Halsey," I asked quickly. "Are you drinking again?"

"No!" she yelled, then smiled at me sweetly. "I would never take a drink. Never. I swear." Halsey Hamilton, princess of the silver screen, reached out and put a dangling arm around my shoulder. She could barely stand up. Steadying herself against me, she leaned on me harder, soon hanging on me with all her weight. I'd lifted grocery bags that weighed more, but still, the unexpected burden made me list in an unattractive way to the left. There I was, dressed in my floor-length golden ball gown, wrapped in the tight embrace of a half-naked girl. I don't care what your views are on same-sex couples, we made an alarming family-viewing-hour pair.

From behind the camera, I heard Allie giggle softly with nervous energy. Both Malulu and Killer looked shocked. And Unja, mouth open in alarm, still had his camcorder rolling.

What was the world coming to? This was tragic. I knew these girls seemed to exist on nothing but a cocktail of fame and pills, and I suspected this party-till-they-dropped lifestyle was never going to stop until they crashed into something cold and hard. As a mother, it disturbed me to see these talented children throw away their lives just to see their faces splashed across one more cover of *People.* I had half a minute of airtime left. It was tough-love time.

"Halsey, you're a beautiful, talented girl. You acted your heart out in *The Bones of War,* and don't play it down, your part took raw courage and heart. They don't give away Oscar nominations like party favors.

You earned it. But, sweetie, something is not right. Look at you. Not only did you make a risky fashion decision today, but now you are clearly impaired."

"Shhhh. Maxooo. Pleassse, don't tell the whole wide world."

Will's voice jabbered in my ear, "Ten seconds, ten seconds, ten . . ."

I put my hand to my ear, gently tugging the infernal earpiece out and said on air through a tight smile, "Keep rolling," begging for more time. And then directly to Halsey, I said, "With all the cameras rolling here, I've got news for you, honey. It is no longer just Victoria's Secret. Can you tell your fans what prompted you, a young and talented actress, on the night of your greatest professional achievement, to make a mockery—"

"Mockingbird?" she asked me, confused. She had become unable to hold herself up and, frankly, neither could I. We leaned more heavily to the left.

"Halsey, I was told you were in rehab for the last four months."

She nodded. "I hate rehab. Wait. I mean, I love it. Or . . ."

"So what the hell happened?"

"I sipped," she said, then laughed loudly. "I mean, no, I mean I *slipped.* He said . . ."

I waited to hear more, but she began to cough. This was outrageous. Had some horrible guy given Halsey alcohol after all she'd been through?

I pressed forward with the interview. "Who did it, Halsey? Who gave you the first drink?"

Okay, isn't this what everyone wants to know? What kind of heartless monster would undermine a girl with such a gifted future? And who was protecting her from these jerks? No one in Halsey's family seemed to be in charge. I took a quick look around to see if Jimmy and Dakota Hamilton were standing by to support their daughter tonight, but they must already have entered the auditorium. Almost the entire crowd had been herded inside by the ushers. I hurried to ask again, "Who did this to you? I want to go out and wring his neck."

Halsey had a pained look. Her smooth brow scrunched. "Don't blame Burkie," she said, her eyes glazing.

Burkie? My head spun. Could Halsey possibly mean my Drew's idiot ex-fiancé,

Burke Norris? Of course I had nothing but contempt for Burke, the self-absorbed lunk, but the idea that he might have offered booze or drugs to this poor kid was dense, even for him.

"He . . ." Halsey put her hand up to her mouth just in time.

Great. This was just what I needed. My fabulous Michael Kors was about to be covered with celebrity puke.

I tried not to shudder on-camera. I suppose if one must be vomited upon, it might as well be by of one of the most photographed young women in America. I could probably get a fortune for it on eBay. What was I thinking? That clip would live on You-Tube in slow motion forever. That would be on my final tribute—not Maxine Delilah Taylor, Tony-winning actress and red carpet fashionista, but Max Taylor, the poor schmuck upon whom teen queen Halsey Hamilton whoopsed her cookies. With my sad obituary flashing before my eyes, and in fear of imminent disaster, I carefully let go my hold on Halsey and watched worriedly as she slid down to one knee.

I put all thoughts of Burke out of my mind for the moment and turned to my task at hand. It was still my interview, damn it, and I had never before let a celebrity slip away. I got down onto one knee, and now eye to eye once more, I asked, "There are lots of teenage girls who look up to you, young lady. For God's sake, what were you thinking?" I held out my microphone, disappointed in her fall from grace. But just like the rest of America, I was also fascinated. Despite the slurred speech and the drool, this was one beautiful and talented girl. Such a waste.

"I wassen thinking, Maxo . . . ," she whispered. A tear leapt into the corner of Halsey's clear green eye, appearing so quickly that I marveled at either the pureness of her regret or the acting talent it had taken to produce it. "I want them to take me serrus . . . seriously." Her other knee collapsed and she was sitting on the red carpet, leaning on one tan and slender arm. Not a dimple of cellulite anywhere on that magnificent body, I couldn't help but notice, and made a quick mental note to call Dr. Bob to ask him about the latest arm procedures. Just then, Halsey gasped up at me, "Help me, Max. I hurt. I hurt bad."

We were now the only story in town.

With the entire invited Academy Awards audience seated inside behind the closed doors to the Kodak, the dozens of abandoned preshow camera crews, reporters, and a daze of photographers from all over the world pushed and crowded close around us to gawk. From farther down the red carpet, cameras from several film crews were trained on us, using telephoto lenses. Even the crowds of fans in the bleachers were riveted, gasping at the scene, pointing at Halsey, craning their necks in our direction, snapping cell phone cameras at us, calling, "Halsey!" and "We love you!"

So I plunked my derriere down on the red carpet right next to Halsey, bringing my mike again to her level. "Of course I'll help you. You could use a good doctor, and my best friend in all the world is a doctor." Okay, Dr. Bob specialized in lifting behinds and Botoxing foreheads, but he would be sure to know the right referral. I made a signal that only a transfixed Doberman could have detected and saw, from the corner of my eye, that Malulu was hurrying off with her cell phone to make the call for help. In the background, the final auditorium announcements were blaring: "Doors closing. No one will be admitted once the doors are closed."

I tried again with Halsey. "Let me get you out of here. You're beautiful, yes, but you're not looking so hot." Damn. What happened to my fun, upbeat pre-Oscars interview with Halsey Hamilton, the shining star of the moment? Instead, I had been somehow cornered into giving an impromptu AA intervention on live television.

Halsey's eyes began closing, and she leaned down on one forearm, curling up on the ground. I couldn't help but notice that the ebony color of Halsey's slinky little bra did work rather well against the crimson color of the carpet. The hot-pink micro-thong, not so much. I made a mental note: if there was the least chance of winding up stripped down to a bra and panties outside of an awards show, basic black was never a mistake. Celebrity is a cruel mistress, and in our line of work these things must not be left to chance.

"Maxo," she whispered. "Come closer."

I looked back up at Danny, who was tilting the camera down, trying to keep the two of us together in the shot, but Halsey's new laid-out, prone position was making it tough. I knew Danny would never deviate from a camera angle that featured over-ample cleavage tumbling out of tight, strapless cups.

Quickly, I did what I had to. I lay down on the red carpet next to Halsey. Part of me, of course, was aware that the viewers at home would sure have something juicy to talk about tomorrow, all right, and wasn't that really the point of my job? But a much bigger part of me was getting alarmed. I was struck by just how unwell Halsey looked. Her skin, beneath the perfect tan, was clammy.

She struggled to talk. "Tell, Derrr . . . tell Dereww . . . I don't blame her, Maxo. I don't blame her."

"Drew?" Why would Halsey, this poor sick kid, bring up my daughter? Drew had done everything she could to help Halsey, hadn't she? What's to blame?

I was becoming more concerned about Halsey. I made another almost imperceptible gesture with my nonmike hand and saw, out of the corner of my eye, Malulu making another off-camera phone call. If she'd read my mind right, and in the four years she had been working for me she always did—that witch—she was calling the paramedics.

"Halsey?" I tried again. The girl's eyes closed. "Last thoughts? Predictions of who's gonna win? I don't suppose you have written an acceptance speech? Where would you keep it?" I held the mike up in front of her slackened jaw. Nothing but drool. And maybe a soft snore. Tele-journalism isn't always pretty, folks.

Okay, on occasion I have done a few dull interviews. Not many, you understand, but nobody is perfect. Until now, however, I had never actually put a guest to sleep. I shook my head. A sad, sad first.

"Halsey!" I yelled, again holding the mike in front of her slack mouth, hoping for one last word, but nothing. I knew our telecast was running way over our show time. I had to give up.

Flat on my back, looking straight up at the camera, I brought the mike back to my face and wrapped it up. "Folks, I could not make this up. A sadder and more dramatic scene of Hollywood excess you could not see. A nineteen-year-old actress who should be inside the Kodak Theatre right this very minute, seated and waiting and hoping to learn if she has won the world's most prestigious film award for her jaw-dropping performance as the Nazi officer's girl in Scorsese's *The Bones of War,* is instead right here next to me, lying on the red carpet. Distressed. Demeaned. And . . ." I looked at the unconscious beauty, searching for one more *d* word, noting her long auburn hair splayed out on the carpet and realized . . . oh my God. She wasn't breathing.

Dead.

3

Best Missing Camerawork

And then there were boots. And legs. And men. And a gurney.

Before I could grab Halsey's wrist to feel for a pulse, we were suddenly under siege. Eight or nine storm troopers in ill-fitting tuxedos nearly trounced upon my up-swept curls in their heartless scramble over my prostrate body to get to Halsey.

Hello? Celebrity down!

In two seconds, flat a series of draped panels had been erected around my camera crew, Halsey, and me, blocking the view of our tragic scene from the crowds of gathering gawkers and especially from the lenses of so many rabid photographers. Pulling the delicate hem of my gown from under the heel of a cheap size-12 oxford, I snarled. These beefy penguins must be a phalanx of security guards and emergency medical techs, and their formal wear was simply Academy Awards–night camouflage. Where the hell had these overdressed EMTs come from?

I tried to get up, but one of the men almost tripped over me and another turned and said, "Do us a favor. Just stay put, would you? We've got enough to attend to right now."

"Halsey, honey," I called out weakly, lying back down as I was told to do, but in the tumult of medical triage, my cry was lost. And not one of the fine, young ambulance men thought to stop and check for my pulse.

I figured this medical unit stands by on Oscar night, available in case some old actor suffers a coronary. At an event where big losers outnumber big winners four to one, hearts were bound to break, and with the mean age of your average Academy member up above fifty, plenty of likely emergency-room candidates were inside the hall. But I guarantee at no time could anyone on the planning committee have imagined that the second-youngest Best Actress nominee in the history of the awards, right after the kid who rode on a whale, would collapse out in front of the ceremonies while being interviewed—I looked around nervously—by *moi.*

I twisted just in time to avoid being trod upon by a size-13 patent leather evening slipper—at least this footwear was designer—as I strained to peer between a dozen moving black-sock-covered ankles for a glimpse of Halsey.

On the one hand, I could try to get up again, but on the other, down on the ground I was much more likely to overhear the kneeling medical techs talking about Halsey's condition. It was a risk, but I was on a story now as well as personally concerned for the girl. Swarmed by a dark, moving forest of manly pant legs, I grabbed a handful of fabric from the next passing cuff and pulled. Its owner didn't notice, so I yanked harder. "Hey," I rasped upward, "is she okay?"

A thick-chested guy shot a quick suspicious look down at me. "What's going on here, Ms. Taylor?"

"Me? Not a thing. They told me to stay put, so I'm staying put."

"Did you give Ms. Hamilton anything to eat or drink?"

"I'm an interviewer, not a caterer. Look, I just asked her about her acceptance spee—"

Another guy looked down at me. "Did you remove her dress or something?" He looked from the barely covered, motionless body of Halsey over to me, concerned.

"It's a long story."

With words like "dehydration" (hah!) and "exhaustion" (right!) called out by designer-shoes guy, the handsome one wearing the only tux in the crowd that didn't look rented, I watched several of the team lift Halsey's inert body onto the gurney. My heart sank. I couldn't see her breathing. Exhaustion. Right. Why, I wondered, weren't the medical techs the ones calling out the diagnoses?

Finally, glaring at anyone who might try to stop me, I stood up. I pulled off my earrings and stepped out of my shoes, my

usual ritual when the preshow telecast is
wrapped. Two hours of grueling smiles
usually ends in a break, but apparently not
this year. I called out to the nearest guy,
"Enough with the BS. What really happened to her?"

"How'd you know her?" asked the thick-
chested EMT. Was he kidding? Didn't he
recognize her or me? Don't tell me they
hired the only person in America who
doesn't read *Star* magazine to work this
event. "You related to her or something?"

Was this guy serious? "Yes," I lied.

"You family?" he asked, sounding at last
concerned.

"Even closer. We're celebrities," I corrected.

The handsome security guy in the good
tux intervened. "Don't worry, Ms. Taylor.
Everything will be fine."

Sure it would. The poor girl hadn't
moved a pinkie in five minutes. I smelled
the unmistakable perfume of public relations.

As they efficiently tended to Halsey,
covering her bare limbs with a blanket, talking to her softly, no one paid me the least
bit of attention. Halsey, of course, was the

one in desperate need of attention. That was obvious. By all means, have twenty young men hover in attendance. But, then, what was I? Chopped liver?

By now, a curtained-off corridor had been erected all the way to the curb. But inside our private cocoon, I could hear the screams of a frustrated press. The white fabric panels popped with a strobe-light effect as the photographers outside the perimeter went mad. A line of uniformed officers stood outside our barricade, shouting down the rabid paparazzi. I glanced at the flimsy walls, then looked back just in time to scoot quickly to the right. "Hey," I yelled as I barely avoided getting trampled by the nasty wheels of the gurney, as the large response crew trundled the body of Halsey away to an awaiting ambulance.

As the emergency-response team hurried off, my dear Killer, who had been a pent-up ball of furry rage in Malulu's arms throughout all the excitement, let out a ferocious yip of teacup-guard-dog fury. As they slammed the rear doors to the ambulance, I heard Drew's voice from behind the security curtain: "What do you mean? Let me in there, you goons. It's my mother!"

My Drew charged her way back to us, her face drawn and ashen, as she looked at me standing barefoot and earringless on the red carpet. "Mother!"

I gave Drew a brave smile. The serene effect was spoiled as the last ambulance attendant tripped over my ankle in his attempt to catch up with his departing mates.

My team had had enough. Allie stood *en garde* with her longest contour brush, while Malulu carefully handed Killer over to Drew and, with arms flying up and splayed fingers stiffened like weapons, instantly assumed the fighting stance for the secret Samoan martial art of Limalama, shifting and swaying at the ready in her bright, lime-green pantsuit, as she eyed the departing attendant.

"How dare they!" huffed Allie, waving her sable-hair makeup brush in agitation. "Max, you must sit down and rest." She gestured to the canvas chair Malulu had set up for me.

"This is no good," Malulu grunted.

"Mom, you're filthy," Drew moaned.

Where had courtesy gone? Where were good manners? People need to say "please" and "thank you" before they grind my cou-

ture into the ground. "Hey, you!" I called after the departing, nice-looking security guy.
He stopped and smiled.

"What's going on?" I demanded. "Did
you get a good look at her? I mean, I don't
want to dwell on the negative here, but I
think that poor, poor girl may be . . ."

"Forgive me, Ms. Taylor. Aren't you a
member of the press?"

That did it. I have been an actress and
a fashion maven for thirty years, but when
they want to stonewall me, they accuse
me of being a reporter. Like I'm Woodward
and Bernstein.

"I'm a style expert," I spit out at him. "By
the way, nice trousers."

"Don't worry, Ms. Taylor, we'll take it from
here." He smiled at me with a smile that
lasted a little longer than necessary between a security-type person and an on-
air commentator. Not that I noticed. "Where
are my manners?" he asked no one in particular.

Hello. Hadn't I just been asking that?

He looked at me, and I wondered for a
second if he was struck by how lovely I
hoped my face appeared from that ad-
vantageous angle. He wasn't.

He was just hired security trying to smooth over a potential PR crisis.

Malulu, instantly protective, rushed over. She glared at him as she, frankly, glared at all men. "You okeydokey, Ms. Taylor?" she asked.

"We'll see," I replied.

At that, Malulu reassumed her shifting, swaying ready-to-attack pose. I really wished she would stop it, but I suppose if I keep an unnecessary bodyguard on the payroll, I shouldn't interrupt her flow.

Turning back to the security guy, I demanded, "Now where did you take Halsey?"

"She just needs a little rest," he said.

What? Everyone was behaving as if nothing were really wrong, but no matter how "exhausted" they said she was, I could have sworn that she hadn't actually been breathing. And no breathing, where I come from, usually means dead.

"Not to worry," the guy said, looking around. "Miss Hamilton is getting help. But even though her collapse was regrettable, we don't need to upset the guests at the event going on inside."

Right. What was I thinking? Let's keep the priorities straight.

Drew interrupted, "What about you, Mom, are you okay?"

"Maybe." I wasn't ready to commit. It's so rare for a mother to get her child's full attention that I felt I should maybe take a moment to enjoy it.

Just then, the private ambulance, parked where only a few minutes earlier Halsey's Hummer limo had been, pulled slowly away from the curb. And so I turned back to the security man. "That's it?"

"Oh, just one more thing. I need to talk to your camera operator," he said, turning to Danny, of whom I'd lost track. Danny was standing back by the edge of the security curtain, stunned.

"What?" Danny jerked to attention, surprised to find the spotlight so suddenly turned on him.

The big-shouldered security guy faked a friendly tone. "I'm Jay O'Neil." He handed each of us a small, white card. It said he was chief of security for GlobalTrac Ltd. "The Academy doesn't want any disturbances."

"You're a rent-a-cop?" I wasn't surprised.

"Consultant," O'Neil said. "The awards are an important international event, as you know. My crew is here to prevent any unpleasantness."

"We wouldn't want another streaker to rush naked across the stage," I joked. "Oh, no. That was the seventies."

"No," he replied, deadly earnest, "we wouldn't. Nor do we want any other unfortunate matter to distract from the celebration this evening. A lot of people worked very hard to get here, and they deserve to be protected from a situation that could go unpleasantly out of control."

What was he suggesting? That I had somehow caused this sad scene with Halsey? How dare he? I'm never at a loss for words. Never. But to that astonishing half accusation, I could get out only one loud and rasping *"What?"*

"So please tell your cameraman to cooperate. I need the videotape out of his camera."

"No, you don't," yelled Drew, defensive.

I bristled. "Are you crazy? That tape is ours."

With all the excitement and worry, I had

lost sight of what we had. I had sudden vi-sions of the great things we might do with that video. A feature on *CBS Nightly News*. A segment on *60 Minutes*. A "hot topic" on *The View.* That insane interview, lying on the red carpet with a drunk Halsey Hamilton, could easily become the hottest five minutes on television. And, let's face it, there was big, big money at hand. I took a nanosecond to dream: paying off some bills. Buying a new coat. Picking up a little house in the south of France.

Look, although this can seem harsh, this is the way the business works. You have to separate the work from the personal. No one was sadder to see Halsey fall from grace one more time than I. I'm a mother. I feel for her. But if she kept making bad choices, and she chose to do it on live tele-vision during my exclusive interview, that tape was news and I had the right to the tape. Besides, I had been on my feet talking off the top of my head for the past two hours. Even during the interview with Halsey, I had to have one eye on the camera, one eye on the monitor, and half my brain thinking of what question I would ask next. Instead of wasting any more time with this hired cop,

Drew and I should be back in our hotel suite, where we always went right after a telecast. Normally, we relax and watch the Academy Awards show—wearing three pounds or so of borrowed diamonds can be tiring—but I was now dying to see what had really happened to Halsey.

O'Neil got serious with Danny. "Take my advice. You don't want any trouble."

"What kind of trouble?" Danny asked, looking worried. The big guy was just a big wimp.

O'Neil kept at him. "I'm sure your network doesn't want to be dragged down into something nasty. Lawsuits are expensive. They won't thank you. Sometimes it gets hard to find freelance camera work in this town, I've heard."

"Well . . . ," Danny said.

Well? Well? That was Danny's tough-guy response to the blithering threats of some idiot with semi-authority? I stepped between Danny and O'Neil and smiled at the fake cop, unimpressed. "Maybe that sort of intimidation works with other kinds of people. People who stay up at night worried they underpaid their income tax. But this is a different world, my friend. Are you kidding? Networks love the gutter. They invented the gutter."

"Please hand over the videotape," O'Neil repeated, still pleasant, but with an edge in his voice.

I smiled even harder. This was so not going to go the rent-a-cop's way.

Danny gulped and looked over at me for moral support. He knew the alpha dog in this setup. Good boy.

I kept on smiling as I started pulling stray pebbles from my hairdo. "It's ours. I'll get my attorney on the phone." Before I could make a gesture in her direction, Malulu stepped out of her martial arts pose and began speed-dialing my lawyer.

Killer, with open hatred, stared at O'Neil's ankle as if it were prime rib. Malulu, always alert to my puppy's moods, stared at Killer. Drew, feeling unsure how far I'd take this confrontation, stared at Malulu. O'Neil, with a little less open admiration for me than he'd shown earlier, stared at me. I, knowing how easily Danny might be swayed to give up our tape, stared at Danny. Danny, unable to cope with the pressure, stared down at his ridiculously old sneakers. No one moved.

O'Neil, not much of a negotiator, re-opened the talks. "Look, let's keep calm. No one is saying you and your daughter ought to be banned from future red carpets, but . . ."

Five minutes ago I would've half-thought this O'Neil guy was cute, but if this was some new twenty-first-century form of flirting, give me the old-school flowers and vodka shooters.

"We've got to go," I said, taking Drew by the hand.

"Yes," said Malulu, relieved.

"Yip," added Killer.

"Sorry, but I can't let you leave until you hand over the videotape," O'Neil said to Danny.

"Hey, no need to get all threatening or anything," Danny said. "See, there isn't any videotape."

"What?" we all said at once.

"Yeah, well . . ." Danny tugged on his baseball cap. "My camera doesn't use tape anymore. When I'm rolling, I'm just sending a live feed back to the truck. The director is in the booth there and decides what shots he wants, and the technical director pushes the buttons. It's a live show."

I knew that Will Beckerman and crew were working in our portable TV control room in a large trailer parked on a side street a block away, where they received the live shots from all the roving camera-men plus the interviews shot by the fixed cameras covering Drew and me. What I didn't know was that they edited the show as it went directly to the viewers watching. Who can keep up with the technical de-tails? Apparently, there was no film or vid-eotape in our camera.

"No tape?" O'Neil said, tapping the large camera mounted on a tripod next to Danny, unconvinced.

"Not here." Danny wagged his head side to side.

"Well, then where?" O'Neil asked, still not losing patience.

"They can record a tape from the live mix."

"They?"

"The guys in the truck."

"You didn't think you should've mentioned that a little earlier?" asked O'Neil, dis-gusted.

Alas, O'Neil was learning what all of us already knew: Danny was a nice steady camera operator, but he'd spent a few too many lost years listening to Santana and smoking pot. O'Neil just shook his head and headed away toward the production truck.

"That's good luck for us," I said, smiling again. "Glam will never give up that tape."

"That interview with Halsey is gold!" crowed Cindy, who had finally been cleared by security to enter our secured area and had completely missed our tense standoff. "Did I deliver or did I deliver?" she asked, beaming. No one spoke. "Okay, I get it. A little shaky on Joaquin Phoenix, yes, I know, but then I pulled through in the clutch, baby!"

"Not bad," I told her. "I doubt dear Sam Rubin will ever return my calls again, but not bad. However, it was Drew who got us that interview."

Danny looked mournful. "Max, we have big problems."

"What?"

"I don't think they ever taped Halsey's spot. You were going way, way over our time."

"I realize that," I said, exasperated. I was wearing a $140,000 watch, wasn't I?

Drew jumped in, looking upset. "Mom couldn't exactly get a coherent word out of Halsey."

Danny looked sick. "See, the thing of it is, Max, we were cut off."

"What?"

"Glam and Will in the truck. They cut the feed when we started to go over time."

"Cut the feed?" I screamed. "What the fuck are you talking about? You mean no one saw my interview?" A bit of dead leaf fell off the butt of my gown, fluttering to the carpet.

Danny said, "I don't think so. My camera went dead, Max. Will must have pulled the plug."

"That idiot!" I shouted. I felt the back of my neck getting as red as the carpet!

"Come on, Max. You know the rules," Danny said in a don't-blame-me voice. "We're never allowed to spill over into the Oscars. We're contractually obligated to stop our show so there's no overlap when the real Oscar telecast begins on the network."

"Of course I know that," I yelled. But that rule just pertained to entertainment, and

Halsey's collapse, right here, right now, had been *news*. After all these years in the business, I was pretty sure news trumped all. What the whole world apparently wanted was to look hard and close at whatever had happened to that poor young woman, including watching her fabulous collapse in a heap in front of us. And what I wanted was to simply save my show for one more year. And all that could have been accomplished if they hadn't turned off the camera.

"Oh, Mom," Drew said, her face ashen.

"No," I yelled. "No, no, no! Those idiots! Didn't they understand? We had *news* tonight! Look, I have a big heart. I would never wish an alcoholic relapse on anyone, but if Halsey chose to have one on live television, on my red carpet, it's goddamned news." I shook my head in disbelief. "We had the most stunning interview in the history of interviews, and they blew it. We had Halsey Hamilton, live."

In a nanosecond the dreams evaporated: I saw a stack of bills. My old coat. A little house in the South Bronx.

"But you had her, Max," said Cindy, throwing her note cards down on the ground, kicking off her high heels, still proud. "Whether you used her or not, you had her, and I got her."

"Mom," Drew said, her voice hushed. "Maybe it's best that we let Halsey have some privacy after all."

"Honey, don't you think I wish she'd been sober? But the fact is America's troubled sweetheart was breaking down, the poor, unhappy child, on live TV, and our director, that idiot, that jerk, that ignoramus, he actually cut us off? I'm gonna kill myself."

"Mom, calm down. Calm down," Drew said.

"Don't tell me to calm down. America lost its only chance to view what really happened to Halsey just as she collapsed. And those idiots in the booth lost what would have been their biggest ratings ever."

Danny shook his head. "No red light, no feed. And no feed, no backup videotape in the truck."

I shook my head in utter frustration.

Drew started to cry.

"It's okay," I said, patting her hand. My dear girl knew what a bitter blow this network blunder had turned into. I pinched her cheek and smiled. "We've had bigger idiots do stupider things, haven't we? And we've always survived." I looked at my little group of staff, hoping they understood. "I'm just getting that awful feeling I sometimes get."

"Indigestion?" asked Malulu.

"No."

"Restless leg syndrome?" Malulu guessed.

"No!"

"What feeling, Mom?" Drew asked.

"About what happened to Halsey."

Drew nodded. "Me too. After all she did to get clean and sober, what could have gotten into Halsey?"

"You saw," I said, shaking my head sadly. "Another misstep."

"But drinking? On the night of the Oscars? Even Halsey would never ever do anything that foolish," Drew said. "I was so sure of it."

"People fool us," I said. Then I thought of that poor girl, probably in a hospital emergency room, cold and all alone when she came to. Or maybe cold and all alone and just . . . getting colder.

"Drewie, I was just wondering. Do you know where Burke is tonight?"

"What?" Her delicate chin turned sharply. "What about Burke?"

"This is not a big thing. I'm only asking. When you and Burke broke up this last time, didn't you tell me he was going away?"

"Don't get on Burke's case, of all things, Mother. He just took some time to sort out his issues."

"What issues? He's a good-looking boy with not enough talent for making a living."

"Why are you starting on Burke, again?"

"Something came up. Actually, I need to talk to him."

"Really?" Drew brightened a little.

Did she think I wanted to talk him into getting back together with her? Oh, my God, no!

She added, "He may be at one of the Oscar after-parties."

"Perfect." Drew and I try to get to most of the big studio parties. With our names on those precious guest lists at the door, we go in, circle the room once, sip a bit of wine, and connect with as many stars as we can. Once you've met socially, it's hard for them not to talk to you on the carpet. "Which party?"

Drew gave me a small shrug. *"Vanity Fair."*

I cursed. That was the one party, out of all the glamorous parties, that never invited us. Each year we get invitations from Sony, Warner Bros., Miramax, and Elton John. But the puffed-up powers at *Vanity Fair* cannot be coaxed or bribed to put our names on their list, claiming that, although we are noted entertainers, for this one night we're competing press.

"Vanity Fair?" I snarled, my eyebrow lifting. "That piece of yellow journalism?"

"Mom," Drew said, her voice lowering, half in resignation, half in fear, "what do you have in mind?"

I had in mind two things: one, that I wanted to take my tight bustier off immediately, and two, that I needed to track down my AWOL hairdresser, Unja, because I'd bet money that he was the only guy with the wall-to-wall home videos of this evening's preshow event in its entirety stuck in his hat. If I knew starstruck fans, and I do, I knew that Unja would never, *never* have cut away from taping Halsey Hamilton's slow, dramatic collapse just because some stupid clock said our time was up and some even stupider contract said we weren't allowed to continue to film. That tape of Unja's would have answers.

But I knew that wasn't what was worrying my daughter. She stood staring at me. "Mom?"

Okay. I also had in mind that Drew and I, before this night was through, would be crashing the most uncrashable party in Hollywood, brilliantly dodging four mammoth bouncers, just so I could finally talk to Drew's no-good ex-boyfriend Burke about a girl who I was rapidly coming to believe might not be waking up from her last plunge.

"Mom?" Drew's voice now held a more frantic note. She'd seen me like this before.

And she knew me. I wasn't going to lose this story, and if all else failed, I had in mind to run over to Cedars, the posh hospital that catered to movie greats, and stalk the emergency room, if I had to, to find out what had happened to that beautiful falling star.

4

Best Stunt Crash

Century City. The roped-off entrance to Craft. The ever-crush of paps and fans along the curb and spilling into the street. It was after-party time.

Drew and I had gone back to the Renaissance Hotel, where Glam-TV had given us rooms in which to freshen up and watch the Oscar telecast. Throughout it all, no mention had been made on-air of the Best Actress nominee who had collapsed on the street outside the theater. Inside, it was one glorious polished celebration, and the show must go on.

While we waited for news of Halsey, with

Drew sending out texts to all their mutual friends, we watched our hotel television set in rapt attention as the awards were handed out, taking copious notes on the stars' fashions for our fashion-review commentaries.

"She must be okay," Drew said more than once. "There's no announcement."

Even when Daniel Day-Lewis was handing out the prize for Best Actress, and they showed all the nominees in their seats, all except Halsey, no mention was made of what had happened on the red carpet—the underwear, the slurring, the collapse. And when the Oscar went to another actress, Halsey's moment quickly passed completely, as she moved from missing hopeful to absent also-ran. Not a good night for Halsey Hamilton. I called in favors, but still no news came to us about Halsey, and so as the award show ended, we left the hotel to find some answers. I was determined to hunt down Burke.

Flashbulbs shot off in record numbers as our limo cruised slowly up to the curb in front of the Century City restaurant that was the new setting for the *Vanity Fair* party. It may have been Dr. Bob's latest dermabrasion that had given me that extra zing, I don't know, but I detected the paparazzi approved of my glow as they seemed near frenzy when Drew and I emerged from our limo in front of chef Tom Colicchio's latest hot spot.

"Max! Max! Drew!" came the shouts as we straightened our couture and faced the cameras.

Since the venerated Morton's had closed, the new location for this most elite post-Oscars bash had become stylish American-cuisine food-star Craft, a spot close to the hearts of the power agents and entertainment attorneys who worked in the nearby luxury towers, probably the only people in town who could afford the joint's $98 Wagyu rib-eye steaks and $21 side order of mushrooms.

"Mom," Drew said, her voice getting that let's-be-reasonable tone, as here and there entertainment reporters in the throng faced their cameras, one hand up to their ears to block the din, broadcasting their live remotes back to a couple of dozen nightly news shows.

"Max!" came the shouts. "Drew! Look this way."

"Smile, darling," I said between clenched teeth. The press were animals tonight. They couldn't get enough of us. How sweet it felt.

"We're not on the list," Drew reasoned as we faced the reporters, this time on the side of the celebrities ourselves. "You know that, Mom. They won't let us in!"

"They'll change their minds." I kept smiling and turned Drew to face another phalanx of photographers. "And if you don't stop worrying, you'll get that tiny frown line on your forehead."

"The one I inherited from you?" she accused.

Touché.

"Max!" yelled Nicholas Tostado, an adorable reporter from KCAL-News. His camera was hot, and so was he. "You were standing with Halsey a few hours ago. What happened to her? Is she all right?"

So. The crazy-wild reaction to our arrival had nothing to do with my new glow. Damn.

Several other microphones were being shoved in our direction. What could I say? That Halsey was a wreck, a girl soaked in booze or high on pills or both? That I had serious doubts she would survive many more of these lapses? I lost some of my radiant smile, debated how exactly to respond, then said, "Tell them, Drew."

Microphones were immediately swung toward Drew, who had the presence of mind not to glare at me on-camera and quickly answered, "We don't know what happened, but we love Halsey and hope she is doing well."

Many more questions were yelled out, but I put my arm around Drew's waist and pulled her toward the door to Craft, where we were admitted to the roped-off entrance outside the front door by a young woman who was still gaping at the huge reaction we had received upon leaving our limo. A table was set up outside Craft where a young man wearing a high-tech headphone tended an impressive leather-bound book. The guest list. At the front door a few feet away stood two massive men wearing earpieces. The bouncers.

"This will end badly, Mother." Drew sprang a tiny frown line. "Remember what happened at Morton's in 2007."

I pointed at her forehead, and she stopped.

"Oh, dear," said the young man at the table when he spotted us approaching. He had the air of a man who was preparing to toss me out on my ass. Believe me. I know that look.

"You got the news," I said with a conspiratorial whisper.

"Ms. Taylor. It's a pleasure to see you tonight," he started. Smooth. Then came the word: "But . . ." Both he and I remembered well our famous tussle in '07. And in '06 for that matter. Only the cancellation of the *Vanity Fair* party in '08 due to the agitation over the Writers Guild strike had spared us this indignity a year ago.

"And you. And thank heavens you know about the story," I confided.

"The story?" He worked for the magazine and the word *story* stopped him.

"Yes," I continued. "You do not have my name on your guest list, do you?"

He shook his head. "No, I—"

"And no matter how many times I have my publicist call your people, we never seem to agree that Drew and I are not in competition with your wonderful magazine. We are, after all, celebrities ourselves."

"That is never in question, Ms. Taylor," the young man said, suddenly becoming very officious. "It's just, as I've explained before, we—"

"You have taken the position that, on this one night only, we are also the competition. Ridiculous!"

"Please don't yell," he said snippily.

"My mother never yells," Drew roared in my defense.

"Oh, dear," said the young man.

"We are here tonight to bring *you* the story," I said. "*The* story, if you know what I mean."

"I'm afraid—"

"Halsey Hamilton," I said in a raspy whisper.

"Oh my God!" he whispered back, suddenly all attentive. "I am *dying* to know what happened. You were with her, Ms. Taylor! Was she wasted or what?"

I turned to Drew. "Sweetie, who's that guy we know at the magazine. The guy who called tonight begging us to come to the party and give him all the sordid details?"

"One of our writers?" asked the man at the table, alert.

"You know," I continued to Drew, "when we said we were giving the exclusive story to *People* magazine when they promised us the cover?"

"Wasn't it that writer," Drew asked, vamping merrily, "that President Clinton hates?"

"Todd Purdum?" breathed the young man at the table, quivering a little at the name of the hard-hitting *Vanity Fair* reporter. He put up his index finger and then began talking into his headset in a whisper.

Just then an overzealous elderly reporter pushed his way past the roped-off barricades and called out to me, "Max, it's nine forty a.m. in Germany! Just a word about Halsey for the *Stuttgarter Zeitung*?" Within five seconds the two towering brutes had bounded over from the entrance to Craft and put the poor German reporter in a headlock.

"Wait! . . . Wait! . . . Wait! . . . Just one minute more, please," begged the young man as he tried to reach someone inside the party to give him the okay to let us in, presumably to be interviewed by this Todd person. All this blasted technology. I had to hurry things along.

"We can't hold this story much longer, honey," I said sadly to Drew. "Look. It's already breaking in *Stuttgart.* And it's not like *Vanity Fair* has shown us any love all these years. Hmm."

"We are the only people who know what Halsey said before she collapsed with you, Mother," Drew offered.

The young fellow sucked in his breath. I turned back to Drew. "You're right. Let's go."

"Please," he called after us.

No one can watch a story walk away. No one. Why hadn't I ever thought of this idea before? *Be the news.* Hell, I could easily have shot Nicole Richie in some nonlethal body part or perhaps slept with Robert Downey Jr. during one of his lost phases and waltzed right into this party years ago.

"Wait!" the young man pleaded. "Ms. Taylor, I'm—"

I spun back to him and said to Drew, "Well, well, well. I think this very nice young man from *Vanity Fair* wants to apologize."

Drew smiled.

"Yes," he said earnestly. "I do."

"For all the years of mistrust and insults?" I asked.

"I am so sorry."

"And?" It was a pretty sweet moment, so I waited for more.

"And . . . ," he said, breaking into a tiny sweat. "I've always been a huge fan of yours, Ms. Taylor. You know that. This little misunderstanding each year, it's always made me sick."

"Me too," I said.

"Just tell me," he breathed. "Halsey. Is she back in rehab? Does she wear hair extensions? Is she still doing the horizontal hula with that fake Hispanic guy?"

I put my finger to my lips. "Yes, yes, and even under the tables at IHOP," I lied three times.

"Jonathan!" the young man called out, his voice ringing with middle management command. One of the beefy monsters came to our side.

"Please escort Ms. Taylor and Miss Taylor into the party."

Just like that. Fourteen years of waiting. Fourteen years of begging. Fourteen years of rejection. A freaking hot story scoops all.

As beefy Jonathan opened the door to Craft, allowing us to pass into this most anticipated party, the young man at the table called out to us cheerfully, "And don't worry. I'll keep phoning. I've got everyone's cell numbers. I'll get Todd and make sure that he meets you for your interview! You won't have to wait long."

Was that a less-than-trusting gleam I saw in his eye?

5

Best Villain

We're in," said Drew, amazed. "You did it."

Before I could respond, Drew and I were swept up among partygoers, crushed in the loud and merry mix of close friends and close enemies.

"Drew!" came a British-accented call from the crush.

With one heavily jeweled hand I held tight to Drew's wrist as her cheek was kissed by the beautiful Anne Hathaway, so pale in her deep-red Versace gown, and my other hand was quickly grabbed up by the handsome Pierce Brosnan, who was wearing a hand-tailored Armani tux but would have looked heavenly even wearing off-the-rack.

"Max, you look marvelous."

Hand? I pulled him down to my level for a kiss. Hey, with half the hunks in Hollywood filled with expensive champagne, I was not about to pass up the opportunities available to a dead-sober single lady. In fact, it was like any other glittering Hollywood affair, except better, because Drew and I had felt the thrill of sneaking in, and that adrenaline high was keeping us pumped.

"Yes, hi, hello!" I waved at the various and beautiful, as I pulled Drew closer and ordered, "Now go find Burke." Who knew how long we'd be allowed to mingle before our butts would be tossed? We had no time to waste.

A black-vested waiter passed, holding a platter of bent spoons.

"I'm starving," Drew said, following the waiter. Upon each silver spoon, its handle bent all the way back around and under, was a sliver of cured fish with a pinch of garnish. We each helped ourselves, but it would take a dozen more tiny such Craft morsels to satisfy us. I grabbed the last spoon, and Drew slapped my hand and took it. Receiving a concerned look from the waiter, we backed off.

"First Burke, then food," I said, pushing Drew along.

"Mother!"

Inside the vast, ten-thousand-square-foot interior, track-lighting-style filament bulbs dangled over the fawn-colored banquettes, lending the gold and beige space a warm amber glow. Along the back, a wall display showed off neatly arranged rows of backlit wine bottles in custom floor-to-ceiling cases. Around us, about three hundred celebrities and industry giants were now laughing and flirting and landing their next films, while at least a hundred more were schmoozing outside on the patio. For this special evening, several giant-screen plasma televisions had been installed around the space, each projecting the live after-party news coverage so we could all check ourselves out on-screen. Not a bad idea in this crowd.

As we pushed gently through the throng, I nodded to Clive Owen, thin and fabulous in a white dinner jacket, while Drew got a quick hug from Penelope Cruz in a shimmering silver Dolce gown, and I scanned the room for any sign of Drew's evil ex-boyfriend. I have an eagle—if nearsighted—eye, and for just a moment I thought I caught a glimpse of Burke Norris's broad shoulders from behind a beehive hairdo that made the beautiful Heidi Klum look as if someone had left a bleached squirrel on her head. But, no, it wasn't Burke after all.

"Heidi! Nice hair," I called out, then whispered to Drew, "Do me a favor. If I ever leave the house looking like that, shoot me or hand me a bag of nuts."

"Max!"

I looked up to see Diana Bates, the third woman I've known to be married to the head of Interscope Pictures, in her backless, teal-colored Dior, waving to me.

"Great dress, Diana."

"Thanks, Max. You look gorgeous."

"Don't start."

"What happened to Halsey?" Diana asked. "She really must be desperate for attention. I mean, she makes that crazy last-second grand entrance to the Oscars? Come on. Guess it wasn't enough for her to be one of five nominees, was it?"

I looked at Diana, stunned. "Halsey? I don't know what you mean. She was sick. I mean, she collapsed for God's sake."

"Exactly," Diana slurred. "She pulls that stunt right before the awards. James was livid. Says she'll never do another picture for Interscope."

I recalled that Halsey had never agreed to do any pictures with Interscope, ever.

Diana went on, "Such a publicity whore." Bitch.

I didn't point out who, in fact, the whore was and just smiled. This town. Diana swirled away in her happy little bubble.

My little Judith Leiber bag began to rattle and vibrate. Cell phone. On the display, a phone number with a British prefix and area code.

My Sir Ian.

"Hello." I tried to cup my hand over one ear to dampen the sound of a few hundred Hollywood celebrants, but I could hear just the faintest of voices. I spied a hallway that led to the kitchen and figured I might find less crowd noise in that direction. "Hello, darling?" I tried again.

"Maxine, my dear, can you hear me?" came the deep voice. "I've had a bloody time reaching you. You never think to consult the list of missed calls on your mobile. So what is a poor fellow to do but keep calling?"

Sir Ian McBride and I had been "dating" for almost a year. While he lived in England and I traveled from coast to coast in the United States, we still managed to clock a great deal of time together. I was always booking work trips overseas, and he had many reasons to come to New York, as his business of buying gems and selling them to the world's wealthiest jewelers kept him hopping around the globe. Although dating a man in the diamond business may sound too good to be true, our relationship was much more valuable than mere gifts. I'd found a man whom I not only adored but was also a terribly good friend.

"Hello, yes, I can hear you perfectly. I'm at a party, Ian," I said.

"Yes, my dear. Of that I am completely aware, as is most of the world. You look marvelous, by the way. I've been watching you on television all morning, haven't I?" With his clever array of live satellite feeds, my dear Ian had obviously been able to follow my movements around town from the comfort of his flat in London, where it was currently tomorrow morning. I noticed a big screen off to my left replaying a video clip of my arrival with Drew at this very party only moments before. Ian, seven thousand miles away, probably noticed it too. "I must say, Maxine, I was more than a little surprised to see you arriving at the big *Vanity Fair* party. Aren't they the bastards who continually try to keep you out?"

"In the past, yes, true . . ." One of the things I adored about Ian was his fabulous business savvy. A brilliant man, he told me wonderful and daring stories about trading diamonds all across Europe and Africa, and over time I had shared some of my professional victories—I hate to brag—and some of my most bitter defeats. With his businessman's habit of keeping careful score of those who have bruised me, he hadn't quite mastered the art of Hollywood amnesia so necessary to finesse the tricky ins and outs of doing business here. Sometimes it's better to forget all the names on one's enemies list. If one survives in this town for any amount of time, it can be a long list. I put on a hearty tone to my voice and said, "We're all friends again. Everything's fine."

"Max, darling." His voice had the sound of a man who knew me too well. "Did you bash into that crazy magazine party?"

"It's *crash,* Ian. And, no. Of course not. I was asked in. What do you think I am?"

"An American," he laughed.

Three waiters, all clad in dark vests and striped ties, passed by on their way to the kitchen.

"I am just a bit worried about you, that's all. My media people managed to arrange a live feed of Glam-TV, and I watched your show. It was all going marvelously well, my dear, but then what on earth happened with that girl, Halsey?"

The question of the evening.

"My God, Maxine. You're lucky she was wearing any clothing at all, or they would have had to place modesty bars all across the screen."

"Were you shocked, Ian?" I was only teasing. Few people could shock my boyfriend, who had a talent for negotiating the price on natural diamonds that belied the civility of his McBride family's well-educated lineage, but I liked to try.

"Maxine, do listen to me this time. I think you had better go home and stay out of the public eye. I am fairly safe in saying that there is rather a large storm of press coverage here in Europe surrounding this Hamilton girl, and I can only imagine it is worse there in the States. You may not realize it, but . . ."

He went on for a bit. Nothing is less romantic than a man who wants me to stay home and avoid the storm. I was just getting ready to say so when I spotted one of the servers, a lovely redheaded girl with a long ponytail, hastily rebuttoning her black vest as she emerged from an alcove in the hallway to the kitchen. And what was this? Immediately following her out of that dark alcove was none other than Burke Norris, who brushed past without noticing me, looking down, as he was, to zip up his fly.

Oh. Really.

I interrupted Ian's mini-rant: "Got to go, love." I don't know why, but when I talk to him I get all "Beatles" in my word choices. "We've got terrible cell reception. I have no bars. Call you lat—" I snapped shut my phone midword, rushing after Burke.

I rejoined the loud party, approaching a tangle of guests standing around the bar, and just heard the last words directed at Burke, coming from some man I didn't recognize.

" . . . the last time I saw her. It's got to be a bummer for you, man." The stranger drained his martini glass. "I mean, you and she were still real tight, right?"

"Are you two talking about Halsey?" I interrupted.

"Max Taylor," said the man, brightening when he recognized me. "Max Taylor. I love your interviews. You are so mean."

Burke, suddenly realizing whom he had brushed past on his retreat from the waitress boff, looked sheepish, while I graciously decided not to lash into him for that ridiculous behavior. I had bigger grapes to squeeze.

"Isn't she *mean*?" persisted Burke's friend, smiling in admiration.

"Is she ever," Burke mumbled.

Well, he had dated my Drew for over a year. During their romance, he had seen both my generous and my fierce sides.

"You look beautiful, Max," Burke said,

revving up the charm. "Your show was great tonight. You and Drew."

"So nice to know you are still a fan." I smiled a not-altogether-friendly smile. "What I really want to know, though, is what have you got to do with Halsey and her drug problems?"

"Whoa. What?" Burke took a few steps back away from the bar and his buddy.

I followed closely. "Halsey was upset about *you* tonight. *You.* What the hell was that all about?"

Burke turned to his buddy for support, but the guy was getting a refill on his martini.

"Tell me," I insisted. A prickle of fear kept me glancing back at the entrance, expecting at any moment to see a commotion of bodyguards and bouncers coming after me, finally having tracked down Todd Whomever and confirmed I had no free pass to this party. "Come on, Burke, don't play games. Something was up between you and Halsey."

"Huh?" he asked, perplexed, a glint of gold in his wide gray-green eyes.

A brain surgeon he wasn't.

Burke Norris was quite a package. On the surface. He had the height—at six feet four he was a foot taller than I was—and the looks: dark, wavy hair that he wore perfectly cut, and shoulders just wide enough to make him walk through crowded bars sideways. He had a permanent five o'clock shadow even a decade after the unshaven look had become passé, yet it perfectly suited his strong jawline and tanned face. He dressed well and smelled good, but as much polish as he had on the outside, in his heart something had always been lacking. He'd been brought up with a little too much unsupervised time in Beverly Hills, and after drifting away from college, he'd found better things to do, apparently, than getting a job. Heaven forbid he should go to work for his father, the pickle king of Van Nuys!

The better Burke looked, standing there in the bar in his Armani tux, the more I hated him, because this good-looking idiot had stolen my daughter's heart and he just wasn't worthy of her. Eventually, soon, Drew's heart would stop aching and she'd know she was much too good for this lout. But to help that healing moment come sooner, I had to find out how Burke was connected to this night's fiasco.

"Did you give drugs or booze to Halsey? Answer me."

"No. Of course not. Why would you think I could ever . . . ?" He looked hurt. His eyes scrunched in a convincing mock-up of confusion and innocence. Right.

"Because Halsey Hamilton, God love her, collapsed at my feet this evening," I whispered. "And as she lay there, she talked about you."

"No kidding." His beautiful face was a cipher. Was he sad? Sorry? Concerned? Proud?

"Were you two dating, Burke?"

"No. Well, not anymore. Really, Max. Halsey and I, we were over as a couple. History."

My head began to ache. Burke and Drew had started out fast—too fast, I always told her—and had gotten engaged after only a month. They had been happy together for over a year. But when things began to go bad a few months ago, Drew could see the end was coming and finally threw him out for good two weeks ago. Since Halsey had been tucked away in

rehab during the entire period that Burke
and Drew had been on the rocks, when
had he and Halsey had this bout of "history"? Had Burke and Halsey been having
a sick, secret affair during Drew's year of
"good times," the year Burke had been engaged to my daughter? He couldn't have!

"So when did it start?" I asked.

"Well, yeah, okay. Back in the day . . ."

I felt a momentary urge to commit murder. Really. Burke Norris was clearly admitting that he had had a short fling with
Halsey, Drew's so-called good friend. If
Drew ever found out, she'd be devastated.
It was in the rules, damn it. When a girl
breaks up with a rat, none of her friends
was allowed to sleep with him. Ever. And
if the sweet girl hadn't even broken up
with the rat yet, but was still *happily
engaged* . . . But when had Halsey ever
cared about the rules?

I reached out and grabbed Burke's arm,
feeling the hard biceps beneath the fine
wool of his jacket. "If you ever tell Drew
about your stupid affair," I began, "I swear
I'll—"

Just then, Big Jonathan, the bruiser
from the front door, walked into the bar.

His eyes held the cool gaze of a commando looking to search and destroy.

I gulped. Time to go. As Burke burbled his regrets about Halsey, and sincere-sounding, soppy apologies, begging to be released one more time in his gilded life from the consequences of his bad choices, I slunk down low and reversed course, steering away from the bar, staying below the radar of the additional three bouncers who had joined Jonathan. The security team was beginning to talk to people at the bar. Burke's buddy was one of them. I thought I could hear my name above the general chatter.

I slunk even lower, limping along quickly toward the other side of the lounge, explaining to a startled Daniel Day-Lewis that I'd gotten a charley horse, damn it. He seemed concerned. But this is Hollywood, so who can tell?

"That's her!" a masculine voice boomed. "Max Taylor!"

I sped through the opening in the crowd, miraculously cured of my phantom leg cramp and ran smack into Graydon Carter, with his large forehead, beefy middle, and clouds of silver hair, the editor of

Vanity Fair himself. He was standing, talking to a pretty woman whose shiny coif was swept up in a great-looking topknot.

"Max Taylor," he said in astonishment. "You . . ."

"Yes, Graydon," I said, smiling warmly. "Me."

The beefy bouncers, exiting the bar area, spotted me standing in the middle of the crowded restaurant, surrounded by TV screens, talking to the big boss. They stopped, agog, uncertain, wanting to snap at me like the guard dogs they were, but then not wanting to bust into the editor's conversation, lest they get put back on their leashes outside the fine event.

"Wondered when I'd run into you," he said, gesturing with his drink toward a big-screen nearby. The pretty, young woman at his side smiled. Of course everyone knew I was here. But he was cheerful; that was something. "And you have quite a story, don't you, Max? The story of Halsey Hamilton's latest meltdown. Not very pretty, but then, you have the smarts to be where the ugly stuff happens."

I loved it. He actually sounded jealous.

"Perhaps," he continued, "it's a story

you would like to share with our *Vanity Fair* readers?" He smiled down at the woman at his side, then said, as an afterthought, "Max Taylor, this is Sibyl Morgan, one of my best young editors."

She said, "You'll give us the story?"

"That's exactly what I was thinking," I said.

"Yes?" he said, smiling a most charming smile as the tiny pin spotlights gleamed off his silver waves.

"If the price is satisfactory, Graydon," I added.

"Now, really!"

I smiled at them both. My private view of the downfall of an Academy Award–nominated party girl was surely worth more than mere entry into a party that, while glamorous, didn't, let's be honest, feed guests more than a spoonful of fish.

"How much?" asked the lovely Sibyl. She had out her BlackBerry and was taking notes.

"A lot."

Graydon scoffed, "We clearly have a difference of opinion on the value of this story. We're not a daily rag, as I'm sure you know. We are a prestigious monthly, and I'm not sure it would even be worth it for us to talk numbers." Pretty Sibyl frowned. They were both suddenly not as amused.

The movie stars and moneymen around us hummed with good cheer, but I was wasting my time here. "I'll be going now. Thank you for your kind hospitality."

"Oh," he said, perhaps startled I had ended our discussion. "Did you get a chance to taste the—"

But I would never hear what astonishing culinary treat I would have no chance of sampling since, at that moment, the crowd around us started hushing one another, and that included us.

An elderly actress seated at the banquette nearest to us said, "Turn the volume up, won't you?" and a young waiter came rushing over to do so.

On the several huge TV screens in the room was featured a close-up of local reporter Nick Tostado. He was no longer standing on the curb outside Craft, where last I'd spoken with him a half hour or so earlier. It appeared that Nick was now positioned in the street in front of Cedars-Sinai hospital, only a few miles away. The party was still too noisy to hear what he was saying, but perhaps his exact commentary didn't really matter. Because the words on the bottom of the screen, under the reporter's handsome image, read, HAMILTON ACADEMY AWARD NIGHT TRAGEDY.

"What? Is she dead?" gasped the older actress.

"No!" cried a woman I knew who used to buy specials at HBO.

"No!" echoed from several overplumped lips around the room.

Yes, I thought, suddenly miserable. My eyes searched the room for Drew, but I couldn't find her.

I had known it all along, hadn't I? No matter how much PR BS was slung, I had known this hadn't been a game or a trick or a stupid publicity stunt.

Halsey Hamilton was dead at the age of nineteen.

6

Best Wrong Move for the Right Reason

Mother?" Drew was suddenly by my side, her eyes shiny.

All the time we had watched the Oscars telecast back at the hotel, I had held on to my concerns about Halsey, never sharing too much with Drew, not wanting it to be true.

"Let's get out of here," Drew said, turning for the door.

"Max," called Diana Bates, standing in her teal Dior, blocking our path.

"Well, Diana," I said, a glimmer of steam escaping, "are you satisfied now? Not a publicity stunt, was it?"

"What?" She put her hand up to her mouth, palm out. "What are you talking about? We're *devastated*. So young. So talented. James had a meeting set with Halsey and her father this Tuesday, for God's sake." She shook her head at me, outraged.

Right.

I pushed on the door and felt a hand hold me back.

Turning, I found Graydon Carter's aide Sibyl Morgan at my side. "Don't forget, Ms. Taylor. You can't sell your story to anyone else without giving *Vanity Fair* the right to bid."

"Oh, really?" I swung around and stared down the perfectly styled young beauty. How quickly my "nothing" story had zoomed in importance. Disgusting.

She smiled. "We're in the middle of negotiations, aren't we?"

"Are we?"

"And Ms. Taylor, when you step outside, don't forget to visit our gift tent. Just a thank-you to our most special guests. Take anything you like. Anything at all." She handed me a blue rubber band that was the magic gift pass. "There are plasmas."

"I beg your pardon?"

"Sonys." She smiled.

Once outside, I could finally breathe.

"Mom," Drew said, her face ashen. "Halsey! This is all so terrible."

"I know, darling. I know. Halsey had de- mons, and they must have been too strong."

"How can she be dead?"

The question hung there in the air of a cold, clear L.A. night.

"Ms. Taylor!" "Max!" "Drew!" "What did Halsey say to you, Ms. Taylor?" The night was lit up with floodlights as dozens of cameramen jockeyed to get their shots in front of Craft on Constellation Boulevard. I took Drew, who was starting to shake, by her elbow and guided her past the en- trance to the swag tent (truly, the ultimate mother sacrifice—Beverly Hills–style) and over to the curb.

"We'll talk more in the car," I said, as our limo glided up in front of us.

I was helped into the backseat by our driver, Jeffrey, then Drew joined me on the smooth black leather seat. She had never been a crier or one to beg for a hug. I had always wanted to give them, always, but

my daughter had more dignity. Now, for
once, Drew didn't pull away.

"This is a very bad night," I said softly.

"You have no idea, Mother."

I pulled back and looked at her, while
Jeffrey asked where we wanted to go next.

"Take Drew home first," I instructed. She
has a lovely house in Beverly Hills, tiny but
perfect, and that's where she wanted to
go even though I asked her to come stay
with me for the night in my suite at the
Hotel Bel-Air, my permanent L.A. resi-
dence.

Drew was really agitated, rubbing her
thin arms even though the heat setting in
the limo was perfect. I looked her over carefully. "Drew, what is it?" My voice was much
calmer than my heart.

"I didn't want to tell you right now," she
said, looking down.

"Tell me? Tell me what?"

"It's Burke."

Oh my God. Well, when wasn't it Burke?
What now? I gave her a little encouraging
look.

She went on, "I just talked to him back
at the party."

"What do you mean? When?"

"Just now, Mother. I was with him when the news came on about Halsey. We were standing together when we found out."

Drew must have run into Burke in the bar right after I had made my escape. Just what had the two of them been cooking up?

"Now, I know how much you don't like him, Mother—"

"What? Don't *like*? I would love the schmuck if he would have been nicer to you. Didn't I buy him that three-hundred-dollar pair of True Religion jeans he wanted for his birthday? And this for a man who probably never prayed a day in his life. But he was bad news, Drew, and—"

"Exactly, exactly," she said, interrupting. "You hate him because of me."

"Let's not fight, honey," I said, trying to hug her again, but she pushed herself away.

We get along gorgeously on-air, but in real life things have not always gone perfectly for the two of us. Since my marriage to her father had ended when Drew was twelve, my daughter and I had had an earthquake to recover from. That her father had ended his own life two years later only made it harder for Drew to see that I wasn't the enemy. Over the years, with a lot of good therapy, Drew had found a way to forgive me, and I had learned to be patient. But at times like this, with this sudden death of someone close to her, and on the heels of her separation from Burke, I couldn't be sure she had ever really forgotten her pain and anger toward me.

And even without all our tragedies, every girl holds an inalienable right to blame her mother.

"What can I do to help, Drew? You know I would do anything on this earth for you."

"Just let me finish this, Mom. I know you have reason to criticize Burke. He's not perfect son-in-law material, I get that."

I smiled encouragingly, biting back all the scathing lines I was thinking.

Reassured, Drew continued, "Here's the thing. Burke, no matter what you think he's capable of, is really a sweet guy. I mean, he's not a guy who would ever hurt anybody. You have to believe that."

My tongue hurt from the biting, but I said not one word; that's how sweet I could be when I tried.

"Anyway, he told me some news tonight that is really horrible. Burke's in trouble,

Mom. He wouldn't tell me any details, but he said he could go to jail. And not because he really did anything wrong. But it would just look bad enough, you know, that he might not be able to prove he is innocent."

I guess I had known it might come to this. Burke Norris had somehow given Halsey Hamilton a lethal dose of something. I just hadn't wanted to think it all the way through to the part where it turned out my baby's recent fiancé was a killer. Oh my God.

"So this is about Halsey?" I asked calmly, trying not to shout, I TOLD YOU SO, I TOLD YOU SO.

"No, no," Drew said, dismissing the thought immediately. "Burke wouldn't have had anything to do with Halsey. I mean, they hardly even knew each other. I don't think I ever saw the two of them talk to each other, not once. No, for some reason he thinks he'll get framed or something. But it wasn't his fault."

Right. I'll bet it wasn't.

"And, Mom, here's the really terrible part. Burke is afraid. Really afraid. And he told me I'm the only one he trusts to help him."

"Wait, I'll go get my violin," I said, unable to hold it in.

"Mother, you promised," Drew warned.

Just then the limo pulled up in front of Drew's lovely Mediterranean cottage. Even at night you could see she had the loveliest garden on the block.

"So, okay," I said, starting again. "Burke is in trouble. And then he asks you to help. But what can you possibly do, precious?"

"He wants me to call a lawyer. Hire someone big and powerful. Who should I call, Mom?"

"Big and powerful? That means expensive."

"Okay. Money isn't a problem. Who should I call? He said call someone tonight, so it has to be one of your lawyer friends that I can call at home."

"Wait, whoa, wait. Money isn't a problem? Is that because you are planning to pay for it out of your own pocket?" Drew had inherited a decent amount from her father's life insurance policy, money she'd only had control of since her twenty-first birthday. She had put most of it into buying her little house, which in Beverly Hills cost a bundle, but now, even only four years later and in a downward market, it was worth substantially more. What money was left after purchasing the house wasn't much, and now she wanted to throw it away on this loser Burke Norris? I sighed. She had real estate sense; what she didn't have was man sense. "You know, manies and pedies don't grow on trees, Drew. If you give him all your savings . . ."

"No, of course not," she answered, upset.

"So you're not going to pay for his fancy lawyer?"

"Well, okay, I offered to." She shifted in the backseat. "But Burke wouldn't hear of it. He told me he didn't actually have cash on him, but he had something of great value, and I could cash it in to pay for a lawyer."

What could Burke have of great value? His drug stash? His little black book filled with solid-gold hookers? His daddy's AmEx card number? "He gave you something valuable?" I inquired, trying not to look too jaded.

Drew swept her hair off her forehead, just the way I like it, and gave me a pretty smile. She pulled my cell phone out of my bag and handed it to me. "If you call your lawyer right now and beg him to see Burke, as a special favor to you, I'll show you what Burke gave me, Mother."

I flipped open my cell phone.

"You'll help clear Burke?" she asked, her voice dropping to a whisper. It meant so much to her, I could see that. Damn it. Damn it. She was still in love.

What can a mother do?

If I said, "No, no, I'll never lift a pinkie to help that no-good, drug-pushing gigolo you managed to fall for," my daughter would have no choice but to pick between him and me. And I had no illusions over which of us she would pick. The mother always loses out in these conflicts. I wasn't a fool. And Drew, so grown-up and independent in so many ways, was still young enough to want to show me I'm wrong; want to prove she too is a good judge of character. She'd fly back to him in a second. He'd move back into her house by tomorrow. She'd show me!

And if I said, "Yes, I'll help clear your exboyfriend," what then? Perhaps I would be able to win her gratitude. Not a little goal, that one. And in the process, we might work on this project together, confiding in each other and sharing in the pursuit. I was often invited over to Drew's house for brunch, or for dinner, but rarely did she ask me to go shopping. Or call me to share secrets. Maybe this would be our chance to start our relationship on a new foot. Our first project, adult to adult: clearing Burke of murder.

Or, at any rate, trying to clear him. If, in the process, we came across incontrovertible evidence that nailed Burke Norris to the death of Halsey Hamilton, what would Drew do? Would she have to shed her blinders and see him for what he really was—a lying, cheating scoundrel who had gone too far once too often? Of course she would. And if she could see him that clearly, wouldn't that break the spell he still held over her?

What did I have to lose? If I denied Drew's request for help, I would surely lose her to Burke, and the farther down the road she walked with him, the more destructive he'd be in her life. Would he clear out her bank account? Have her borrow against her house? I looked at my beautiful and distraught daughter and sucked in my breath. Would Burke marry her to deflect the shitstorm that was about to rain down on him? I couldn't let any of that happen.

"You'll help us, Mom?" my trusting daughter asked me.

I pressed speed dial, and the swift touch-tones sang out from the earpiece of my cell phone. "I'm helping," I said, semi-smiling. "We'll get Sol Epstein."

"He's a killer!" Drew said, her voice instantly bright and happy.

"The deadliest. And what did you say Burke is going to use to pay our killer?"

I heard Sol's home voice-mail announcement as Drew reached into her evening bag and pulled out a little silk satchel. As I waited for the pretaped message to finish, Drew opened the drawstrings and tipped the bag upside down, emptying the contents into my open hand.

The interior lights of the idling limo were picked up and splashed into a thousand flashes and twinkles as dozens of perfectly cut diamonds spilled into my palm.

"Sol, it's Max Taylor," I said into the tiny cell phone, my voice even raspier than usual. "Pick up, Sol. I've got trouble."

7

Best Supporting Costume

Back to the Bel-Air Hotel, Ms. Taylor?"
Jeffrey asked, after we watched Drew unlock her front door and close it behind her
again. Every other night, Drew is perfectly
capable of letting herself into her own
front door without a parental guard dog
watching, but I couldn't turn off my inner
mom.

"No, Jeffrey." I looked at my borrowed
Piaget: 1:18. "Take me back to Craft."

"Yes, ma'am."

"Don't call me ma'am," I said for the
hundredth time. "Save that for the queen."

He chuckled from the front seat.

Ten minutes later, we were back at the sleek, modern building, the familiar crowd of paps still yapping out front, floodlights glaring. Several of them dashed over to look inside the back window, realized they had already gotten enough shots the first time I'd arrived, and backed away.

"Please, one more picture, Max," yelled one of the photo crew as Jeffrey opened the back door.

"Leave me alone already," I said, putting my hand up in front of my face. "I looked much younger a couple of hours ago. Shoo."

Just then, Christian Bale appeared in the doorway to the restaurant, leaving the party with a group of friends including Matt and Kevin Sullivan from MTV, and all the cameras swiveled his way.

I dashed over to the swag lounge set up off the entrance and walked through the doorway. Inside, a security guard wearing a tux stood by.

I held up my right hand, allowing gravity to slide almost half a million dollars' worth of borrowed gemstone bracelets up my arm, and displayed the thick, blue rubber band that was stamped with the words VANITY FAIR SUPERGUEST.

Mr. Tuxedo stepped aside, smiling, allowing me to pass. I was the lone customer in Ali Baba's cave of riches.

Tables lined the tent walls, piled with luxury items, some desirable; many not so much. A PR rep, a skinny, young thing in a plunging, silver halter dress, offered me a Prada tote bag for my loot, and I walked to the nearest table and picked up a Coach green leather glasses case. Cute. I looked up at the PR girl, and she gestured to the table in a most generous way. I picked up two more in turquoise and peach and tossed them into my bag. Malulu would love these.

It had been a stressful day. Our red carpet telecast had been great this year, sure, but had it been great enough? The constant demand for higher ratings had put pressure on Glam-TV's programmers, and the stress of staying on top trickled down to me. True, I had several incredible gets—the accidental confession that Gwyneth was trying for another baby was an exclusive!—but in this business it's the numbers that count, and were ours high enough?

I spotted a pretty leather strap with the Gucci-logo G's. "What's this?"

The thin girl smiled. "A cell phone strap. Would you like one?"

"At least."

She pulled a new Gucci box out from behind the table.

"I've got a hairstylist and a makeup stylist," I explained.

The girl pulled out a second box and handed it over without a murmur.

"Very nice."

"You are a superguest, Ms. Taylor. It's our pleasure."

"Well, then give me one more, would you? I've got a very demanding acupuncturist as well."

The smiling girl complied.

On the ride back to Craft, I'd checked my home messages and found dozens of calls. So many friends who wanted to find out what had really happened with Halsey on the red carpet. So many news directors begging for an interview. I'd have to play this carefully. I didn't want to sell the story to some sleazy outlet just because they offered a fortune, but then, I couldn't afford the luxury of selling cheap, either. This was the business I was in, and I had so many staff members' mouths to feed, not to mention a career to resuscitate. Over and over.

"Do you like candles?" asked the girl.

"I love candles," I said seriously. "Who doesn't?" I followed her to another table that held an assortment of fragrance items.

"Have you seen these? Juicy Couture Home Fragrance Rocks."

"Ahh," I said, sniffing the amber rocks. "What's that scent?"

She read from the label, "Watermelon, Mandarin, Pink Passion Fruit, Marigold, Green Apple, Water Hyacinth, Crushed Leaves, Tuberose Absolute, Wild Rose, Princess Lily, Caramel Crème Brûlée, Vanilla, Precious Woods, and Patchouli."

"I never get enough patchouli."

"Let me get you six sets. You can use them in any room in the house."

Oh, the good times I'd missed in all the years I'd been excluded from this party. But who was I fooling? They didn't roll out this many goodies for just any guest.

"What's your name?" I asked my hostess.

"Heather. Heather Donaldson."

"Heather. Pretty name. Tell me, Heather, how many of these blue wristbands were given out tonight?"

"Oh, not many, Ms. Taylor. Really, you are only the third superguest I've served all evening."

"Only three?"

"Well, there were other hostesses on duty tonight. But I've only served two others besides you. And they were both nominees."

"Oscar nominees?" I was impressed. How badly did *Vanity Fair* want my exclusive story?

"Yes. And not just any nominees, like documentary filmmakers or soundmen. Actresses."

"Wow. So tell me, what sort of merchandise did they take? Candles?" I looked down at the table in front of me. "Icepods?" While I was there, I picked up several of the crystal-encrusted iPod cases.

She shook her head and giggled. "Follow me."

She led me over to the side of the tent

where an open hallway was barred by a blue velvet rope, then opened the passage to let me through. In this special side room, I soon discovered, the real prizes of the evening were stashed.

"You must take the seventy-inch Sony HDTV flat panel," she offered. "It's their newest Bravia."

"Plasma?" I breathed. I knew little about technology, but this one looked insanely expensive.

"No. Something newer and better. But I'm afraid there is a limit of one."

I smiled. That one was going home with me.

I opened a leather portfolio that held pictures of a luxurious weeklong trip for six at a five-star resort in Portugal. My eyes widened. "Tell me, will Angelina and Brad be vacationing here too?" I asked, tempted to grab the vacation paperwork and run. "Because with all those kids, it could be a nightmare if you got the room next door."

Heather giggled. "No, Ms. Taylor. You'll be safe from their kids. Brad and Angelina don't go gifting." She sighed. "But Uma is planning to go."

What fun! Comparing tan lines with a body like that. I put the portfolio down. Then picked it up again. Why wouldn't this be the ideal place to send Drew if I needed to get her out of town fast? I plunked it into my overstuffed Prada tote.

"Here, let me," Heather offered, and took the heavy bag.

"I'll just browse, if you don't mind?" I asked, riffling through a variety of items that ranged from a pair of $1,000 Black Diamond Havaianas flip-flops to a $5,800 certificate for free LASIK eye surgery.

"Want them all?" asked my coconspirator. Who could resist? She stacked one of everything into my tote and started filling a fresh one.

I loved to share the wealth, gifting down my giveaways to all my closest friends. I counted in my mind who would get what, and the list was long. I came to the Glam-TV crew and figured I could easily give the jeweled flip-flops to my cameraman, Danny. If they were too much for him, his wife would love them. Then I thought about Cindy Chow. What to do?

Cindy had bobbled one too many gets tonight. I loved her, but her clumsy handling of several stars might make the difference in our losing the show next year. What sort of gift do you give to a woman who may just have loused up your career?

"What's on that table?" I asked Heather, pointing to the back corner.

"Oh, nothing good," she said, waving her hand dismissively. "Shower Soother pellets from SudaCare and a Tide stain-remover pen." She giggled.

"I'll take them," I said, finding it a fitting reward for the girl who let George Clooney get away. Next year, I can guarantee she won't be so careless.

"What about the real stuff, the jewels?" I asked.

"We can't give them out," Heather said, crestfallen. "I mean, the jewelers have made their own arrangements with certain stars. Sorry."

The young ones, I figured.

"But I can show you the Best Actress undies," she offered, dimpling.

"What do you mean?"

"Victoria's Secret is a sponsor. And each year they design a special custom bra for the Best Actress nominees."

My ears pricked up. In the dizzying world of freebies, I found myself suddenly sober. "A bra? Is it black?"

"Uh-huh. But that's not all. It's worth a smoking twenty thousand dollars."

"For a brassiere?" I'd maybe pay that much for the right boobs, but for a piece of fabric and baling wire?

"Yes! It's really stunning, and I actually have one here if you'd like a peek."

I stood there, suddenly sure I would soon be shown the exact same bra that Halsey had been wearing. I mean, why else would Halsey have shown up to the Oscars in just a bra and panties if she didn't think the special gift had been some sort of required uniform.

Heather pulled a cord, and a little hot-pink velvet curtain in the corner opened. Behind the curtain was a white wire mannequin. And on the form was the exact same black, satin, strapless bra I'd seen Halsey Hamilton wearing on the red carpet.

There was only one difference: the bra that Halsey had been wearing was sleek and unadorned.

"Isn't it a knockout?" Heather marveled. "Can you imagine Dame Judi Dench wearing one of these?"

The Victoria's Secret Best Actress bra displayed in front of me had something Halsey's garment didn't. It was covered in dozens of tiny, perfectly cut diamonds—$20,000 worth of them.

Man. Could Burke Norris *be* any guiltier?

8

Best Location

The Hotel Bel-Air, with its luxurious fifty-two rooms and thirty-nine elegant suites, each having a private garden entrance, is nestled along Stone Canyon Road in the plush hills of L.A.'s Westside—the money side—and is popular with the Hollywood elite looking for the perfect hideaway.

The hotel didn't start its life, however, quite so friendly to we entertainment folk. Its history reaches back to 1922, when Alphonzo Bell acquired more than six hundred acres, named it Bel-Air, and enhanced the upscale neighborhood-in-the-making with new roads, utilities, a country club, and lush vegetation. In 1946, a hotel entrepreneur from Texas purchased eighteen acres, including the Bel-Air Stables, and built a resort, transforming the grounds into beautiful gardens, adding Swan Lake, and building a sparkling pool in the exact spot of the old stable's riding ring. Alas, back in celebrity-fearing 1946, the hotel began its fabled history by blackballing movie people. But that was then, and this is now. Today, you couldn't hoist a cosmo from your lounge chair around the Bel-Air's famous oval swimming pool without spilling a few drops on an A-lister's chiseled torso. Over time, the hotel had become accustomed to our scandalous behavior and also our useful habit of getting the studio to pay for all damages in full.

Here, among the Hotel Bel-Air's leafy eighteen acres, Hollywood rumors have swirled. Supposedly Marilyn Monroe spent a lot of time hopping between rooms 133 and 33. Here, legend had it, Lauren Bacall flooded the hotel during a long-ago Academy Awards weekend. And here, the most discreet concierges in the world can rustle up anything you need, such as an entire wedding, at a moment's notice—witness the seventeen-minute ceremony they instantly produced for Ronald Reagan's daughter, Patti, and her yoga instructor. I figure if a hotel can get you laid, clean up your mess, or get you married, it's got my business.

When I'm not home at my apartment in Manhattan, here is where I stay. Among the ninety-one perfectly decorated guest rooms scattered across the manicured grounds, my preferred accommodation is their lovely Herb Garden Suite, so named because it looks down upon the hotel's charming eight-thousand-square-foot herb garden. With a full bedroom for me, plus an adorable extra side room, I'm able to keep Malulu and Killer with me at all times. And the kitchen, living room, dining room, and two baths also come in handy. I love everything about this suite—*my* suite— and it is always a little tricky to get the darling management to make sure it's free when I roll into town on a job. For Academy Awards weekend, it's murder. I practically had to arm wrestle Will Smith to the floor this year to keep my reservation.

By 10 a.m., Monday, my head had yet to touch the pillow, and I walked into my own private 1,650 square feet of bliss at the Bel-Air, wobbling ever so slightly from thirty-six straight hours of smiling. Killer rushed up to me, looking as if he would love to jump up, but at that point one more ounce of push might have toppled me over.

"Not now, Killer," I warned, lifting a finger. "Mommy needs a vodka."

"Here you go, Mrs. Livingston," said Malulu, using my real-life name, entering the living room from the direction of the small kitchen. She'd clearly heard Killer's happy yips and now handed me a freshly whirred, bright pink smoothie in a cut-crystal highball glass.

I looked at it. "Is this what I asked for?"

"Of course not, Mrs.," she said, beaming. "Good juice. Fresh. All healthy with fiber."

I glowered at her in her cheery rose-colored pantsuit. "There's a lot of nice stuff over there in those goody bags for you," I growled, waving to the several totes I'd dropped at the front door. "But when they deliver the Sony, hands off. That baby is mine."

Immediately after leaving the *Vanity Fair* swag lounge loaded with gifts, I went back to work and continued on my traditional

Oscar-night whirl of appearances. This one event offered me, as the big night's fashion commentator, dozens of network gigs, and they came with their much needed appearance fees. At two thirty in the morning, I had to zoom across town to make it to the local FOX and CBS stations. Allie, my makeup stylist, was already there to freshen up the dead, but during the night she'd lost track of Unja, and as the minutes ticked by, he never made it to the station. I always have Allie keep a wig around for just such an eventuality, and, in less than six minutes, we had added enough lip gloss, blush, and hairspray to fend off reality for at least another hour or two.

For the next forty minutes, I helped edit our Oscar-arrivals fashion footage, pointing out where to highlight the wows and the bowwows, then I slipped out of my glamour gown, changed into a pewter knit top and classic black slacks, turned my borrowed jewels over to the bondsman who had met me at the studio to retrieve the valuables, cleared my voice, and from 4 to 6 a.m., gave two dozen down-and-dirty interviews starting with Regis and Kelly, which were broadcast live to the East

Coast so New Yorkers could have all the latest Oscar fashion scoop at breakfast time.

For those earliest interviews, I worked alone, letting Drew stay home and catch a little sleep. She usually did the entire shift with me on Oscar night, with her coming into the editing bay to rewatch the clips with me and argue over who had looked the absolute worst, but then we'd never had a close friend of hers die before, and we'd never had her ex-boyfriend involved in the mess either. Drew had wanted to wait at her house, anxious to get the call back from Sol Epstein, and I only prayed she got a little sleep and had no bad dreams.

The live interviews went well enough. I always make sure each one is different— talking about different stars. Everyone loves to see the beauties and the beasts dressed and bejeweled. But this time, all I did was spend the next few hours fending off the two questions everyone had to ask: "What happened to Halsey Hamilton?" and "What were her last words?"

"For that," I told my various audiences all night and all morning long in a conspiratorial whisper, "you'll have to watch our prime-time special." Of course I was bluffing. We had yet to make any such deal. But I thought I should put the idea out there. Why not dream big? "But for right now," I would always conclude, knowing exactly how to let down the hopeful on-air hosts and put a stop to their probing questions in just the nicest way, "we have too much sympathy for the family to say any more."

At seven o'clock, Drew, looking no more rested than I did, met me at ABC-TV as we were leaving their Burbank studio. We rushed over to do the live feed for NBC, and still we were not done with our work as we spent an hour doing live radio interviews. Finally, Drew and I were driven over to Glendale to finish up at Glam-TV's studio, changing again into new outfits to do the chatty mom-and-daughter commentary for our one-hour *Oscar Fashion Disasters* special set to air later in the evening.

The word came down at Glam that everybody had loved our red carpet show. Loved it. The best show ever. And if I could tell you how many times I'd heard those very words just hours before getting the call saying my show was being canceled, I might have smiled a little brighter at the compliments. Instead, I questioned everyone I saw, "But why did they cut away from our interview with Halsey? Answer me that?"

And no one could understand, from the studio wardrobe man to the vice president of programming, why our young director, Will Beckerman, hadn't at the very least let the cameras roll and tape the footage instead of just bloody pulling the plug. Asshole.

By the time our unruffled driver, Jeffrey, returned Drew to her house and me to the Hotel Bel-Air, I was just getting my fifth wind.

"Good?" Malulu asked, as I held on to the evil pink concoction she'd handed me without so much as taking one sip.

Okay. I tried it. That's what guilt can do to me. "What's your secret ingredient? Sardines? Peanuts?"

"You go to sleep now, Mrs. L?" she asked, bustling to pick up all the things I'd dropped when I'd entered.

"No. Too much to do. You have my messages?"

"I do. But you sure you . . ."

I sank down on one of the pair of flower-upholstered bergère chairs, one with a straight back, and held out my hand. How could I rest when the world was calling?

As Killer softly jumped into my lap and settled himself gently, and Malulu brought over my BlackBerry, I checked out a thick handful of messages. The personal calls were many. Ian had called twice, and I knew he'd want to hear I was home safe and sound. I tapped out a quick e-mail to him and signed it with my usual row of *xoxoxox*.

Several friends were on the prowl for gossip, but I only took the time to call back Dr. Bob, who seemed most interested in the specific details of Halsey's collapse, but whether from a medical standpoint or that of just another shocked avid fan, I couldn't quite tell. Halsey's flawless youth had held a hint of fragility, a combination that kept most of the world spellbound. Even those of us who knew her and her troubles felt the pull of her talent and beauty.

"I remember seeing her around my house," I told Dr. Bob, "when she was only twelve or thirteen."

"Oh, Max. That's right. She used to tag around after Drew, didn't she?"

"I'd look at that gorgeous kid, and I worried that her parents would need to keep a careful rein on that girl. Only twelve, and she had more cleavage than I did."

"But I fixed that."

"Those parents," I said, ignoring Dr. Bob. "When Halsey was only twelve, they had her starring in pictures with much older boys. I think she began dating that Alberto character back then, and he must have been twenty-two at the time. Now you tell me what a twenty-two-year-old man wants to do with a twelve-year-old."

"It's tragic," Dr. Bob agreed. "Who's looking after you, Max? This has got to be hitting you hard."

"I'm fine," I said, just as Malulu entered the room with a fresh stack of messages.

"You need time to process all of this."

Dr. Bob was probably right. We made plans to meet for dinner later, after I'd had time to rest, and I rang off to get through my growing pile of messages and the newly arrived e-mails Malulu had just printed for me.

I put aside the numerous well-wishes from my fans and friends over another in-the-can red carpet show and put into a separate pile the news-biz hysteria over Halsey's death, then read all the way through a most unexpected e-mail from the president of a popular home-shopping channel, a man I'd been begging to meet for a year. He was suddenly anxious to discuss with me my proposal for a line of jewelry I'd wanted to design. How wonderful! I told Malulu to forward that one to my attorney and business managers; then I eyed the rest.

"Mrs. L," Malulu said, "the phones are crazy today. Please." She waved at my pile of messages. "Some of these people call you back three times."

The fan mail and friends would have to wait, it seemed, because every news or entertainment outlet in existence had found me and was begging for me to give them an exclusive on the real story of this year's Academy Awards—my last words with Halsey. As the early twenty-first century would have it, an infinite number of cameras had been trained on the poor young thing last night as she collapsed on the red carpet and brought me down with her. But that, apparently, had only whetted the world's appetite. From the thousand cell phone digital recorders in the hands of gaping fans in the grandstands to the extreme zoom lenses of the international press corps, so many people present at the Oscar arrivals had some angle on that sad drama. But with Halsey slurring and whispering only to me, not a one of them had been able to record a sound.

I was the only one on the planet who knew what Halsey had had to say.

How unfortunate that Halsey had merely talked in wasted riddles and ramblings, and, really, how disturbing that the only phrases that seemed to make sense mentioned my own daughter, Drew, and the infamous nickname of Drew's Burke, whom many in their young crowd called Wyatt Burp. I considered the impact of the story on a parched media if I told those details now. How quickly it would ravage Burke's reputation. Even if he had somehow miraculously been blameless in the events that had brought down Halsey, his name would forever be mixed up in the scandal. I toyed with that tantalizing thought: finally, Burke Norris would be made accountable for his worthless soul. And then I sobered up. Even if an outraged but silent mother might be drawn to the idea of making such a loathsome idiot suffer for all his past sins, how quickly would such a story gather fury and, in its terrible wake, blast my own darling Drew and her good blameless name, possibly forever?

I could hear the suite's two phones ringing incessantly in the background, Malulu's patient Samoan lilt taking names and numbers from some relentless reporters, such as Devon Jones, for the fourth time that morning. There was a huge story here. Everyone from Barbara Walters to perezhilton.com was after the truth, and I was the only one on earth who had it. And I, such a staunch advocate of the truth, would take a few hours longer, at least, to gather my wits and decide just how best the truth would have to be spun.

An hour later, with Malulu's help, I'd worked through 179 messages, deflecting requests from news agencies from as far away as Tasmania (where they loved their celebrity gossip) to the little local paper in Manhattan Beach (ditto). This is not the right time to speak about dear Halsey, I texted, e-mailed, and said in a sotto voce rasp, sadly. Perhaps later. No matter how rabid the dogs of the media could get when they were hot after a story, I could handle mad dogs. I calmly wrapped myself in a cloak of dignified silence. I was sweet. I was respectful. I said, "No." They had never heard of anything like it. All of them calculated the cost of the story upward.

"Fun," I said to Malulu as I disconnected with the president of CNN-TV.

The doorbell rang, and Malulu ushered in the fourth flower arrangement of the morning, all red roses and white hydrangeas. "Larry King," Malulu read from the card as she bent over to place the huge vase on the floor next to the fireplace.

"He's a smart one," I noted, admiring how the red roses complimented the deep-red velvet love seat in the living room. "His producer had researched the color scheme of my suite. I love him dearly, but here we are sitting on a million-dollar story, and I can't give away Halsey's last words for a measly plant?"

"It's da thought dat counts," Malulu advised me, not getting my joke. Again.

The doorbell chimed once more, and Malulu rose to answer it. Instead of more sweet-scented bribes, my lovely daughter floated through the door. Killer stood up on my lap and wagged his tail.

"Drew, I thought you were going to go home and lie down."

"I tried." She threw herself into the deep down cushions of the cherry-red love seat. She had changed out of her early-morning on-camera dress into a pair of jeans and a thin white sweater. "But how could I sleep?"

"I know what you mean, I'm too amped. And it's not just the Oscars." Again, one of the suite's two phones rang softly in the background. I pointed. "People don't stop calling."

Drew nodded. "Same at my house. I tried to turn my phone off, but then I was waiting to hear from Sol Epstein. He finally called me half an hour ago."

"He did?" I looked up.

"The good news is, he said he'll work with Burke."

"He's a smart lawyer. Good."

Drew still looked strained. "For *now*. That's all Mr. Epstein would commit to."

"Okay. That's something." I always try to stay upbeat. As the kids say, why be a hater? Even though in this case, I had every reason. But I was getting sleepy, and that makes me forgiving.

Drew shook her head. "And then I kept getting calls from Burke. He wants to know if I sold the diamonds. Mr. Epstein needs a retainer check. Ten thousand dollars. Today."

I had just been drifting off for a second. Not napping, but not fully charged. That last comment snapped me back like a triple espresso. If Burke had somehow contributed to the death of Halsey, even if Sol Epstein could prove it had been an accident, Burke certainly wouldn't be able to claim he just accidentally walked off with thousands of dollars' worth of Halsey's diamonds. How had he come to take them? Had she paid him for drugs using her bra jewels? Had he been tempted by all that flash and easy money and somehow simply ripped them off? No matter, when the police found out Burke took the diamonds, he would be in a new world of trouble, and when they learned he gave the Victoria's Secret diamonds to Drew after Halsey's death, and that Drew ran out and sold them for cash . . . My head spun. Would that make my Drew an accessory to something really awful after the fact?

"No!" I said, then stopped and calmed my voice. "Don't worry about all that fuss just yet. Let's stay calm, honey."

"But Burke's defense?" she said, almost near tears. And this is a young lady that doesn't cry.

"It's only money, sweetie." Let me tell you, that's not an easy line to deliver and make believable. But I did it. "Why do you think we work so hard? I'll pay Sol's retainer. Leave it to Mama."

Drew sat up, alert. "You will? Oh, Mom. That's amazing. I mean, what was I going to do, anyway? I had no idea how I was supposed to sell fifty loose diamonds. I mean, you can't just list them on eBay, can you?"

Just then Malulu waved a phone receiver at me in her sweet Samoan way. "Mrs. L."

It wasn't like her to interrupt. "Not now, Malulu. Take a message. I can't talk to anyone."

"On the phone," Malulu said, her voice now a pitch so low I don't think I'd ever heard her use it before. "It's the police."

Drew's eyes grew wide.

Malulu was fiercely loyal to me, but she was a stickler for rules and the constabulary. She had her work visa laminated and was known to whip it out and show it to meter maids on Rodeo Drive. In fact, she was ridiculously impressed with anyone wearing a uniform. Honestly, I once wore a nurse's costume in a skit and she began treating me with new respect. In New York, I had to ask her to stop inviting Boy Scouts up to the apartment. Now, with a policeman on the phone, I could see her loyalty was becoming strained. No one wants a Samoan woman who knows Limalama karate to feel the pains of cognitive dissonance, believe me.

"Mom," Drew said, her eyes darting. "No. What if they're looking for Burke?"

I waved at Malulu to hang up the phone. Killer, who had been dozing in my lap, stood up and began to growl.

"But, Mrs.," Malulu said, faltering, her Samoan accent getting stronger as she faced her own dilemma, "what can I say to the mon? He the police!"

"Tell him Mrs. Livingston has had a very long night of work, and I'm resting now. Cannot be disturbed. But I'll call him . . . you know the rest." Really, I had to think of just about everything for everyone or the whole world seemed to fall apart.

Malulu shook her head and muttered to herself, and I took this as an omen that in order not to make a liar out of my Samoan bodyguard, I had better go straight to bed.

"Drew, I can't stay up one second longer. Would you like to stay here and curl up on the sofa?"

Malulu made whooshing gestures, aiming toward the bedroom, and I followed her general whoosh.

"Can I come with you?" Drew asked.

My daughter was usually the cool one, a sophisticate, a graduate of a top Ivy League college. But for once, she seemed to want to stay close to her mother. I was thrilled.

We both climbed up onto the giant bed

in my bedroom, made quite a show of both turning off our cell phones, and then, fully clothed, crawled under the cool Italian linens.

I watched as my daughter closed her eyes, then I laid my cheek on my own smooth pillowcase. "Drew," I said, enjoying the unexpected closeness of our makeshift sleepover, "everything will turn out fine. Now the only mystery I have yet to solve is where"—I yawned in a dainty way—"the hell is Unja."

"What did you say?"

I continued dreamily, "Unja. Isn't it funny that the only man with Halsey's collapse on-camera from our own best vantage point has sort of disappeared?"

The bed jostled, and I opened my eyes. Drew was sitting straight up. "Do you think Unja's tape could somehow help Burke? I mean, Burke keeps calling me, Mom. He's afraid that any second now the police may want to question him. And he's frantic. A man like Burke is sensitive. He'll lose it in jail."

"You never know," I said, starting to drift off. "Paris hung in there for almost a month."

"Burke will not be able to cope. If the police find him before we can somehow clear his name, I'm not sure what he might do. At least they don't know where he is staying right now, thank God. That's the good thing."

"Umm," I mumbled, drifting off into a much deserved siesta when a light tapping was heard at the bedroom door. I felt a slight shift as Killer stood up in bed. A door opened almost noiselessly in my dream.

Drew whispered, trying not to disturb me, "Shh, Mom's sleeping, Malulu."

"Sorry to bother you, Miss L," Malulu whispered to Drew. "It's the police, Miss. On the phone. They ask to talk to Mrs. L, and I say she resting. They ask to talk to you, miss, but I say you resting."

"Very good, Malulu. Thank you," Drew said, relief in her voice.

I tried not to snore.

"But when they ask me where Mr. Burke is, I just say I don't know."

"Of course you don't," said Drew as I almost but not entirely snoozed off.

"I just tell them," said Malulu proudly, "they should go check over at your house,

Miss L. I told the detective check and see if Mr. Burke is over there."

"Mother!"

"Was that not a good thing?" asked Malulu in her stage whisper. "That mon, he is the police!"

"Mother!"

I opened one eye. Naptime was definitely over.

9

Best Plot

Somehow I managed to steal a few hours of sleep that day from the deepening dread that surrounded Halsey's demise, but only a few. Drew, of course, flew out of my suite so fast her size-2 butt was a blur of dark-rinse blue denim. She couldn't get back home soon enough.

We both knew why she was in such a blind hurry but didn't say it out loud. A mother must have some sort of boundaries with her adult child.

When it came to quasi-criminal-aiding-and-abetting behavior, I guess we both instinctively recognized a line that shouldn't be crossed.

I don't want to know what sort of feverish calls were being made to alert America's newly Most Wanted that the jig was up: Malulu had sent the heat straight to Drew's little crime hideaway in Beverly Hills. If I couldn't stop my dear deluded daughter from rushing to the bum's rescue, then, frankly, the less I knew about any of that, the better. If you can't stop a child from risky behavior, my advice, dear parents, is, avert your eyes.

Before she ran out, Drew begged, "Mom, promise me we'll help Burke. We'll be able to clear up any stupid misunderstandings. You know, stop the insanity." She stepped into her spiky, patent leather Audley of London heels. "Things will be all right. Promise me."

"Of course," I croaked, still half-asleep.

"You're exhausted, Mom," she said, stopping for just a minute to assess.

"No, no. I'm fine." I think my eyes may have been stuck shut as I said this, but she chose not to notice. We agreed to meet at ten that night after my dinner with Dr. Bob, then she sped away.

At seven, somewhat rested, showered, and freshly dressed, and feeling a lot more like a real human being than I had in the previous twenty-four hours, I opened the door to my suite.

Dr. Bob, compact, tanned, and natty in a cream-colored suit with an open-neck shirt, stood in the doorway holding a golden Ballotin of Godiva. I suspect he brings me chocolates in the optimistic hope there will be a liposuction in my future, but I am too gracious to point this out.

"Chocolates!" I would be handing these straight to Malulu in the morning.

"Thirty-six piece." The large assortment. He had spared no expense. "For healing your poor psychic wounds," Dr. Bob said, concern in his voice, as he entered the suite.

"Sheree will not be joining us tonight?" I inquired of his wife, who had been the benefactress of so many of Dr. Bob's little ministrations. She was drop-dead gorgeous but always had a little bandage on her somewhere.

"Just recovering from a touch of work," he said apologetically. "She would have loved to join us, but . . ." He turned and faced my living room. "Wow. Look at the flowers."

"That topiary clipped in the shape of a rhinoceros is from Oprah," I said.

"Impressive." Dr. Bob smoothed one hand over his tanned bald head and gave me a gleaming-white smile. "They all want you, Max."

"Yes. Sure. Did they *all* send flowers and potted rain-forest creatures last year? No, they want the story."

"Same thing," he said nonchalantly. In Hollywood, it was hard to tell the difference.

Dr. Bob and I met ten years ago when I needed a little work done. By *work,* I hope you understand I mean "enhancement." And by *enhancement,* I hope you realize I'm talking plastic surgery. It began as a professional consultation: me, the thirty-nine-year-old comedienne ready to begin yet another new phase of my career, this time interviewing celebrities on the red carpet at that long-ago Academy Awards show; Dr. Bob, the same age as me exactly, with a reputation for being the best cosmetic surgeon in Beverly Hills. Only, none of his big-star clients would ever acknowledge they knew him, let alone that they had begged him to lift their sagging derrieres and inflate their deflated bosoms. It seemed I, alone, was the one big name willing to go out in public with my friend Dr. Bob.

Why not? Everyone on earth had seen all of us celebs "before," so who does anyone think they're fooling? Look, some of us may not be the biggest beauties out there, but we do have to look presentable. It goes with the profession. A little nip. A little Botox. A little body contouring, arm-lift, breast augmentation, nose job, and full rhytidectomy. Whatever. Sometimes it's called for, so get a grip. Everyone knows what goes on behind closed surgical-suite doors. So what's the big secret?

I love the work I've had done. And I love Dr. Bob's company. He knows all the same people I know, likes all the same restaurants, on all the same continents, and he never patronizes me with courtesy laughs. That's a true friend.

"Well, you must know the story about Halsey's death is all we're getting on the news today. Who even cares what won Best Picture? And there is all this pirate video of Halsey lying down on the red carpet with you."

I had not had a chance to watch the news all day. "How did I look?"

"Amazing. Lying down actually draws the skin of the face backward, allowing gravity to give you a lift, did you know that? Makes us all look so much better in bed."

At least those of us on the bottom. I tucked away that bit of advice.

"But, Max, it will be a frenzy of reporters tonight. Do you want to call room service? You know, eat in? Lie low? Keep away from the press?"

I looked at him as if he were demented. "I am wearing all my best jewelry to stay inside my hotel room? I don't think so."

We took Dr. Bob's Jaguar and had our usual fight over where to eat. He offered Mr. Chow's for Chinese, but I just gave him a look. Everyone knows Mr. Chow's is the favorite haunt of Hollywood's oldest stars, accent on the *old.* It's not that I object to Dr. Bob trolling for new clients over a meal, no matter how much he protests he is not looking for sagging jaws among the tables, it's that I hate the thought that someone might for even a second get the mistaken impression that *I* fit the age profile of the typical patron.

Dr. Bob then suggested the Ivy, which is, of course, fabulous for lunch, but otherwise, why bother?

I said, "Let's just go to the Grill," by which I meant the Grill on the Alley. Not that you could actually find a Dumpster or a bum hanging around the Grill, but it is an alley of metaphoric significance, since it occupies some stratospherically high-rent real estate on a Beverly Hills passageway tucked away behind Rodeo Drive where all the biggest agents in town go "slumming" on their endless expense accounts.

"Perfect," said Dr. Bob, steering his Jag down Stone Canyon Road.

We settled into a dark leather booth in the clubby interior, fielding comments from the hostess and one of the patrons, who each told me how much they would miss Halsey and offered their support. This is how nice the public is to me most of the time.

It was a joy to be out and about. I noticed the dinner crowd was fairly light on this Monday night, then I got a call from

Drew, and we agreed to meet back at my suite in a few hours.

Dr. Bob ordered a Marked Man, a cocktail of Maker's Mark bourbon and sweet vermouth, for himself, and a blood-orange martini for me. When I began to protest, he shushed me. "Think of the vitamin C, Max."

"But—"

"Medicinal purposes."

How can you argue with your doctor?

We had a great, long dinner, Dr. Bob starting with the half-cracked Dungeness Crab and I with the Endive, Spicy Pecans, and Romaine with Gorgonzola Salad, which I insisted they bring only half of an appetizer size and still couldn't finish. We moved on to our main courses: for me the charbroiled Lake Superior Whitefish, which was really cooked to perfection; while Dr. Bob talked about his planned move to vegetarianism in the near future, then ordered the House Special Prime Filet (bone in), medium rare. As I unwinded with my second blood-orange martini, we caught up on events big and small since the last time I was in town, including what I was going to do about this latest mess with Drew reat-

taching herself to Burke, and were interrupted only once, by an agent I used to
know at CAA, a charming shark who
seemed surprisingly interested in what I
was doing these days.

"What will you do about this Burke situation?" Dr. Bob asked, as we sat back
and read the dessert menu as if it were
porn.

"That's the question, isn't it?"

"You can't tell Drew you mistrust him."

"Of course I can't. She'll hate me."

"Sad but true. Kids." Dr. Bob had nine-
year-old twins and could relate only up to
a certain level. When the time comes for
him to try to get them into the Harvard-
Westlake School with their one measly C+
in pre-algebra, and he has to go begging
on hand and knee, then he'll start to get
the true picture. When they both decide
they want to become snowboard instruc-
tors in Aspen for a few years instead of
going to college, then he'll really begin to
understand.

I continued, "If I'm right about Burke's
involvement with Halsey . . ."

"And I know you've got him pegged,
Max."

"Drew will never forgive me for being right."

We agreed: I couldn't tell Drew how I really felt, if only to keep peace with my headstrong girl until she could see for herself the incredible depth of the shallowness of Burke Norris.

In frustration, I read about all the delicious desserts I would not be ordering: the New York Cheesecake, the Rice Pudding, the Double Chocolate Layer Cake. All those capital letters. All those calories.

I ordered hot tea with hopes the caffeine might begin to counteract all the Grey Goose vodka that was buzzing around my brain. Dr. Bob had coffee, black. I absentmindedly added two pink packets of Sweet'n Low to my teacup and stirred.

"Ms. Taylor," said the hostess, now at our booth, looking apologetic. "Just a word of caution. We understand there are two photographers outside the entrance. I believe they must have been tipped off that you are dining here tonight. I am so sorry."

I instantly brightened. After all, I was wearing my new Armani skirt, and my hair had turned out rather well.

"I'm shocked!" I responded in a disgusted rasp. "Who would do such a thing?"

"With all the cell phones," she whispered, making a small gesture toward the dining room at large. "And you are such a big star . . ."

"Say no more," I said, taking a look around the room. It was true, many of the guests were quickly averting their eyes, startled to see I was looking their way.

The hostess moved off, and Dr. Bob asked, concerned, "Do you want to leave by the side entrance?"

I stared at him as if he'd lost his mind. "As if!"

Just then, making a small commotion, the calm at the entrance of the Grill was broken as the door opened. Punctuated with the flash of bulbs outside, my own darling Drew hurried in. As her eyes became accustomed to the dim lighting, she spotted the booth at which we were sitting and came over to join us.

I emptied a pink packet of Sweet'n Low into my teacup and stirred, worrying a bit at how thin Drew looked and how tired. Normally thin was a good thing, but without any rest, even a twentysomething such as Drew could begin to look drawn.

"Honey," I said, moving over in the booth to give her room to sit down. "You look frightening."

"Hello, Mother. Hi, Dr. Bob."

"And here you are, you joined us," I said, surprised. "I thought we said—"

"I just couldn't sit still any longer. Everything is closing in on us."

"Us?" I put the teacup down.

"Well, not me. Burke. He's a wreck. I ran back home this morning and told him he simply had to leave right that minute. Until we figure this whole mess out, he has to lie low. Then thirty minutes later, the cops came to my door."

I clutched my napkin. "Did you lie to the police?"

"What else could I do? Burke needed time to hide somewhere else. I told them that he and I had broken up almost nine weeks ago."

Good. That was the truth.

Drew continued, "And that as far as I knew, he'd left town and gone to Alaska."

That one, I'm not so sure they bought.

"So," I said, putting the ugly cards on the table, "they want to arrest him?"

Drew was speaking fast. "They didn't tell me that. Honestly, I don't know exactly what is so terrible. Burke didn't do anything wrong, but it seems Halsey owed him some money so maybe the police heard about that."

I sat up straight in the booth, stirring a packet of sweetener into my tea with a heavy silver spoon. "Now this is news. Halsey *did* know Burke, you say?"

"Yes. I guess. It's no big deal. So they did know each other—or, *knew* each other—but not very well. Anyway, Burke is frantic because he went to see her in rehab one lousy time, and now maybe the police might connect him to Halsey's troubles."

Of course any rational human being would, at this point, scream the question, why in all hell would the police suspect some nice innocent person of a heinous crime against an acquaintance just because of one friendly visit? It simply didn't make sense. Something much bigger and much worse must be up, even if Drew didn't see it. Maybe they had found out about the old affair. The diamonds. Halsey's drugged-out behavior right before her death. I, however, kept my mouth shut.

Drew took my hand. "You don't really suspect Burke could do something terrible, do you, Mom? I know you have issues with any guy I date. That comes with the territory. You're so protective."

"I will not apologize for wanting to make sure you're safe," I said mildly, sipping tea.

"But you don't think Burke could do something criminal, do you?"

That was the question.

Dr. Bob looked at me and sent me the sort of ESP message that could only come from a good friend who spends his career making people look better than they should: lie.

"I absolutely hope *not*!" I said. It seemed to be enough to settle Drew down.

"Here's the plan. We have to go to that rehab center," Drew said, filled with productive energy. "They must be open twenty-four hours, right? I mean, what if people want to check themselves in during the middle of the night? We can go right now, Mom."

I stared at her and gave my head a little jerk.

She turned anxiously to Dr. Bob. "Oh, sorry. What am I saying? I mean, when you two are done with your coffee." She turned back to me. "Okay?"

"Drew, it is not okay to go barging into East Kishniff in the middle—"

"It's only Pasadena," she interrupted.

"Okay, we can't go all the way out to Pasadena at ten thirty on a Monday night and expect to find anyone there who can answer our questions."

"Of course we can." Drew turned to Dr. Bob. "Can't we? Aren't they like hospitals, Dr. Bob? Open twenty-four/seven?"

"Not my specific area," he said mildly. "But I have so many clients who have been through it all. Would you like me to make a few calls?"

"Would you?" Drew asked.

I watched my dear friend pull out his cell and join in the madness, then I turned back to Drew, asking her seriously, "And what, darling, are we trying to find out from this rehab facility at this time of night? Do you think they'll be willing to talk to us?"

That seemed to stop Drew. "No. That's true. I've been watching *TMZ* all day long, and even Harvey Levin hasn't been able to get anyone at Wonders to talk."

"Of course not. This type of publicity could kill them. Beautiful, famous patient leaves their care and is seen, soon after, completely blitzed and then . . ." I didn't want to finish that thought and spell out Halsey's sad ending, even to make a good point, so I just went on, "Some 'wonder'! Not good brand recognition. No one there will talk to the press, you can bet on it."

"And to them, we're the press," moaned Drew, grabbing my cup of tea and taking a distracted sip. "Eww!" she sputtered. "Mother, really! There have to be like thirty packets of sugar in this tea."

"Sugar! Never. Wash your mouth out with soap. It's Sweet'n Low. No trouble."

She flashed a worried look over my head at Dr. Bob and went back to her original thought. "How can we get in there? How, Mom?"

"Let's get logical. First, why do you have to go there? What do you hope to find out?" I asked, as Dr. Bob speed-dialed through

his preset phone numbers, calling and tex-
ting clients who may have been to Wonders
in the past few years.

Drew held her hands out, setting the
scene. "We start with the knowledge that
Burke is telling the truth. He had nothing to
do with Halsey and her troubles. So we
should talk to anyone at Wonders who
could have seen her visitors coming or going."

"Sounds good," said Dr. Bob, like one of
the Scooby-Doo gang right before they enter the spooky carnival fun-house at night.

"Right," Drew went on. "They would
know that Burke had only shown up there
that once, like he said. And they might
know what other regular-type visitors
Halsey had while she stayed there. If anyone is going down for hurting Halsey, we
can at least get an idea of who the cops
should really be talking to. What do you
think? Maybe a talkative patient in an ad-
joining room?"

Oh, right. Like that person should be
easy for us to get to, seeing as private rehab patients at superelite facilities such
as Wonders are held in such strict secrecy
that I half-suspected Osama bin Laden

had been hiding out at Betty Ford all these years.

"Any roommate or neighbor patient of Halsey's would probably still be at Wonders right now, since she only just left yesterday, right?"

"Good thinking." If we could ever see them.

"Or we could talk to the admitting nurse or whoever signs patients in? Or maybe an orderly?"

"Do they have orderlies these days?" I mused. "Or did that era end after the shock-treatment scene in *One Flew Over the Cuckoo's Nest*?"

"Mother, are you playing with me?" Drew asked, her voice now dipping into that low and dangerous region.

"Of course not. If you want to drive out to Pasadena tonight, let's do it. We can only try."

"Wait up," said Dr. Bob, punching his cell phone to disconnect from his last call. "Not so fast. It seems they do not have open visiting hours at Wonders. Every visit must be coordinated in advance with the staff."

"Figures," I said. We paused in our conversation as the waiter brought over a new pot of tea, and I stirred in a few packets of sweetener.

"But good news for us," Drew said. "That means that Wonders will have records of everybody who visited and when. And those records will prove that Burke had only very, very limited contact with Halsey."

"Yes," I said, not mentioning if that "very, very limited contact" had been just before poor Halsey overdosed and died, it could be enough to put the guy away for a long time. And, come on, why would Burke be so worried about the police if there weren't something damning to be found? I tried to stifle that certainty and keep myself open to all possibilities, for Drew's sake. "However, even if we call and ask for an appointment to meet with the staff of Wonders, what are the chances they will agree to talk to us?"

"I'm afraid almost none," said Dr. Bob.

We both turned to him.

He ran his hand over his tanned scalp and said, "I just talked to a good friend. A patient, actually. Her first husband had a problem with painkillers and spent some time at Wonders, and my friend is still bitter to this day. The doctor who runs the place is someone called Dr. Deiter. He kept my friend away from seeing her husband for two months. She was thinking of getting a court order just to get in and see him on a visiting day or something. And she was the one paying the twelve hundred dollars per day for him to stay in Wonders in the first place."

"They finally let her in to visit?" I asked.

"When her attorney threatened that she would stop paying his bill, they relented. But by then, it was too late. Her husband had fallen in love with the Korean facialist who came by the Wonders spa three days a week, and that was that." Dr. Bob shrugged.

"Rehab," Drew said, realizing, perhaps, that it wasn't going to be quite so easy to flash our way in and sleuth our way around.

"Isn't there some other way to get in?" I asked. The whole point, I figured, was to let Drew see, with her own eyes, what this man Burke Norris was all about. Well, okay. The answer to that could well be waiting at Wonders, where any number of nurses and manicurists and herbalists and therapists may have seen Halsey Hamilton in some wicked embrace with the man Drew insisted on defending. There was really no backing off now. If we were going to do this thing, we'd have to barrel through.

Dr. Bob shook his head. "There is simply no way in, Max, short of a . . ."

"An intervention?"

They looked at me, one appalled and the other enthralled. My doctor. My daughter. And if only I could rustle up an addiction, I was as good as admitted as a patient into that rehab palace called Wonders this very night.

10

Best Performance by a Liar

Drew asked brightly, "Do we need to bring in a professional interventionist?"

"What?" I coughed. "That's crazy talk. I'm not about to fight the idea of going into rehab, am I? No, I'm prepared to go in quietly with my dignity intact."

The waiter brought us more tea and coffee as the dinner crowd thinned out and several after-theater parties strolled into the Grill on the Alley for dessert and a few celebrity sightings. I was noticed. What else is new?

Dr. Bob said, "Drew's right. A professional substance-abuse counselor will know exactly how to get you into Wonders on an emergency basis. We need to call in someone to mastermind this intervention who has the right connections."

"Now, wait a minute," I said.

"Don't worry, Mom. We'll get the best."

I wasn't worried. I just hadn't made up my mind what I should be addicted to, yet.

As Dr. Bob speed-dialed through a few more numbers, I tried some ideas out. "Pain meds?" Truth was, I hated pain medication. I was the first one off the stuff when I had my little procedures, preferring clearheadedness and a couple of Goliath-strength Tylenols to anything more toxic.

Dr. Bob said, "Please don't, Max." A tiny furrow of concern formed on his tanned and lineless face.

He didn't want it thought that any patient of his would be so unwisely looked after that he or she might develop that particular addiction. I could tell he was sensitive in this area, so I gave it no more thought.

"There's always booze," suggested Drew.

"Yes, alcohol," seconded Dr. Bob.

"Now, wait just a second there," I objected. "This is all well and good, faking a little addiction to get the inside scoop at the rehab clinic. But I have to go on for the rest of my life, kittens. If it should ever leak out that I had trouble with booze, and I mean *ever* . . . well, people will whisper and poke each other every time I take a sip of wine in public for the rest of my days."

"That's true," agreed Drew, and she said to Bob with a touch of disappointment, "we can't expect Mom to take that kind of hit."

"Damn," said Dr. Bob, seeing the problem and, multitasking, trying another number on his cell. This time it appeared he'd connected with someone on the other end of an emergency help line. "Oh, hold on," he told us as he made some quick arrangements with the person on the other end. I heard him mention Wonders.

Drew looked at me with a gleam in her eye. Was it admiration? Was it gratitude? Was it just a reflection off the table candle? I'll never know. She said, "Mom, you are completely awesome."

"I know, darling."

"You just rock. I can't tell you . . ."

I don't like a lot of fuss. Really, what was I getting ready to do that any mother wouldn't gladly offer to do for her daughter? No big deal. So I waved off Drew's ridiculous compliments and took a moment to check my BlackBerry to see if I had any urgent messages.

I was startled to read a text from Malulu, sent an hour before, saying I'd missed a call from Dakota Hamilton, Halsey's mother. The woman begged Malulu to contact me. Tonight.

I quickly dialed the number in the message, alarmed at how much pain the poor woman must be in. "Halsey's mom," I explained to Drew as I waited for my call to be answered.

"Hello," came a blowsy female voice after the fifth or sixth ring. "Who is this?"

"Yes, hello. Is this Dakota?"

"Oh, it's you, Max!" Dakota had recognized my voice immediately. "Oh, Max. What has happened to my little girl?"

Now, wasn't that the question of the decade. "Dakota, I'm so sorry for your unimaginable loss. Have they told you anything? The hospital. Did they find out what was wrong?"

"Cedars said it was an overdose, Max. Don't tell anyone else that, please. The emergency-room woman said Halsey had taken too many pills. By the time they brought my baby in, they couldn't save her."

"Oh, how horrible." Would any parent be able to bear that verdict? Especially a parent who hadn't been quite strong enough, all along, in the discipline department?

Dakota Hamilton went on, "But it's a lie. She wasn't doing drugs." Her voice rang out in anger, in its slightly loopy tone, so outraged. "That other doctor told me so, the one at her clinic. Halsey had been clean for months. Really. Clean and sober. I just can't stand all the television people saying she'd been drinking again." Dakota's voice seemed to be slurring a little, so it was hard to be absolutely sure that she herself hadn't been easing the pain with something strong, but I suppose any parent could be excused for using medication to slide herself through such an ungodly nightmare.

"They're not going to do any more . . . tests?" Even I didn't have the heart to use the word *autopsy*. But if the police suspected foul play?

"No, thank God. They pumped my baby's stomach, Max. They took her blood. They found a lot of drugs in her system. But since she had this bad history with pills, Jimmy is doing his best to get it officially listed as an accident. You know, hush things up so no one starts thinking she wanted to kill herself." She sobbed into the phone.

"You poor thing. And the coroner is agreeing?"

"Thank goodness, it's being taken care of, Max. There is no question of the time of death since she died in the hospital. There is no question about what caused her death. It was the damned pills."

"I'm sure no one wants to cause you any more grief." Since the doctors would certainly have checked for needle marks, I assumed none had been found. They had the sort of riddle that couldn't be solved by an autopsy. No medical clue could say why Halsey had overdosed.

"Look," Dakota said, "the reason I'm bothering you so late at night—it's Jimmy. He told me you were the last person to see our little Halsey before she . . . before they took her away in the ambulance."

"Yes."

"And I just couldn't understand what happened to her beautiful dress. Did she tell you anything about that?"

"No, Dakota. I asked her, but she never said a word about why she was so undressed."

"I see," Dakota said in her soft, slow way. "Well, her daddy and me were just wondering that. I mean, I told Jimmy it didn't make any sense. Halsey and I had picked out this one special gown from all the designers who were giving her dresses. At first, she was going to wear a darling peach-colored Elie Saab, but at the last minute some other new designer offered her daddy a lotta money so our precious could wear *his* strapless gown to the Oscars. Best Actress nominees get all the really pretty dresses. You see, I never even got to see the one she chose, Max. Her daddy told me Halsey loved it, though."

So Halsey's manager/father had been working a deal to get a payoff from the designer of Halsey's Oscar gown. It figured. But why had the gown disappeared? Perhaps her limo driver might have an idea.

Had she been dressed when he picked her up? I'd have to find out.

Dakota said with a sigh, "I'm sorry I bothered you so late at night, Max. I just remembered how sweet you always were to our Halsey. How cute she was back in middle school when she used to follow your Drew around. She always wanted to be just like your Drew. I better let you go."

"Give my sympathies to Jimmy."

"Oh, Jimmy isn't here," Dakota said. "Out talking to some men. That's Jimmy. Always doing business. Even on a day like today."

"And how is Steffi holding up?" I asked, thinking of Halsey's little sister, now about the age that Halsey had been back when Drew and I first met her.

"Oh, she's great. Just signed on to do her first big movie. Costarring with Zac Efron. We're thrilled for her, of course. But then, now . . . this."

I shook my head. What could I say? I quickly rang off and told Drew what I had learned. The family seemed to be still underwater, but that wouldn't stop them from making deals. How sad.

Dr. Bob held a hand up, and we fell silent. "Yes," he was saying into the phone. "Yes, she's sitting right here, and things have gotten into a terrible state. . . . Yes, I'm talking about *the* Max Taylor, so I can't exactly mention the specific substance here over the phone, but we want to do this intervention just as soon as possible." He listened, and we stayed quiet. "Okay!" He put a hand over his cell and whispered to Drew and me, "I've got the guy on the phone. He says this sort of spontaneous substance-abuse intervention is most unusual. Normally, he likes to meet with the 'intervention team,' that's Drew and me, in person for a few sessions before we have it all out with the addict, in order to counsel us on what to expect, and, you know, buck up our strength and resolve."

"I'm plenty strong and resolved," said Drew.

"I told him that," Dr. Bob said, still holding the cell phone's mute button. "Normally, he likes to be at the intervention himself, to give encouragement and, you know, break up any fistfights or whatnot. But he agrees we must strike right now while the iron is hot, as it were. And we have you here now,

Max, and we are resolved to intervene, so I persuaded him to lead this intervention by phone, as it were. At his usual fee plus fifty percent, of course."

"Right now?" I was suddenly frightened. I had yet to come up with one good addiction, and soon—well, tonight in fact—I was to be locked down or whatever they do to really messed-up addicts. "Are you sure we shouldn't wait until—"

"Mom, stay focused," said my completely calm daughter, taking charge. "Dr. Bob, what does he say we should do first?"

Dr. Bob listened to the man on the phone, then said to me, using the exact tone of voice I use to talk Killer into walking into the vet's office, "Okay. Maxine. Listen to us. Recovery from addiction is possible. There is hope. There is life beyond the pain."

I nodded.

Dr. Bob listened to his phone some more, then repeated, "Do you realize that you are addicted to . . . uh . . . your substance?"

I said, "Sure."

Dr. Bob said into the phone, "She realizes it." He listened, then looked up at us, holding his hand over the mouthpiece. "You're supposed to resist us," he hissed. "It's not realistic."

"Oh, come on." I picked up my sixth cup of tea and noticed it was too cold.

Dr. Bob shook his head and said, "Look, Max. This is the number-three celebrity interventionist on the West Coast. If he wants you in Wonders, he gets you in Wonders. Now resist us, please, or we'll lose him."

I couldn't believe this.

"*Resist us,* Mother," Drew ordered. "For God's sake. Like that isn't your modus operandi for everything I've ever asked of you in my entire twenty-five years?"

"Oh, good grief. I have to resist?" I asked Dr. Bob.

"Look," he said, still covering the mouthpiece and talking fast, "the number one and two guys are out of town at some sort of health expo in Vegas, and celebrity interventionists don't grow on trees. Nobody else may have the juice to get you into the rehab clinic of your dreams tonight."

I raised my voice, "Damn it! I don't have any problem at all!"

The couple in the booth next to ours

looked over. I met the eyes of a well-padded woman dressed in a cream-colored St. John suit from several seasons back whom I immediately recognized as a do-gooder mother volunteer from Drew's old prep school, a woman who had headed up all the fund-raisers. I particularly recall her phoning us each year asking us to donate to the school's annual fund, and if I may say, we donated plenty. Her name was Mrs. Harmony and she seemed delighted to recognize me and smiled.

"Resist harder," Drew begged.

I cleared my throat. "Oh, this is terrible. I can't believe the shame!"

"That's it," whispered Dr. Bob in encouragement.

He spoke into the phone for another moment, and I added an impromptu "The shame! The terrible shame!" Then I upped the decibels and shouted, "I can't bear the burden!"

Before I realized it, the hostess had hurried over to our booth. "Is there something wrong, Ms. Taylor?"

Our waiter arrived immediately, bringing a fresh pot of hot water. "I'm so sorry."

Drew smiled up at them all, including

Mrs. and Mr. Harmony, who were craning their necks from their booth to see what the fuss was about. "Not to worry," Drew said. "We're just holding a little substance-abuse intervention here. Please go on about your business. Shouldn't take too much longer, I hope."

The hostess melted away. The waiter left the pot of water. The Harmonys looked shocked.

"Let's hurry this up," I suggested.

Dr. Bob covered the phone again and said, "Here's the hang-up. He said there are three things that we can use to pressure the addict into confronting her truth: facing jail time, the imminent possibility of losing a spouse, or a comatose career."

We looked at each other. No jail cell was on the horizon since I had not committed any crime, unless participating in a fake intervention was against the law. I had no spouse to leave me. So that left the career.

"Sorry, Max," said Dr. Bob, then he began to tell me just how my career was at this very minute tumbling over a cliff and going straight to hell, and if I didn't give up abusing my "substance," I could very well be next year's pathetic has-been, not even fit to open a car wash on the good side of any town. Ouch.

"Don't destroy your career, Mother," Drew said, her voice quavering. "You are so talented. You have so many wonderful years ahead. You are so damned funny, Mother. And to throw all that you've built up—all your fans and all your brilliance—away, not to mention the money you are earning, over that horrible . . . *substance*! It's just such a waste. You are a star, Mother. You are a talented and strong woman. And soon, you will be reduced by your horrible, disgusting substance to absolutely nothing! Oh, Mom," Drew said, her voice a little too loud. "We have to help you."

In the next booth over, Mrs. Harmony clutched at Mr. Harmony's sleeve. In the dim distance, I thought I might have seen the momentary rustling of hands reaching for cell phones all across the room.

I hung my head and muttered, "You are right. I can see that now."

"You must seek treatment, Max," said Dr. Bob, clearly being well-prompted by the third-best intervention counselor on the West Coast.

I looked at him for approval to agree. He nodded his head at me.

"I know you're right," I said, but then added in a bursting wail, "but do I have to go away?"

Dr. Bob grinned as he listened to his coach. "Absolutely," he told me firmly, following the phone interventionist's directions. "And we have picked out the perfect place for you to recover." He listened a bit more, then mouthed the word: "Wonders."

It worked.

Drew mouthed, "Perfect."

Dr. Bob explained in a whisper, "He's calling in your special reservation right this minute, and as your doctor, I'll write up the diagnosis, and then Drew will sign you in."

"You've saved me," I said loudly. "You both love me so much; you saved me."

Drew scooted over in the booth and gave me a big hug.

Dr. Bob gave us both the thumbs-up.

And the restaurant burst into a nice cheery round of applause as two dozen eavesdroppers joined our private moment of redemption and joy.

11

Best Drama

I need to get back to the hotel and pack," I said to Drew and Dr. Bob, as I pushed on the Grill's front door.

Outside on the pavement, three dozen crazed paparazzi began screaming our names.

"That's not possible, Mother," Drew was saying, following close on my Moschino heels. "You've got to go straight to re—"

Drew bumped into me, dazzled into silence by the sudden burst of late-night floodlights and the attack of flashbulbs. The clicking and name shouting were a shock after the quiet of the restaurant. We never get this sort of attention from the media. Not on a Monday night. Never.

"Drew! Max! Over here!" one of the regular guys from *TMZ* called to me from behind his videocam. "Max, who's the lucky man?"

"A new lover?" asked another pap. A burst of strobe lights went off as I turned to see the always dapper Dr. Bob exiting the Grill.

"Or is he Drew's new boyfriend?" called another one.

"No," I said, laughing. "This gentleman is my old friend Dr. Robert Hopeman, the best surgeon in Beverly Hills. He's an artist. Spell his name right—H-O-P-E-M-A-N."

One by one, the strobes stopped reflecting wildly off the ruggedly bald head of Dr. Bob, and the reporters returned to us.

"We all admire you, Max," continued the *TMZ* reporter. "Admitting you've got a problem is the first step. Would you care to talk about it?"

"Problem?" I stared into the bright lights. They knew! "No, no, boys. You have been misinformed. I don't really have—"

"Max!" a woman's voice cut through the

garble of other reporters on the scene. Devon Jones? Why had *Entertainment Tonight* sent one of their star anchors to ambush me in this alley in Beverly Hills at 11 p.m. on a quiet Monday night? Devon, her blond hair recently coiffed, gave me a concerned look. "We know the truth, dear. *Everybody knows*. You don't have to lie."

Dr. Bob pulled up in the Jag just at that moment, and Drew opened the back door for me, and we both piled inside. As we pulled away from the entrance, we could hear Devon talking loudly to her camera, wrapping up her piece. "And the sad news doesn't end. First Halsey Hamilton succumbs to her addictions. And now, dear comedy legend Maxine Taylor . . ."

As we pulled farther away, I exploded, "That bitch!"

"Mom, it's okay." Drew patted my hand. "You are a big star. Of course the world is going to take notice. She's just doing her job, spinning her story."

"But did you hear? She called me a 'legend.'"

Dr. Bob and Drew both got quiet.

"I do not intend to budge from 'star' to 'legend' for at least another thirty years," I yelled back at the fast-receding curb, where no one could hear me. "How old does that whore think I am?"

Drew grabbed my hand just before my emphatic gesture made it outside the car window. "But the good news is, they are all buying our little story."

"About the substance abuse," agreed Dr. Bob as he cut away and headed east down Wilshire. "And so now we're going to Pasadena."

"No!" I had sobered up a lot since we had hatched our scheme. What the hell had we been thinking? Those damned blood-orange martinis. "Let's get a grip. No one panic. Just take me back to the hotel."

Drew withdrew her hand as Dr. Bob looked at me. I stared him down. Slowly he turned his car around and began heading west. In the dark of the car interior Drew asked, "You are not letting me down, are you?"

"It's a crazy thing to do." I waited for her to agree. "Come on, Drew."

She sat there in silence for a while. When she began to speak, I had to lean forward to catch her words. "When Burke and I were first dating, he brought me one yellow rose." She looked up. "Just one."

I nodded. I don't think Drew had ever before told me any stories about her boyfriends or her romantic life. It was one of the subjects she kept closely locked away. Perhaps, because I make jokes for a living, she needs to hold on to her privacy. Perhaps she just never truly trusted me again after the divorce from her father and after he later died. But I held my breath, hoping for more.

"Well," she continued, "I thought it was sweet. I mean obviously he could have bought me dozens of roses—he had the money—but he chose just that one perfect rose. We were falling in love, and I hadn't felt anything like it before, Mom. Even with Cameron in high school, when I was sure I was in love. And even with Asher . . ."

Drew had been a popular girl in high school and later at the University of Pennsylvania. She dated plenty. I had liked her high school boyfriend, Cameron Dewey, even if I thought he was more likely to get snapped up by Ford Models and move to Europe to do exotic photo shoots than get serious about my daughter. And Asher, her main boyfriend senior year in college, had been nice, but a guy who spent every summer in Washington, D.C., trying to work his way into a political job just couldn't give Drew the attention I thought she deserved. But that's me, the mother, talking. I held my tongue now and listened.

Drew said, "He really loved me, Mother. He said the yellow rose was me because it was beautiful, but also because it was a little sad. A little lonely."

My heart ached. Had my Drew known that sort of pain?

"And he said he wasn't good enough for me. He said he knew I would never be able to love him the way he loved me. But that he always would. No matter what happened." Drew blinked quickly, no tear falling. "So I told him we would make it work. And I would never let him down."

"I see."

"And I won't, Mom. No matter that we couldn't seem to stay together as a couple. Lots of things got in our way. Life isn't simple."

"Don't I know."

"So we're at a terrible time. Who knows

what may happen in the future? Burke and I may get back together, but maybe we won't. No matter what happens, I'll be there for him. I promised him. I know what it feels like when someone you count on disappears, Mother." She stared at me as if in challenge.

I let it pass. Every child has slights she holds on to, doesn't she? Every family has a certain burden of past misunderstandings.

Drew continued, "Burke was the one who held me when I felt lonely until I didn't feel lonely anymore."

I reached over and gave my lovely daughter a quick hug. I know it couldn't take away the kind of loneliness she had been speaking about. Perhaps we all have that loneliness in us but are too hung up to admit it.

By then, we were heading up the dark canyon roads back to the Hotel Bel-Air. Dr. Bob steered the Jag up a half-hidden side road to the curb right in front of my suite, so quiet in its garden setting.

"So." He turned back to face us from the front seat. "Should I wait here in the car for you to pack? I'll just call Sheree and let her know what's up."

"Not tonight, Dr. Bob," I said.

Drew pulled herself free from my hug.

I said, "Don't worry, Drew. I'll go to Wonders in the morning. I'll check myself in, and I'll turn that place upside down looking for all the deepest secrets that Halsey may have been keeping. Whom she was sleeping with, whom she was fighting with, whom she confided in at the clinic, and how she could have ruined her sobriety. If Burke is innocent of any wrongdoing where Halsey is concerned, I'll get the facts, just like I promised I would." And if he wasn't innocent, I'd find that out too. Yellow rose or no yellow rose, I'd protect my daughter from that joker, even if she couldn't protect her own heart.

"Thanks, Mom."

"But I have just been called a 'legend' on national television, and now this 'legend' needs her rest. Just give me a few good hours, then Malulu will pack my things in the morning and we'll be off to rehab."

"I'll come back and get you," offered Drew, whether from thoughtfulness or from the instincts of a warden who may have a twitchy prisoner, I couldn't say.

I kissed her cheek. "Okay. Come at ten."

Dr. Bob said, "Well, I'd better call back the interventionist right away. Get him to move the reservation for check-in to tomorrow."

Drew took my hand again. "I really appreciate you going through with this, Mom. And don't worry. Wonders is located in a fabulous old Pasadena mansion up on the Arroyo. The rooms are supposed to be to-die-for gorgeous. You'll check in. You'll have a facial. You'll chat with the women you meet there. They'll love you. You're Max Taylor."

"Okay, honey. Don't oversell. The only reason I'm doing any of this is because I love you." I opened the door of the Jaguar.

"Oh, dear," said Dr. Bob into his cell phone.

We both looked at him.

Drew whispered, "Is that the interventionist?"

He nodded to us, then said into his phone, "I don't think she's backing down. No, she really isn't . . . Denial . . . Yes, I hear you." He shrugged his shoulders to us. "No, not after she made so much progress admitting her addiction, I see." He put his hand over the mouthpiece of his

cell phone and said to us, "We've got problems. They don't want to see you back-
slide when you are so close to detox."

This was nuts. "Tell them I need to pack
my bag. Take a shower."

Dr. Bob shook his head as if none of
that had been working.

"Good Lord!" I whispered to Drew.

Drew held up a finger and got Dr. Bob's
attention. "My mother wants to pray. She's
going to be praying all night long."

Dr. Bob relayed the message to the interventionist on the phone, and we waited.
Then Bob said, "Good. Splendid. Yes, we
don't want to upset her spiritual . . . um . . .
flow. No." He gave us a thumbs-up. "I
promise. I'll camp out in front of her hotel
suite all night. . . . No? Okay, I'll go with
her into her suite and stay on her sofa." He
listened. "I hear you. I certainly won't allow
Max to have any access to her substance
until we can bring her to Wonders in the
morning. . . . Good. Thank you so much."

Drew shook her head in admiration as
Dr. Bob disconnected from the call. "The
third-best celebrity intervention counselor
on the West Coast—he's a ballbuster."

Dr. Bob nodded. "Don't kid yourself.

These guys are cutthroat out here. You're a big get, Max. He'll be making a move up to number two on the basis of your recovery alone."

"So, Mom," Drew said sternly. "Stay off your damned *substance*!"

Dr. Bob looked stricken. "Which reminds me—what substance is it going to be, Max? I have to write up a diagnosis tonight."

They both looked at me.

"Can we just say I'm addicted to . . . Sweet'n Low?"

"Mother! Be serious!"

Dr. Bob raised an eyebrow. "Sweet'n Low? You mean the little pink packets?"

Drew stared. "You plan to say you're addicted to artificial sweeteners?"

"Well"—I looked at both of them defensively—"I have been meaning to cut down."

12

Best Exit

I heard Malulu Vai calling my name, her bell-like voice echoing through the vast and gilded Great Hall in Buckingham Palace. Her Samoan-accented "Mrs. Livingston!" floated over the parquet floors, past Prince Philip, past Queen Elizabeth—who was at that very moment smiling and nodding over a rather clever joke I had just made—past my exquisite Harry Winston emerald earring, through my ear canal, and down, down into my brain. *"Mrs. Livingst—"*

I opened one eye. It was pitch-black

outside my window. The readout on the digital clock next to my bed read 4:17.

"Sorry, sorry, Mrs.," Malulu said, bending over me as I lay tucked sweetly under the lace-edged Frette sheets. "It's a big emergency. On the telephone. So sorry, Mrs. L."

Oh my Lord. Had they arrested Burke? Never mind Burke, had they arrested *Drew*?

I shot awake, swatting at several pillows, stuffing them all behind me as I sat up in bed. "Who's on the phone?" I asked, my middle-of-the-night voice sounding not a bit croakier than my middle-of-the-day voice typically sounds.

Malulu took over the job of tucking in pillows and straightening the comforter. "It's your Mr. Lukes."

I tried to open my eye. My manager was on the phone at 4:17 a.m.?

Steve Lukes had achieved that rarefied personal talent manager status where he had only a few clients now, all of us working hard. He'd dropped several dozen midsize names over the years and specialized in representing only his closest pals.

Steve and I had been together forever, through the good times and the meh times. He was larger-than-life in personality as well as in his waistband, the sort of man they built Big and Tall men's stores for, and a good day for Steve was checking the sale rack and finding Hawaiian shirts in size XXXL.

Steve had been out of the country for the past ten days, off on some cockamamy vacation on tiny Bazaruto Island. He was having the time of his life, I'm sure, but I was becoming less and less happy. Look, I had a storm of publicity to manage, a ton of interview requests, and where was Steve? His latest vacation destination was a pristine speck of sand forty kilometers off the coast of freaking Mozambique. It was so far off the map that Steve had virtually no cell reception, was in a time zone that made me dizzy trying to compute it, and, to top it off, held the promise of fairly atrocious, shell-laden souvenirs to come.

Malulu turned on the bedside light and handed me the phone.

"Emergency?" I squawked at Steve, skipping any intros. "It better be that you are being currently turned over a spit." I imagined headhunters, and it gave me a little satisfaction.

"Maxine, my lovely," said Steve, his cheerful booming voice coming through the phone receiver as loud and clear as if he were calling me from Brentwood. "Malulu tells me it's O-dark-thirty over there by you in Bel-Air. Sorry to wake you."

He was sorry to wake me?

He piped on, "Don't worry, my darling. I have been making merry plans for you, even whilst on my vacation." He proceeded to tell me all about the mind-numbing difficulties he had overcome in dealing with the avalanche of offers that were simply pouring in on my behalf. "Here I am, all the way around the world, and you are so hot, Max, the world is barking at my door, desperate. They found me here on Bazaruto and will not leave me alone."

"But, Steve, how is this possible? You keep telling me you have no phones," I said, suspicious that he had miraculously been accessible to everyone but me for the past week and a half.

"My iPhone is worthless here!" he beamed across the ether. "There are no phones at all in my simple hut above the sand, but has that stopped the world, Max? I have been tracked down. The poor manager at the Indigo Bay has simply had to turn over his office to me for the past twenty-four hours. You are hot, my darling!"

"How hot?"

"They want you to do the next Bond movie hot."

I gasped, now fully awake. "As M?"

"They're thinking up a new letter," Steve said airily. "There have been calls from all four networks. There are guest shots. There are pilots. Do you want to host a game show, my love?"

"What's going on?" Only two days ago, I was fairly sure I was going to have trouble negotiating with Glam-TV for the next three years of *Red Carpet Specials*. But game shows? Pilots? Bond, James Bond?

Steve explained, "You are sitting on the hottest story in the world. Hell, Max, even here in Africa everyone is speculating about what happened to Halsey. Do you know?"

"I will know a lot more in a day or so."

"Good. The more you know, the more valuable the deal I will make for you to spill it all. Don't say a word to anyone until the deal is done."

"That goes without saying."

"And then, my dear Max, your wonderful and brave admission of addiction." I could hear the awe in his voice clearly. "You are braver than Amy Winehouse."

Wait a minute. He was lying on a hammock under a palm tree in the middle of the goddamned Indian Ocean, and he had already heard about that? "You know?"

"It's so damned hip, Max. You are fresh. You are youthful. You're going to *rehab*. Do you have a tattoo?"

"Yes, of a large, hairy man being roasted by natives in coconut oil."

"Hell, I wish I'd thought this up myself. And your timing couldn't be more perfect. Look, you go and dry out. Get all better, sweetie. And leave all the deals to me."

"Uh, Steve, do you actually think I'm on drugs? I mean, we've worked together for twenty years. Have you *ever in your life seen me . . . ?*"

"No need to explain. You certainly fooled me."

I punched a pillow. "I'm not an addict,

Steve. This is just . . . well, it's just a little game."

"A game? You sly fox. You are a genius. I always knew it. But, please, just keep that your little secret and have some fun in rehab. I'm about to make some major moves, and I don't want you spoiling anything by showing up somewhere, God forbid, sober."

"Okay."

"Will you do Larry King before you check in?"

"No, Steve."

"Where are they taking you?"

"Wonders in Pasadena."

"Make them give you the Passion Fruit room," he advised. "Morning sun and not near the noisy tennis courts."

"You know the place?" I asked, amazed.

"Sweetie, don't ask."

We talked a little more business, then I hung up. Wide-awake now, I decided I might as well get up and pack my bags. Ah, what to take for a few days in recovery? This was a new wardrobe challenge. I thought my gray velvet yoga pants and hoodie might hit just the right note of sorry-but-sporty and jumped out of bed to find it.

A tap at my bedroom door, and then Malulu peeked her head in. "You still up, Mrs. L?"

"I need my luggage." I opened my underwear drawer and considered which bra looked the most penitent.

"Yes, I get your bags. But you have another phone call now. It's Sir Ian calling from England. Dat mon he is very worried, I think."

Ian. Oh, shoot. How was my proper British boyfriend dealing with the breaking news that his lady was, unbeknownst to him, hitting bottom? I should have called him. I should have warned him.

I rushed to the extension next to my bed. "Hello, is that you, Ian?"

"Who else would it bloody well be? You have a problem, a serious problem, and you don't tell me? I'm hurt. Did you think I would condemn you? Well, I certainly would not!"

Five minutes of soothing and explaining usually do the trick between Ian and me.

This time it took ten. Then I threw myself into the packing chores while Malulu, unable to sleep while I was still awake, went off to do a bit of baking.

Killer, unaccustomed to any activity at that time of morning, lay out at my feet and snoozed.

Three hours flew by, and I was seated at the dining room table, nibbling on freshly baked scones, when I heard the chimes at the door to my suite. Killer raised his little head and growled. I felt a momentary clutch in the pit of my stomach. Drew arriving to take me away.

But instead, Cindy Chow, wearing white jeans in February, was ushered in, and Malulu offered to pour her a cup of coffee.

"Max, I'm so sorry to barge in on you like this. At such a time. I mean, you have much more important things to worry about."

"What, me worry?"

"Well," she said in a little voice, "it came as quite a shock to me. But I saw Devon Jones's piece about your personal struggle on ABC this morning."

"Sit down. Have a scone."

"Anyway," she rushed on, "I know things could have gone a little better on the red carpet." She watched me put down my scone. "Okay. A lot better. But I went home and watched our show all the way through—"

"You mean until that bastard Will pulled the plug on my full interview with Halsey?"

"Yes. What was with him? The moron! Yes, until then. And you were wonderful, Max. Of course, that goes without saying. In fact, I think you may have been the funniest I've ever seen you. And maybe that was due to the fact that so much was, you know, whirling around." Cindy's euphemism for her inability to hang on to an A-lister made me cough up a little piece of scone.

Cindy looked at her French tips. "I know I let you down."

"Yesterday's news," I said kindly. I had always liked Cindy. But, to be brutally honest, I had to ask myself, had her fangs dulled a bit? Putting sentiment aside, I would have to think carefully about who would best fill the wrangler position for next year's red carpet show.

"I'm here begging, Max," she said, putting her hand over her pink stretch T-shirt, over her heart. "Begging for another chance. Can you find it in your heart to let me try again?"

"Listen, Cindy, things always work out. You know what I'm saying? Maybe Glam won't even pick up my option to do next year's red carpet. It's that kind of town. Who knows?"

"But you're so hot right now. What about the new celebrity fashion series you're going to do for ABC?" she blurted out. Even I hadn't heard of that one yet. Oh, rumors of my newly ignited "heat" must be spreading like wildfire across the back lots, setting off little sparks, since everyone in this town needed a job.

I eyed her carefully. "But that reminds me. There is something you could do to help me out."

"I can? What? Anything I can do, Max."

"Tell me exactly what you saw in the backseat of Halsey's limo."

13

Best Transportation to a Fashionable Detox Clinic

There she was, Max. Bra. No gown. Humming."

I looked at Cindy, curious. "What was Halsey humming?"

"'I Kissed a Girl.' You know how that one goes? First thing I thought was, 'This girl is high.'"

"Because . . . ?" I asked, leaning forward.

"*Because*? Because she was high! You saw her. I mean, *no clothes*. This was a girl who could have literally worn any dress in the universe that night. No designer, no price tag, was out of her reach. And instead she chose to show up in her bra?" Cindy laughed in pain at the wasted fashion op. "So that's it. She was just sitting in the backseat."

"No. Give me details."

Cindy nodded. "Well, the leather was zebra-stripe, black-and-white, you know—"

I held up my hand. "Details about Halsey."

"Right. She was undressed. Just like you saw her. She was kind of sprawled out in the back there. Very relaxed. And I said, 'Halsey, are you ready? Max is all set.' But she . . . well, Max, she asked me if I wanted to come on in and give her a big kiss."

"You don't think she was making a serious pass? She'd been humming that song the kids all like. She was joking."

Cindy said seriously, "Whatever. If it meant getting Halsey Hamilton for you, Max, I would have gladly kissed—"

You have to give Cindy props for trying to boost her own stock in the retelling of the story.

"So," I interrupted, "in the back of the

limo, any signs of bottles or needles or pills?"

Cindy shook her head quickly. "No. I mean, the limo had a bar, but I didn't notice any open booze bottles lying around."

"No food? No drinks?"

"Oh, she was drinking some bottled water, I think. Yeah, she had a big bottle of Voss water, which was just about empty. But that was it."

The doorbell to the Herb Garden Suite chimed, and Cindy and I were joined by Drew, looking energized and happy. While the two girls were chatting, I grabbed my cell phone and redialed Unja's cell for the twentieth time since we'd become separated after the Oscars. Again, no answer. I couldn't even leave my twentieth pleading message because, naturally by this time, all the message space on his service was full.

Malulu, dressed in a bright orange pantsuit, entered the dining area with Killer in her arms, and I noticed she also had his lead.

"Oh, good," I said. "You're taking him on a walk. He needs a little fresh air."

"No, Mrs. Livingston," she said, "Killer have an appointment."

Killer stopped wagging his tail. "He need to go to, you know, dat place."

"The V-E-T? We can drop you off on our way out of town," I offered, checking with Drew.

"Of course. We have a ton of room. I got us a limo, Mother. A really large limo to take you to that place you're going to this morning."

A morning of unnamed places: Killer was going to the V-E-T and Mommy was going to R-E-H-A-B. Perfect.

"Malulu," I said, "did you pack up a big box of brownies? I want to bring them with me."

"Yes, Mrs. I make a big batch. I wrapped them up with the satin bow, like you like. I get them now." She bustled off, holding tight to Killer.

Drew said kindly, "I think they have gourmet chefs at the . . . place, Mom."

"The brownies aren't for me," I said, insulted. "I want to bring something with me when I go over to the Hamiltons'."

Drew eyed me closely. "What's this?

You know we have an appointment at the *place*. Why are you going to—"

I put a hand on her arm. "We'll stop off on the way. A condolence call. It's the least we can do, right? Now, someone, get my bags."

Cindy Chow leapt up and called, "I'll get them." She had spied the four Louis Vuitton monogram canvas bags at the door, a virtual fleet of *LV*s and stylized stars and flowers floating across a brown/green sea, and hurried to hoist the packed Keepall, pulling its natural-leather shoulder strap across her chest, and extending the handle on the roller Trolley bag.

"Mother." Drew narrowed her eyes at the luggage. "The Steamer Bag?"

"I may have overpacked," I admitted. "Why not look one's best?"

Outside, the day was beautiful as the sun shone brightly onto the cobblestone paths winding among the pink buildings. The scent of the lemon trees mixed with the aroma of mint and rosemary from the herb garden outside my suite's door.

"The driver had to park in front of the main entrance," Drew explained. As she led us down the path past the hotel's lake, two large swans drifted by.

"This hotel is amazing," Cindy said, handling all four of my bags without complaint. "It has such a history."

I said, "Well, not Boston Tea Party history, but Hollywood history. And that's much juicier. If these pastel walls could talk, do you know what they'd say?"

Malulu muttered her guess: "Sex, sex, sex."

Cindy giggled. "Anyone really famous?"

Drew said, "Mom knows all the dirt."

"Well," I offered, "I read that Ted Danson and Whoopi Goldberg . . . whooped it up here."

"Mother!"

"Oprah Winfrey threw her fiftieth-birthday slumber party here. And Nancy Reagan was a lunch regular."

Drew prompted, "Mom even knows Nancy's lunch order."

"Cobb salad with low-fat dressing, no blue cheese," I offered.

Malulu said, "Dat's what I must order the next time. Dat first lady is tin."

"'Thin,'" I translated when Cindy looked up. "They say Tom Cruise and Nicole Kidman met here in secret to hammer out their divorce details. And all the legends used to stay here—Grace Kelly, Cary Grant, Elizabeth Taylor . . ."

Malulu walked along beside us carefully leading Killer by the leash. "I love dat Liz Taylor."

Ah, yes. Malulu would. Only because of Elizabeth Taylor and a wacky fan who went overboard to impress her did Malulu and I meet four years ago. Call it fate. The nut job wrote Liz several hundred love notes on Brut-scented stationery and sent them all here, to the Hotel Bel-Air, addressed simply to "Ms. Taylor," and the huge sack of perfumed devotion was mistakenly delivered to me the next time I checked in. The times being what they are vis-à-vis wack-job fans and celebrities, I naturally thought I was being stalked by a crackpot with atrocious taste in men's aftershave and was advised to hire a full-time bodyguard, as soon as possible. Enter Malulu Vai, my karate-chopping Samoan savior. Then later, when we came to our senses and discovered I was not the target of any fool's fondest longing, Malulu stayed on with me. Just as it was meant to be.

The five of us—Cindy, Drew, Malulu,
Killer, and I—passed a young couple
heading back toward the lake on our trek
across the grounds, and I remembered
another tidbit from the past. "You'll love
this, Malulu. I heard that Liz and Dick knew
how to keep room service hopping. The
Burtons had a standing order for two bottles of vodka with their breakfast tray."

Drew looked up at me. "Are you sure?
I thought that happened at the Beverly
Hills Hotel."

"Honey, don't wreck a good story."

At the curb in front of the main entrance
to the hotel was parked a large, white
stretch limo.

"A Hummer?" I said, looking at Drew as
if she were out of her mind. Nice way to
make a quiet arrival at detox.

"Not *a* Hummer, Mom," Drew said, smiling. "*The* Hummer."

Cindy had slowed her pace. "This is
Halsey's limo."

Drew whispered to me, "And Halsey's
driver. I got lucky. It was available, and so
was he. I knew you'd want to ask him some
questions. Find out about Burke, Mom. If
Halsey's driver didn't see Burke anywhere

near Halsey on Sunday, then we are home free."

I stopped and stared. The driver of the limo stood by the door, and by the tousle of his thick, brown hair and the gleam in his smile, I would put money down that he worked his driving gigs around his auditions.

"Cute?" asked Drew under her breath.

"You hired Patrick Dempsey's stunt double to take me to rehab? What woman wouldn't be thrilled?"

Drew beamed.

I watched the hunk help Cindy load my luggage into the limo, while Malulu and Killer took care of some last-second "business" before they headed into the vehicle, and I pulled Drew aside. "Honey, I hate to ask. But those diamonds that Burke gave you. I've been thinking about them. Did you leave them back at your house?"

"No. I didn't know if that was safe."

"Good, good." The last thing I wanted was the police to return to Drew's house with a search warrant. Drew had sent Burke away, so that was good. But if the police looked around her house and somehow stumbled over the stash of Halsey's

Best Actress bra diamonds, would they assume Drew had been in on the heist? "Do
me a favor," I said. "Go in and ask Mori if
you can put that little bag into the safe." Every guest at the Bel-Air could use the guest
safe-deposit boxes. And if the police were
looking for the jewels, they'd be more likely
to check area banks to see if anyone connected to the case had been seen going
into their vaults. Who would think to look
here?

As Drew dashed into the hotel's main
entrance, and the hunk finished loading
my bags into the limo, I pulled Cindy aside.
"I can't go into details, but something very
important has come up, and I must get in
touch with Unja."

"I'll find him," Cindy chirped. She would
do anything to work her way into my good
graces. I found that comforting.

"Find him and find his camera. I need to
see the footage he shot of the red carpet.
All of it. Get it to me as soon as you possibly can."

"Okay, got it. It's done." Cindy ran off
without another word, bounding down
into the hotel parking lot.

Drew emerged from the lobby and gave

me a thumbs-up. Good. The jewels were safely tucked away. Malulu, Drew, and I all lined up at the side door of the stretch Hummer. Now, normally, an H2 Hummer is an SUV of impressive size. With the two-hundred-inch stretch modifications, it was gargantuan.

The driver-for-hire gave me a gleaming smile, and my dear protective Killer, not far away, began to snarl at him. Malulu held on to Killer a little tighter as the driver looked deep into my eyes. "Ms. Taylor, it is a pleasure to drive you. My name is Barry, and I'll be all yours for the day. Whatever you have in mind."

What a thought. I had a forbidden daydream. I fantasized about how Barry might look standing up on a ladder, reroofing a patch of Drew's red tile that had been causing her sunroom to leak. A good roofer costs a fortune. Ah, but back to reality!

Inside the Hummer, I already had a headache. The old-time Vegas glitz of twenty feet of zebra-striped upholstery was reflected in the mirrored ceiling, mercilessly doubling those damned stripes into infinity. The subwoofers and amplifiers hidden under the seats pounded out the latest hip-hop sounds, while the neon strips along the ceiling were flashing through a rainbow of unnatural colors, pulsing to the beat. Three TVs and a DVD player stood at the ready. I sat there, mouth open, taking in the sight of all the lava lamps, lightning disks, acrylic bars, and fiber optics. Above the music one could not even hear Killer as he barked his heart out.

"Barry, make it stop," I begged. "For the love of all that is holy, make it stop."

"You don't like it?" Barry asked, then closed the back door and sprinted to the front. A few seconds later, all sound was halted. The aqua blue neon light that had bathed the entire interior in its unearthly disco glow was cut, and the two sunroofs were opened.

"Much better," called Drew to the front.

"Dis is crazy," said Malulu, trying to contain Killer, who would not stop barking at Barry.

I looked over the interior in the new calm and still shuddered. "So this is where Halsey spent the last afternoon of her life." We all got quiet then. All except Killer. "Killer, sweetie," I said, looking for a treat in my purse. "Darling boy. Quiet now." He did as I asked, but kept his eyes on Barry, who was now sitting up in the driver's seat, steering the limo away from the curb.

I turned to Drew. "Could we be any more ostentatious?"

She said, "We have a method here, Mother. Stay the course. I just know that Barry will tell you everything. I think he really likes you."

I laughed. "Oh, please. He's a driver-for-hire, Drew. He really likes . . . tips."

Malulu said, "Killer is not very happy, Mrs. L. He usually loves everybody, right? But dis new driver? Dis mon he no like."

I waved away her concerns and scooted up the long, long center aisle, shifting from banquette to banquette, to get to the front of the limo. Drew followed me closely, and so Malulu scooted along as well, holding on to Killer.

"Oh, Barry," I said.

Naturally, he couldn't hear me, and I had to get the hang of the hands-free intercom before communication could be initiated. Really, this limo needed to come with an instruction manual, which I would still refuse to read.

"Barry," I tried again, into the intercom.

Barry looked in the rearview mirror and gave me a brilliant smile. "Something you need?"

"We need to make a quick stop. We're not going to Pasadena."

Drew shot me a wary look.

I amended, "Not *right away,* I mean. First, we need to stop down the road." And I handed him an address to a house above Sunset.

"Oh, okay," Barry said. "You're going up to Halsey's place. Cool."

Halsey's mom, Dakota, had asked me to stop by, and, of course, we had known her daughter for many years, even before the crazy years. It was the right thing to do. But in addition, I had a wild hope that if the people who were closest to Halsey were angry enough, maybe someone in the family would tell some stories about Halsey and Burke. It was just possible.

Maybe we'd hear a bit more of the real story from Jimmy Hamilton, Halsey's dad and manager. I bet he knew the romantic history of his daughter, and I hoped he would talk. Drew would finally hear that her former love had been an unfaithful rat, but she would at least hear the terrible news from someone other than me.

And after that, who knew? If she was disgusted enough, I might even be able to cancel my trip to Wonders.

On Halsey's street, a winding road up a leafy canyon, there were dozens of reporters surrounding her house, at least ten vans, with their telescoping uplinks up high, blocking the street, and a madhouse of photographers standing in groups on her lawn. Just another day in Beverly Glen.

When we pulled up in front of the house in the disco-Hummer, paparazzi hell broke loose. I took the large box of freshly baked brownies from Malulu—she had baked 150—and instructed her to stay inside the limo with Killer until Drew and I returned.

"You no need bodyguard?" she asked, staring at the group of reporters crowding around our limo, hurt.

"Watch your soaps," I suggested, pointing at the array of screens.

Drew said, "I have an idea to get us into the house."

After Barry walked around the Hummer and opened our door, we stepped outside and faced the crowd with smiles.

Drew said, "We brought you hardworking guys something." She held up Malulu's perfectly wrapped package.

As four dozen starving paparazzi gratefully ripped into the box, Drew and I hurried up the walkway and into Halsey's house unscathed.

14

Best Escape

Arriving empty-handed, Drew and I were let into the tall, sunlit entry hall of Halsey's ultramodern, steel-and-glass home by her sister, thirteen-year-old Steffi. We couldn't help but stare. She'd grown a lot since we'd last seen her. Tanned, and with the same wide-set, oval eyes and fresh smile as her late sister, Steffi Hamilton looked so much like Halsey it was eerie. Steffi had white streaks bleached into her dark hair and sported a tattoo of a mermaid on her shoulder, but, despite that, anyone could see she would be a beauty. She was almost as tall as Halsey, but standing in front of us in tiny white shorts and a skinny, blue T-shirt, she was wafer-thin where Halsey had been curvy.

A man's voice, from the back of the house, bellowed, "Steffi? Who the hell is at the door?"

"Daddy," she screamed, without even turning around, so that her voice thundered in our faces. "Shut up. I'm here with Max and Drew Taylor." Then she smiled at Drew and touched the bottom of her gauzy shirt. "Hey, this is real nice. Is it Dolce?"

"Actually, Nordstrom Rack," Drew said.

Steffi nodded seriously. "Cool."

Into the large, slate-tiled entry hall came Jimmy Hamilton, his pale, pink dress shirt, with the top three buttons unbuttoned, tucked into expensive jeans. He was in his stocking feet and was carrying, I noticed, a bar glass filled with half-melted ice. "Well, hey there, Max. Drew. Isn't this nice of you to drop by and visit."

I cleared my throat. "We wanted to tell you how devastated we are. If you need anything, Jimmy, you or Dakota, please just let me know."

He smiled. "That's kind. Yeah, that's real

kind." He stood there looking at us, and the longer he smiled, the more uncomfortable we became. "Of course," he finally said, "if you really wanted to help, you might have seen to it my little girl Halsey didn't die." He shook his head. "But, no. You weren't too helpful when it really might have done our girl some good."

"Now, wait a minute." With all the years of escalating problems to which Halsey had fallen victim, did he actually think that I, in thirty seconds on the air, could have stopped the momentum of Halsey's freight-train rush toward tragedy?

Drew grabbed my elbow and whispered a warning, "Mom," through her polite visiting-the-grieving-relatives smile.

Jimmy smiled his little smile. "I'll wait all the minutes in the world if you can give me my daughter back."

Steffi pouted. "Well, I'm right here, Daddy. Duh."

Jimmy said, "My famous daughter, I mean, kitten. Can they give us Halsey back? Her mama is crying in the back bedroom, and I can't even get the woman to come out and fix me a drink. Our whole family is in misery. So if Max Taylor wants to help, she should have done something at the Oscars, shouldn't she?"

Drew began backing up, pulling me gently by the elbow. "So sorry, Mr. Hamilton. I loved your daughter too. But now Mom and I have to be leaving."

Jimmy looked at Drew, then hit his head in an exaggerated gesture. "Oh, yeah. You gotta take your hopped-up mama to go dry out somewhere, isn't that your racket? I watched the whole lousy story on *Nightline,* who, by the way, were supposed to devote their entire hour to our dead Halsey. Did you know that? The producer promised me. One solid hour. But, no. They just had to cover your fucking recovery story, Max. So thanks to you, Halsey loses again, doesn't she?"

I took a deep breath. The man had been drinking too much, no matter how early in the day it was, and the man had just lost his daughter. Love and guilt. The horrible what-ifs. And let's not forget—the loss of a family's source of income. Grieving in Hollywood could get twisted.

"Well," I said to Steffi, "please tell your mother we stopped by. Very sorry."

Jimmy roared at us, "She wasn't an easy girl to raise. You know that, Max. My girls are headstrong, and let me tell you, you just can't beat that out of them. Halsey was over eighteen, and she had no idea of how much trouble she could get herself into. The men, all those damn parties. You think it's all my fault, don't you? That's what everybody is thinking. Where the hell was her dad when Halsey needed him the most?"

My hand had been reaching for the doorknob, but I stopped. That was actually quite a pertinent question. Drew shoved me gently, trying to keep me moving, but I wanted to hear what else would spill out of Jimmy Hamilton. "So," I asked, "where were you, Jimmy?"

"I was inside the goddamned Kodak Theatre, that's where I was," he shouted. "With Halsey's mama and all the other goddamned nominees. When Halsey didn't show up on time at the red carpet like she was supposed to, how the hell did we know what was wrong? She must have just chickened out, that's what we thought. Don't you think I called her cell phone like every five minutes? She didn't pick up."

"But," I said, "while all the rest of the world thought Halsey was still in rehab, you knew she was coming to the Oscars." He should have been with her, I thought. Who would leave a vulnerable girl alone?

"Of course I knew," Jimmy yelled. "I planned this whole big entrance back to Hollywood for her, didn't I? I had the dress deal and the limo deal and all that stuff nailed down. And I made sure everyone we were working with kept their mouths shut so her big surprise entrance there on the red carpet would be a fucking miracle."

"So you're the one who made it all happen."

He wanted to be admired for managing the hype machine, but I could only see extra pressure placed on a girl who was already fragile.

"Hell," he continued, "I'm the one who told Halsey she was going to give just one exclusive interview out there on the carpet before the Oscar show started. Less is more, I told her. Make the public drool for your next words."

Steffi, standing to the side, spoke up. "I always listen to you, Daddy. I don't give any inter—"

Jimmy didn't let the girl get the whole sentence out. He put his hand up and, still looking hard at Drew and me, continued, "So where the hell was Halsey, our little Oscar-nominated star, that night? She stood us all up. Her mama and I went on inside the hall and took our seats. What else could I do? I figured I would just have to pick up her Oscar statuette myself when her name got called."

But she didn't win. Jimmy Hamilton was one disappointed man. All that bitterness was eating him up. Perhaps when the truth of his girl's death sank in, when he was over his anger at how the world had cheated Jimmy Hamilton, he might finally be ready to cry over the life that had been lost, the daughter who would never come home.

"I'm sorry for your loss, Jimmy," I said, and whether he thought I meant about Halsey's Best Actress Oscar or the end of her life, I figured he could interpret my words any way that most mattered to him. Then Drew and I left.

Outside the house, in the dazzling sunshine, standing in the street, a field reporter from a New York tabloid called, "Max, Drew,

those were the best brownies I ever ate."
The gaggle of cameramen laughed and
agreed as Drew led us down the front walk
to the waiting limo. Then he said, "Help us
out here, ladies. We'll make sure you look
good. But give us something. Did you see
the family? How are they holding up?"

I figured Drew and I had just absorbed
about fifteen minutes of abuse—why not
talk to the press? We stood where he suggested, in the good light, and a dozen
sleepy broadcast stringers came to life and
trained their cameras on us.

"It is horribly sad," I said into a dozen
microphones, my voice in its lower regis-
ters. "But they are a close family. They are
together. They will get through this unimaginable pain. But let's send them all
our prayers."

Drew kept a straight face in front of the
cameras, but almost giggled as she and I
entered the limo, with Barry shutting the
door behind us. "Class."

"Never try to stoop lower than the low-
lifes," I advised her. "Believe me, it simply
cannot be done. Take the high road."

Drew saluted. As she and I settled ourselves onto the glaring faux-zebra cush-

ions, my darling Killer wagged his little tail in ferocious happiness. I asked, "Did you miss Mommy?"

Malulu smiled and said, "The men outside love my brownies, Mrs. Livingston. I watched them eat every one."

It was always best to travel with gifts, always, and I thanked Malulu, again, for her hard work. Who knew when we'd need the celebrity press to be on our side? The story with Halsey was far from over, and in the frenzy to broadcast new speculations and rumors, the reporting could bounce many unflattering ways. What were those words Halsey had said? *She didn't even blame Drew*. I shuddered and put that outrageous thought out of my mind. As we pulled away, the stringer from *Us Weekly* waved, and I waved back.

By giving one short statement to the press and sharing one measly box of brownies, the vultures now owed us one, and we might need the favor.

I had one more errand to attend to, and then, I realized, I would be heading to Wonders. I began thinking of all the questions I should ask once I got there. Questions about Halsey and Burke. In just a few

minutes, we slid out of the hills and, I realized, looking out the large, tinted windows,
had arrived at the office of the V-E-T.

I gave Malulu a significant look, as we
had been through this trauma before. She
may or may not have caught my signal.

Barry pulled the gigantic stretch SUV
into the small lot that served the Beverly
Hills Veterinary Clinic and also an upscale
Thai restaurant, both of which were located
on a quiet side street off Wilshire. When
the vehicle glided to a stop, I held my
breath. The windows were tinted, after all,
so the view was obscured, and I had great
hope that our previous unhappy visits might
be forgotten.

But Killer, alas, is no fool.

He had no intention of visiting the V-E-T
that day. Or any day. As soon as the limo
came to a halt, my tiny Yorkie started
squirming and pulling this way and that.

He really is the smartest dog in the
world.

Malulu didn't want to crush him, of
course, and in Killer's frenzy to get free of
her grip, his little legs wildly dug into her
sides as if he were trying to retrieve a favorite bone. She loosened her fingers for

just a millisecond, but that was enough. Killer broke free and began ping-ponging around the enormous interior of the limo, bounding off the lava lamps, the ebony bar console, and miles of fake zebra-skin.

"Killer!" I shouted, as my tiny darling flew past me. "It's okay, sweetheart!"

Unaware of the chaos in the backseat, Barry chose that exact moment to open the limo door, presumably to let Malulu take Killer out, but at that point, my freaked-out bundle of fluff sailed right out the open door, never even hitting the pavement until about ten feet past the astonished chauffeur.

15

Best Performance

Two hours later, we were all completely exhausted. Malulu and Barry had fanned out across Wilshire Boulevard after having checked out every single building and alleyway on this side, while Drew and I had literally bent down and looked under every car parked in a six-block area.

"Mom," Drew said, looking at her watch. "I have been getting calls all morning from Wonders. They think you are a no-show. Even our interventionist thinks you've gone into deep denial again. I know this is breaking your heart about Killer, but maybe we should leave. Just hear me out. We can be in Pasadena in an hour. Malulu will find Killer . . ."

I stared at her.

"Okay, I know. You can't leave. But Killer might hide out for hours and hours. And the time . . ." Drew shook her head in frustration. "Don't you realize that Burke is just hanging by a thread? I've gotten six texts already. The police are looking for him, Mom. They've been over to his dad's office. They went to his sister's house in Calabasas. They've gone out to Manhattan Beach and talked to all his friends that have houses there. And now that Killer has run off, you are clearly unable to focus on our plan to help Burke."

We were seated again in the back of the limo, taking a break from the search, sharing a bottle of Voss water from the mini-fridge in one of the bars. I held a cut-crystal glass filled with ice and water against my hot forehead. "We'll find Killer pretty soon. God willing. He's a very good boy. I don't believe for a minute he would run into the street. He's probably nearby, just calming down." I prayed that what I was saying was true. He was a good boy. But the V-E-T had unnerved him.

"I hope so," Drew said, sipping straight from the clear-glass bottle.

"And I promised I would help your friend. A promise is a promise."

"Thank you, Mom."

"Hey, Ms. Taylor," said Barry, poking his head into the parked Hummer limo in the lot behind the vet's, where we were sitting with the back doors wide-open. "Don't worry. We'll find your little guy. We've been up and down these streets like a hundred times, but we'll keep looking. Your body-guard, Malulu, has been going door-to-door, telling everyone to call her cell number if they see him, but nobody has. I told her to take a break, but she just won't stop."

"They build them hearty in Samoa," I said.

Barry nodded. "Anyway, I'm going right back out. I just wanted to let you know what's up." He ran his hand through his thick, brown hair. No matter how many hours he'd been chasing around in the heat of the day, his gel stood up to the torture. "I can't tell you how sorry I am," he said for the third time that morning. "I could kick myself. I should have grabbed Killer when I had a shot. Damn."

"Here, sit down. Take a rest."

"We'll find him soon," he said, climbing into the back of the limo and sitting opposite us, where I suggested.

Killer didn't want to be found. That was clear. I wouldn't put it past the dog to wait us out until after the vet's business hours were over. At 5:05 p.m. we'd see Killer saunter up to the limo. I smiled to myself, hoping I was right.

"Let's talk about something else. Something that will help get my mind off poor Killer."

Barry nodded. "Sure. Whatever you want."

I said nonchalantly, "When you drove Halsey Hamilton to the Oscars, was she drinking or doing drugs in the backseat here?"

He blinked. "No, ma'am. No. Not even a beer. Hell, I already told all this to the police and to my boss. I cleared out every bottle in the on-board bars before I went to pick her up. Mr. Hamilton is the one who made the arrangements with my boss, and he was very clear about what he wanted, so I made damned sure the bar was G-rated. There was nothing in there but soft drinks and mineral waters and juice. Shit. She was doing just fine, Ms. Taylor. Ask the police. They checked it all out."

Drew looked at me. "Then she must have been wasted before she got into the limo that night." She turned to Barry. "Couldn't you tell?"

Barry shook his head, not quite sure how to answer. "She looked great to me."

I put my hand up. "Let's start at the top. Where did you pick her up?"

"I went to get her in Pasadena at nine a.m."

From Wonders. I wanted to ask more, but wasn't sure how far he would go. "You don't mind me asking?"

"Why should I? You're human, right? Everyone is asking me about Halsey. My agent is working on a deal with *OK!* magazine, I think. It's pretty hot."

"Good for you. Then maybe you would tell us: did Halsey come out of Wonders with a guy?" Okay, it wasn't an innocent question. I looked over at Drew, wearing her cream-colored peasant top over a pair of tight brown jeans, who suddenly realized where my question was casually leading. But what choice did I have? Drew wouldn't believe anything bad about Burke until she faced a few cold, hard facts. Perhaps here was the first one.

"Halsey was alone," he said.

Drew smiled at me and asked Barry, "Where did you drive Halsey when she left Wonders?"

"I took her home. To the house above Sunset. And then I just waited. That's what I get paid to do." He smiled.

"There must have been a lot of people coming and going to the house all day," I said, and Drew gave me a glance.

He cleared his voice. "I don't mean any disrespect, Ms. Taylor, but I may be signing a big-money deal with *OK!,* and I don't know how much more about it I should really be telling you. I mean, is this for your TV show or something?"

Drew moved across the center aisle and sat next to Barry. She said daintily, "Barry, if I were a driver who worked with celebrities, and I had managed, through my own negligence, to lose the tiny darling dog that meant more than life itself to my celebrity client, I would try to do everything in my power to distract that worried client. Everything. Wouldn't you?"

Barry looked at the carpet and mumbled, "I'm awfully sorry about all this, Miss Taylor, I am," as I mouthed to my daughter, *Class.*

"So," I said briskly, "who did you see going into Halsey's house that afternoon?"

"Well," he said, thinking about it, "kind of the usual crew. I've driven for her a few times before. Halsey's hair and makeup people came in. And some fashion stylist carting in a bunch of new dresses. Plus there were other folks taking care of the rest of the family. You know. And then a limo came to take the rents to the awards."

I looked at Drew and she interpreted, "The *parents.*"

Probably all part of Jimmy Hamilton's master plan for maximum impact: Halsey arrives at the red carpet alone in this mammoth limo. "So then all the other people went home."

"Well, not her friends," Barry said. "That guy she used to date was still there, I'm pretty sure."

I stopped pouring Barry a glass of water and stared. "What guy?"

Barry smiled, reaching for the water. "I don't know his name. But he drives a little Audi sports car."

"An Audi?"

Drew looked up at me. "That Audi could belong to anyone, Mom. I mean, they sell hundreds of them. Thousands."

I pulled my bag open and withdrew my wallet. As I had been packing for rehab this morning, I found a picture of Drew and Burke from two Christmases ago, the happy new couple, and folded it in half so that only Burke's image showed. I turned this shot of Burke, smiling into the camera with his arm around an unidentified shoulder, toward Barry. "Was this the guy who was driving the Audi?"

Barry took a look. Drew held her breath. I waited.

Barry said, "Sorry. I hardly looked at the guy when he went into the house. But I think the Audi guy I saw was not as big as this dude."

Drew exhaled and said, "So, let's get back to when Halsey was leaving for the Oscars."

I exhaled, too. This might have been enough. If Drew discovered Burke was with Halsey on the afternoon of her death, it would prove he had lied to Drew, perhaps lied about everything. But we weren't there yet.

On the other hand, Burke drove an Audi TT. It wasn't a rare car, but it wasn't that common either. In time, I reminded myself, we would stumble across something really conclusive, and my dear daughter's eyes would be pried open. I would stay focused on helping her see the truth, even if it meant that I had to check into rehab to do it.

Drew picked up the questions. "So what was the story with Halsey's missing evening gown?"

Barry shook his head, his big smile reappearing. "Making a big entrance, I guess. Didn't matter what that lady wore, she looked hot. Going to show her dad something, that's what she said to me. But she came out of the house really late. I had to concentrate on just getting us to the Kodak. I mean, I was driving on Sunset Boulevard going seventy. But we made it."

None of it made sense. Halsey wasn't drinking. She didn't seem high. She was playing a game with her outfit. My goodness, if the girl hadn't actually died the other night, all of this would actually be believable. I squinted at Barry, wondering if he was a much better actor than I'd given him credit for.

Malulu came up to us, huffing a little as she reached the open door of the limo. "Mrs. L. I am sure that Killer didn't get far. I think it is better if you all stay in one spot. I think Killer might return here after his little walk-around. And he will not be too frightened if he sees it is only me coming to look for him."

"Thanks, Malulu, but you need to rest. I'll go looking now."

Malulu gave a snort. "As if," she muttered, then took off at a trot down the side street. Barry, not to be outdone by a tall, large woman in a bright-colored pantsuit, took off after her. But Malulu stopped, turned Barry around, and ordered him to stay behind. Sheepishly, he returned to the limo and, leaving us to our privacy, got into the driver's seat.

Drew had been quiet.

"What's the matter, Drewie? We'll find Killer. He's just—"

"It's not Killer, Mom. It's Halsey. That day of the Oscars. Something doesn't seem right."

I reviewed what we'd just heard. "Isn't this just what we thought must have happened? She stayed behind while her parents took their own limo to the event. She must have taken some pills or been drinking." I left out, for the moment, any question of who the young man in the Audi was or what he might have had to do with Halsey's erratic behavior. And death. Let this all sink in for Drew in its own time.

"Mom," Drew said, reaching for my arm, her eyes bright. "Wait, wait, wait a second."

I waited.

She looked at me. "Remember when Halsey's dad said he'd been calling Halsey all night, trying to find out why she was so late to the Oscars?"

I nodded.

"Maybe they were fighting, you know, and when she saw his phone number on the incoming calls, she chose to ignore him."

"Makes sense," I agreed. "Unless she left her phone at home that night."

"But remember? She texted me right before her car pulled up to the theater. To arrange our exclusive interview."

"Of course."

"So the question is—where is that phone now?"

It was curious. With the minuscule garments Halsey had on that night, we'd have certainly seen a small, rectangular, phone-size bulge somewhere on her if she'd been carrying a phone. And she hadn't had an evening bag. So . . .

Drew looked around the interior of the limo, taking in the dizzying sight of animal print gone wild, along with the shiny surfaces of two bars. "In here?"

I hit the remote-control button to open the privacy window, hit the intercom switch, and said, "Barry. Could you tell me one more thing? Who cleans the limo after an event?"

He turned in his seat to talk to us. "I do, Ms. Taylor. Why?"

"Did you find a phone when you were cleaning up after Halsey's last trip?"

"No, ma'am," he said, his eyes clear and

his voice steady. "Not too much in the limo that night. Some papers and junk like that. Empty water bottle. Not much, really."

I thanked him and closed the window again, giving us a chance to confer in private. Drew was getting excited. "Halsey must have had her phone with her in the limo that night. I know it. Her little Prada phone—she loved that thing. They've only come out in Europe right now, but she got one anyway, of course. A gift from some royal sheikh, she said. Covered in diamonds. Custom."

I got down onto the floor of the limo. "Okay, if it's covered in diamonds, I'm searching for it."

Down on all fours, looking behind every banquette, I rubbed my hands over the thick, white shag carpet. Drew looked at me and sighed. She sank down on the floor and took up the hunt on the far side of the limo. She giggled, "This is absurd."

I squeezed my hand far behind the bar, where it was pushed up against the wall. I felt something hard, pulled at it, and came up with an ancient pretzel. "If I knew any of Malulu's curse words in Samoan, I'd use them."

"Mom, this limo has been vacuumed within an inch of its life. I can't even find lint behind the seats." She sat down on the shag carpet.

I sat down too and faced her. "Drew. You have Halsey's phone number. Call it."

She looked at me, and in an instant she pulled out her phone and hit a few buttons.

We waited in silence.

And we heard nothing. No little ring. No little tune. Nothing. I looked at Drew, and she pointed to her phone. "It's connecting, I hear her ringback thingie."

Damn. This type of thing worked so well in the movies.

Drew flipped her phone closed.

"Wait." I reached up on the seat for the remote control. I hit the button for the privacy window, which noiselessly opened.

Barry turned in his driver's seat and looked back at us, now sitting on the floor. "Is there something I can get you, Ms. Taylor?" he asked, suppressing a smile.

"No, no." Then I casually gestured to Drew, pointing to her cell phone. Pointing. And pointing.

She finally pushed the redial button.

In ten more seconds something amazing happened. We could faintly hear the muffled opening notes of a far-off cell phone.

"Rihanna," Drew said, listening hard. "'Shut Up and Drive.'"

I froze, trying to hear the almost-impossible-to-hear bars of music. Just then, Malulu returned to the back of the limo and, with the ears of a hunting dog, cocked her head to the side and asked, "What's dat tune?"

"A cell phone," Drew whispered.

"Dat's not from in here," Malulu said, pointing to our passenger cabin. "It's from up there." She pointed to the front of the limo. Just as I had imagined! Barry, that old liar, had Halsey's Prada cell phone somewhere up by him. Was it coming from his pocket? But by then the music had gone quiet.

In the little parking lot that our Hummer limo had dominated all day long, hogging three spaces, a patient Volvo wagon with two Weimaraners in the back was waiting for a spot. A Benz with a Siamese in a carry-case had just pulled out, and the

Volvo was inching into the tight spot. Before we knew it, Barry was clambering out of the driver's seat, and the three of us, Drew, Malulu, and me, were barreling out of the back.

"Ms. Taylor," he said as the Weimaraners cut behind him, and we blocked his path forward.

"So," I said, "you don't know where Halsey's phone is?"

"Me?" he asked, doubling his dimples.

I turned to Drew. "Hit call again, sweetie."

Drew pulled out her phone, and in a few seconds we heard the sound of Rihanna singing "Shut Up and Drive," this time a little more distinctly, but not actually coming from anywhere on Barry's person.

I looked at Barry closely. "Open the glove box, please."

Barry could drive naughty starlets to grand events with the girls wearing nothing more than their undies. He could handle drinkers and druggies, I supposed, and even celebs on their hands and knees in the back of his limo searching for God knew what. But Barry had had enough.

He looked left and right, then jumped over the Weimaraners in the parking lot and took off running as hard as he could.

Malulu Vai, with some ancestral instinct for the chase, saw the quarry run, and there was no stopping her. As Barry bounded up the street heading toward Wilshire, Malulu Vai loped after him and picked up her pace.

I saw that Barry had left the keys in the ignition. I grabbed them. Sure enough, a tiny key was most likely to fit into the lock on the glove compartment. I handed it to Drew, who fit it into the lock, and voilà! As Barry the driver zigged left and sped out of sight; as Malulu Vai zigged left and raced west on Wilshire; as the lady with the Weimaraners untangled the leashes of her barking dogs; Drew turned the key in the lock, and the door on the Hummer's glove compartment popped open. Inside were a handful of crumpled papers and other random trash, a Thomas Bros. book of road maps, and a slim, gem-bespeckled Prada phone, from which Rihanna was still singing "Shut Up."

"He had it all the time," I said. A phone like this one—the jewels and the star's private phone numbers—could be worth twice his annual salary driving a limo. And this particular one, from a mysteriously dead celeb, more than five times what the guy made, including superstar tips. Pure greed had taken over.

Drew looked at the other rubbish in the glove box: the gum wrappers, the empty Voss bottle, the note cards that had been torn in two. "Mom, I think this stuff was all from Halsey." She picked up one of the cards. "Oh, Mom . . ."

I grabbed it and read, "'I would like to thank the Academy of Motion Picture . . .'" I looked up at Drew. "So sad."

She nodded.

"Victory!" came a familiar voice. "Victory, Mrs. L!"

Outside, running back toward our limo, was a triumphant Malulu Vai.

I was impressed. "You caught Barry?"

"No, Mrs., I let that scumbag go. Good riddance to that one. I got better news!" She opened a large metallic shoulder bag and pulled out the prize.

Killer said woof.

16

Best Prison

Until that very moment, I never knew that my bodyguard was licensed in the state of California to drive a limo. What luck! As Malulu pointed the enormous white SUV, finally, eastward toward my fate in Pasadena, her foot heavy on the Hummer's gas pedal, I poured chilled designer water into a small cup for parched little Killer, the naughty boy who had, we found out, been living the high life in Barneys New York on Wilshire while we had been scared witless about his safety. At the luxury department store, two attentive girls working the Fendi handbag boutique on the main floor had temporarily adopted him when he suddenly appeared in their midst before lunchtime. According to Malulu, they fed him smoked oysters from their own lunches and hid him from the handbag manager, hoping a distressed owner might eventually turn up to retrieve the little doll and, in gratitude at how well he'd been looked after, maybe fall in love with a little-over-$1,000 something at the Fendi counter. After all, the girls there work on commission. Malulu, taking their hint, had dutifully put this season's large tote in metallic gold on my account and thanked the girls profusely. So it goes. And to think it was only because Barry had skidded through the doors of that particular department store in his attempt to shake Malulu that we came to be reunited with our dear, always pampered Killer. Isn't fate something else?

And after all of Malulu's tireless dashing around that day, searching for my wayward pup and chasing after a double-crossing chauffeur, I was certain a golden Fendi reward was in Malulu's future.

Now, in the back of the limo, Killer collapsed in a tired heap while Drew's cell phone and my BlackBerry didn't stop jumping. I took a series of calls, from Ian, who had irrationally begun to go all he-man protective after my fake confession of an itty-bitty weakness (No, don't jump on British Air. I'm fine.); from Cindy Chow, who had heroically tracked down Unja, finally finding him wrapped in cowhide in a leather bar on La Cienega (Quick, meet me at Wonders with Unja's camcorder. All is forgiven.); and from dear Dr. Bob with the latest news (Holy shit! The cops just arrested Burke Norris in connection with the drugging death of Halsey Hamilton!).

I put down my BlackBerry as the limo came to a gentle stop, and Drew received a new text message. I could tell exactly what news she was reading by the tears that leapt into her eyes. "Mom. They've arrested him. He was the last one to see Halsey right before she got into the limo. So it was his Audi the driver saw there. All her stylists said so. And the police say they have some evidence he was involved with drugs at one point. I don't know anything about that. But I know he didn't kill anyone, Mom."

"Oh, Drew." What could I say.

"You've got to find something at Wonders. Some really strong evidence. Something that will clear Burke's name."

From the front seat Malulu called out, "We here, Mrs. L," and before we could react, the door to the limo flew open and a chorus greeted us. Literally.

A welcome committee of therapists and former addicts who made up the professional staff at Wonders swarmed the limo, pulling me out, and, accompanied by a pretty young lady playing a ukulele, sang me their welcome song. They were all dressed in pale yellow, and they swayed to the music. The words *morning, steps,* and *rejoice* figured prominently.

Oh dear Lord. I'm in hell.

Drew jumped down from the limo and called out to them, "Wait. Something terrible has just happened. Seriously. I need a few minutes to talk with my mother in private."

"Ah, Miss Taylor," said a tanned man in his midthirties, stepping between Drew and me. "We don't ever point fingers in anger or use accusing words like *enabler* around here. We wouldn't do that. But we'd like to gently suggest with love that this time at Wonders is strictly for your mother, isn't it?"

Malulu, taking no chances, had locked Killer inside the limo for the few minutes it took to unload my luggage, and I turned to the man whose name tag read HUCK. "No, really. That's my daughter. That's fine."

"It will be soon, Max," he said with a friendly smile. "Soon."

I looked back at Drew as I was gently pulled toward the large Mediterranean-style mansion on the Arroyo by the singing yellow people. I knew what was upsetting her, of course. Burke Norris had been arrested for murder. I strongly suspected they had arrested the right man—I mean the police had all those CSI labs and fingerprints and tests. But Drew was in shock. Shouldn't a mother really be with her daughter for such news? "I am here for you, honey."

The man named Huck shook his head with a little smile. "Well, someday you will be. But for now, Max, don't you think you need to be *here for you*?"

"Huh?"

The chorus of happy singers began a round of some new song that centered on the words *here for yourself*.

I didn't often lose my temper, but this group of singing counselors had gotten on my last nerve. "Hold on to your hats, people," I said, simmering. "I'm not going anywhere."

Drew angrily brushed at her cheeks, wiping away the tears. "Mother," she called, halting my explosion. "Remember why you are checking into Wonders? Remember our plan? It's more important now than it ever was."

Huck smiled as the little group of welcome staff applauded Drew. "That's much better," he commended my devastated daughter, her tears falling as I hadn't seen them do since her father died. "We feel all sorts of emotions when we come to Wonders. We let the pain out, Max."

Oh, brother.

No time for hugs and good-byes, I was told, it was instead time for beginnings, and so I was hustled off, my luggage handled by one of the staff members, to the receiving center on the main floor without so much as another backward glance at Malulu, Killer, or my dear daughter, Drew.

Well, I was here to do a job, so I would try to do it. Either I would discover some solid fact that might help Burke defend himself, or I wouldn't. I figured I'd give it a day, meet anyone who had been close to Halsey, get a facial or whatever might be the treatment du jour, then check out.

The interior of the main building in the Wonders complex looked like a boutique hotel, and I was led into a nicely furnished Country French office where guests were processed in. Huck, who was handling my entrance to Wonders, sadly noted that Dr. Deiter *himself* had been looking forward to greeting me, but that he had expected me earlier in the morning and was, alas, unavailable this afternoon. In his place, Huck was happy to tell me all the official paperwork had been completed before I arrived—the diagnosis documents had duly been faxed by Dr. Bob, my interventionist had called in with the proper referral, and the bill for $35,000 plus tips for the thirty-day rehab package was awaiting my credit card—Visa or MasterCard?

I knew I'd only be there a day or two, at most, so I handed over the plastic, looked over the evening's gourmet menu and made a few selections, and was offered a complimentary upgrade in rooms. Music was playing softly from the courtyard, where, I was told, Jocelyn, the ukulele artist, was having a small concert for whomever wanted to listen. I signed whatever forms Huck put in front of me and leaned back in the high-backed chair. Perhaps I had been a bit tense these past few weeks. Well, more than a bit. Who among us rush-rush-rush type As couldn't appreciate such a lovely place to relax, where the world couldn't hunt you down? I could see the appeal of it for a girl like Halsey, who couldn't go buy toothpaste without the picture of her and her new tube of Aquafresh Triple Protection showing up on the cover of some rag.

Huck stood as a woman in her late thirties entered the admissions office. "You're in good hands," he said, turning me over to the lady in, of course, yellow. "Our counselors here at Wonders are the best."

The woman, dressed in her flowing, pale yellow dress, had a freckled, clean-scrubbed look and feathered, pale yellow hair to match. She was holding a package and a clipboard and beckoned me to follow her. As we left the office, she wheeled a shiny, brass luggage cart, the kind they have at the Ritz-Carlton.

"Hi, I'm Jonnie, and I'm an alcoholic and

a cocaine addict." She smiled at me brightly. "Nice to meet you."

"Hello."

"And you are Max, right? We just received a package for you. Delivered by messenger." She put the small shoe-box-size package on top of my neatly stacked Louis Vuitton luggage. I noticed the word URGENT stamped on the front, and the return address was marked *Cindy Chow.*

Redeemed! Cindy had pulled an impossible get out of thin air at the last minute. She'd delivered Unja's camcorder, judging by the size of the package. As soon as I was alone, I planned to watch all of Unja's up-close and personal red carpet footage. He might have caught something Halsey was doing or saying Sunday that I had missed in my jumble of performance duties and adrenaline.

Pushing the loaded cart over beautiful, old Mexican pavers, Jonnie led me down a hallway and into a room that had been outfitted as a doctor's office. She left the brass cart in the hall and suggested I take a seat in one of those chairs that have a blood-pressure cuff attached.

While the machine was compressing

and decompressing, Jonnie said with a warm smile, "So, Max, what is your drug of choice?"

I guess we weren't in Kansas anymore.

I shrugged. "I'm not sure how to answer that."

Jonnie kept her happy smile. "With the truth? We don't bite."

"Maybe later," I said, retrieving my hand from the cuff.

"Now then," Jonnie said, staring down at a clipboard. "When was your last drink, Max?"

I thought about it. I had water in the limo. Then I remembered where I was. "You mean liquor?"

She nodded and pulled out what looked like a small digital device from a drawer.

"Last night," I said, recalling the blood-orange martinis.

"How many drinks, do you recall?"

"Two." Then, under Jonnie's further stare, I made an amendment. "Three."

"Right. Get light-headed? Pass out?"

"No, of course not. Three drinks with dinner. I was visiting with . . ."

Jonnie motioned with the digital thing.

"This is a Breathalyzer. Ever been Breath-alyzed before?"

"No, of course not." What a question! "I don't have a problem with alcohol, for your information."

Jonnie smiled. "Okay." She reached into the drawer and pulled out a new mouth-piece and began fitting it on the hand-sized unit. "So, I just need to double-check to make sure—you haven't had any alco-hol in the past fifteen minutes?"

"Gee, no."

"That's good. Because it can really mess with the test results." She held the Breath-alyzer up about four inches from my mouth. "Please take a deep breath, Max, and then breathe out nice and steady for five sec-onds, if you can."

This was all so wrong. But Drew had asked for my help, and I was here for her, wasn't I? I thought about Halsey and finding out the truth. She certainly deserved that. I thought about the secrets that might be whispered to me down these protected cor-ridors. I thought about Steve, my manager, arranging all sorts of news specials and tell-all books for me, and I just had to sigh.

All this drama made me want a drink.

17

Best Check-in

The Breathalyzer beckoned.

To break into the inner sanctum at Wonders, to find out all I could about Halsey and Burke, I was probably going to have to do a lot worse things than simply breathe into a tube. I was a woman on an undercover mission, after all. What would Cinnamon Carter from *Mission: Impossible* do? I bent over the tube and blew.

Jonnie looked at the readout. "You blew a .00 BAC. Nice," she chirped.

Damned right.

"High on anything else now, Max?" she asked, putting away the equipment.

"No, Jonnie."

"Good, then we can skip the detox clinic and take you right to in-residence care. You'll be on my floor, which is awesome. We're called Butterfly Wing, and we have a group song, which is great. You'll learn it tonight."

Oh, joy.

"Our daily schedule is posted in your room. Every minute is accounted for. It may seem that there's a lot to learn—but don't worry. You'll be staying with us a nice, long time, and pretty soon you'll get the hang of it. You're on your way, girlfriend."

All this cheeriness was bringing a slight case of nausea. But I was undercover now. I needed to get into character. I said, "Thanks, girlfriend," and met her waiting high five. Oh, Lord. This might just kill me.

Down the hall again, we turned at the main lobby and walked toward the back patio, where the ukulele music had just ended. No one was outside in the courtyard or farther down the lawn, near the pool. Jonnie pushed the brass luggage cart and said, "It's quiet time. Soon we'll have small groups. You will get so much out of group, Max." Then she gestured for me to step inside a doorway at the end of the original building's new wing.

Inside, she announced, "And here we are: Butterfly Wing. Your new home. Isn't it nice?"

We stepped down the hallway, and Jonnie turned the doorknob to room 122. "No locks," she said as the door swung open. "We don't need them here. All is safe and trusting at Butterfly."

"But the main doors? To the outside world? Locked?"

A tiny furrow appeared in Jonnie's forehead. "Well, of course."

The new construction of Butterfly Wing was meant to evoke a bit of the old-time glamour of the main house, but didn't quite make it. The floor tiles had an even, manufactured appearance, their uniform, dark-red color not quite the gracious, worn terra-cotta of the pavers in the mansion. Room 122 was large and sunny, though. Two beds were made up in yellow sheets and fluffy, white damask duvets.

Jonnie gestured to the window. "View of the Arroyo. Upgrade to private bath. Nice, huh?"

"Very nice." It looked like an upscale bed-and-breakfast, with a sliding French door that led onto a small patch of patio. I tried this exterior door. It didn't budge.

"I'll get security, if you like, to unlock that for you," Jonnie offered, watching me jiggle the handle. "But of course, they do lock it up at night."

"Right."

Jonnie pulled the cart with my luggage into the room and said, "I don't want to make you feel bad, but I'm going to go through your things."

As I stood there in shock, Jonnie put one of my bags up on the bed and began to sift through everything I had packed, her hands quickly dipping into every pocket, sliding along every hem. "Any necessary prescribed medications—blood pressure, allergy—need to be checked in with us. We keep them locked up in the medical clinic, and we'll dispense them to you as prescribed, so no worries. Any unauthorized pills, narcotics, alcohol, or other substances will be taken for your own protection, as I'm sure you are aware since you just signed the authorization form."

I did? I hadn't taken the time to read every line.

She neatly stacked my lavender, satin Christian Lacroix robe and pajamas on the bed. "We can work together, if you like. When I'm done with things, just go on ahead and put them in the drawers. We'll be done in no time."

I stared. "This is absolutely necessary?"

Jonnie had finished with the first bag and was opening the second. "We want to make certain that everyone who enters Wonders is safe."

As she worked through my clothes, I meticulously refolded every item and placed each one back in the original suitcase. I was not staying long.

As I zipped up the first suitcase and moved it next to the closet, Jonnie put my third valise up on the bed and smiled. "So far you're doing great," she said. But I noticed she had begun to collect an assortment of items.

"What have you got there?" I asked, refolding a pale green Tory Burch cashmere sweater and placing it back into my second bag.

"A few books." Jonnie smiled up at me. "You know the rules. No reading material that isn't focused on recovery."

It's a sad world when a person going through the pain of learning to live without his or her addiction is also forcibly kept from reading Mary Higgins Clark. "Where is the harm?" I asked politely, still trying to be the perfect prisoner.

"Lifestyles." Jonnie sighed. "We don't want to glamorize certain lifestyles, not while we're here working so hard. And books can offer an escape from our troubles." She smiled. "That may be good for us in our home life, but not here, where we need to face our troubles and concentrate on getting well."

"This place is tough."

"You don't know the half of it," Jonnie said seriously. "Now, would you please open up your handbag, Max?"

I did as she requested. Jonnie took many of the items out and scrutinized them. The tiny silver pillbox filled with antihistamines was the first thing she grabbed. My tiny spray bottle of Opium perfume.

"The name?" I asked, watching her stow it with the other contraband.

"The alcohol. You wouldn't believe how many of our girls in Butterfly drink their perfume."

I thought that one over, then, before I could stop her, she palmed my cell phone.

"No, no, no. I need that. I'm in the middle of a very tricky negotiation. Networks are involved, you understand? And my manager is out of the country."

"The concerns of the outside world are not our concerns," Jonnie said in the tone of voice I imagine a mother superior uses when talking to naughty nuns. "We are here, Max, for one purpose only. To help you heal yourself. You must focus on that. And cell phones are only a distraction. Ah, I see you have a second phone." She pulled out Halsey's pavé-diamond Prada phone. "While you are here at Wonders, you must be truly *here*."

"Here," I parroted, showing what a good student I planned to be, because this sunny drug counselor, the one who was psychobabbling me into a coma, might have been Halsey's counselor too for all I knew. And I had to behave.

I still had no clear idea of how the staff at Wonders were organized, but I planned to find out. I had noticed two wings off the main building, with signs in the lobby pointing one way to Butterfly Wing and the other way to Dragonfly Wing, where, presumably, they stashed the men on the opposite side of the complex. As one of the counselors in Butterfly Wing, Jonnie was my first contact with someone who might have the inside scoop on Halsey and any of her visitors.

Jonnie continued talking while I faded off a bit, plotting my big plans. When I came back to the present, she was finishing up her well-meaning spiel: "Don't you see? This is the best time of your life, Max. This stay at Wonders is all about you."

No, actually, this stay was all about Halsey Hamilton and whatever she was doing in the days before her death. I nodded as if suddenly enlightened. "So true." I sat down on the empty bed and dropped my voice. "I don't know if I can make it here, Jonnie. I'm so unsure."

Jonnie stopped looking through my change purse and came over to me, concern on her face. "Of course you are going to make it. You can do it, Max."

"I don't like my odds right now," I said, shaking my head. "Look what happened to Halsey." I kept my head shaking. "Poor sweet Halsey. She was a close friend to my family, you know."

Jonnie froze. Her words suddenly became measured. "We are all so disappointed in that."

"Yes." I turned to Jonnie. "Halsey's relapse into using all that crap she was on and her terrible death . . . it may be a message. Maybe Wonders isn't really a safe place for me after all. What do you think?"

She looked at me, worried, as if it was all suddenly sinking in. "Is that why you wouldn't even unpack?"

"I'm seeing things more clearly now," I said, improvising. "It might make more sense for me to try a different rehab clinic that has a—how can I put this gently?—a better track record. Less deaths. No offense. But I'm getting a sudden strong feeling that I should take my . . . um, *addiction* to a more successful center. Betty Ford. Promises. Maybe that place on the Big Island . . ."

"Oh, Max," Jonnie said, sounding stung,

"Wonders is an amazing place. Miracles happen here every single day. Dr. Deiter is amazing. I don't think you need to worry."

I was giving the performance of the season. Befuddled. Wary. Vulnerable. Substance-recovering. Shy. "Then please," I begged, "can you explain it to me? Halsey lived here for months. Months. And now . . . she's gone. You must have known her well, right?"

"I was her personal counselor," Jonnie said quietly.

I nodded. Bingo. "After all the good work you must have done with her, what on earth would make her go back to using?"

"I shouldn't talk. Privacy is everything to all of us at Wonders."

"I really want to stay here and get better," I lied. "And now that I think about it, I'm sure my successful recovery here could help Dr. Deiter when it comes to convincing other celebrities to believe in Wonders again."

Jonnie bit her lip.

"I mean, after your—let's face it— disastrous failure to help Halsey, anyone would ask what I'm asking. You must tell me what went wrong with Halsey's treatment so I can believe the same tragic ending won't happen to me."

"I know it seems bad, but when you learn more about recovery, you'll know that anyone can have a slip. We love our clients, but we cannot walk their road for them. We say it all the time around here: Addiction isn't a party that goes on too long. Addiction leads to death."

"That's encouraging."

"Max, I'm only telling you what you will learn in rehab no matter where you choose to stay to recover. Most slips, fortunately, don't lead to such a terrible conclusion. But it is always possible, and I've seen it happen too many times."

"But Halsey stayed here at Wonders with you guys such a long time." I looked at the empty bed I was sitting on. "This must hurt business."

Jonnie looked upset. "I knew we'd feel the backlash. Halsey's relapse. Halsey's death. Those headlines are not going to die down for months."

"Years."

"It's just not fair. We help a thousand people find sobriety and lead them back to the wonderful lives they had lost through addiction, but then just one famous person has a slip in public . . ."

"Tell me what happened to her." I sat down next to Jonnie. "I need to know. Maybe if I understood how such a thing could have happened to Halsey, I'll be better prepared to face my own demons. Perhaps I won't have to leave here after all."

Jonnie looked as if she wanted to tell me, but she shut her mouth and shook her head no.

"Let's take a hypothetical patient named Hope," I said. "Tell me about why Hope would leave Wonders in the morning, all sober and excited, and end up dead on a hypothetical red carpet by nightfall."

"I don't believe she ever intended to take another Soma for the rest of her life," Jonnie whispered. "I truly don't. I have known a lot of addicts, Max. Hell, I'm a recovering addict myself. I know the lies, and I know the denial, okay? But Hals . . . Hope was as clean as they come while she was here. She didn't ever want to go back to being out of control. I would have bet my life she'd never use again."

"But we addicts can fool you," I said, commiserating.

"Or someone gave her a pill, and she didn't know what she was taking. One pill, one sip of alcohol . . . when you have a chemical dependency, it only takes one, and then you can't stop. If someone gave her that first drink . . ."

"You said she was taking Soma?" I had heard the name of that drug before, but couldn't remember where. Had that been the prescription my manager, Steve, was given for his bad back?

"It's a muscle relaxant," Jonnie said. "Do you take it?"

I shook my head. Ah, ever the substance-abuse counselor.

"It's really a horrible problem these days. Very popular with the young kids. They get their hands on the pills and mix it with alcohol and down out, you know? And it's crazy hard to kick, that stuff is so addictive. Sometimes takes them weeks in detox."

"So Hope's doctor prescribed them for her? How stupid."

"No. Oh, no. She had her own supplier. She didn't need to get her name written up on a prescription. Celebrities can get anything, can't they? They've got people to get it for them. And Soma is available down in Mexico without a prescription. They buy it in bulk. Her so-called friends ran down to Mexico all the time and picked the pills up by the hundreds."

I opened my mouth but no words came.

Burke and Drew had taken trips down to Mexico. All those last-minute romantic trips he sprang on her. Just a little business to take care of, he'd told her. Then the rest of the time for the two of them. How happy she had been.

Jonnie shook her head, her pale yellow hair fluttering against her cheeks, and looked at me. "Poor choice of friends."

Poor Halsey. Poor Drew.

18

Best Ensemble Cast

"Oh, gosh," Jonnie said, looking at her watch. "Look at the time. We only have ten minutes until small group, and we can't be late."

"Right," I said, still reeling from the shock that my daughter, dear Drew with her big sympathetic heart, might actually now be seen by the police as an accessory *before* the fact—accompanying a drug runner across the border—as well as *after* the fact—helping a guy she believed could have nothing to do with Halsey's death. How could this be happening? It seemed the harder I worked to dig Drew out from under this mess, I only managed to dig her in deeper.

Would the police believe that she had no idea what Burke was up to when they crossed the border with, I now suspected, cases of illegal Soma in his trunk? Or would they just see a pretty and successful young star and rush to lump her into Halsey's category, another girl living in the fast lane who'd skidded off the road? My Drew! The good girl! They wouldn't even want to understand. And neither would the wolves dressed in paparazzi clothing.

"Now, Max, we're almost ready." Jonnie gathered up the stash of items she'd confiscated: my vial of perfume, all the Madeline Bean mysteries I'd wanted to reread, my sainted BlackBerry, Halsey's blinged-out Prada phone. "Could you please open your package?" Jonnie handed me the box that had come by messenger from Cindy Chow.

"Oh, this? It's nothing. Just a little something I asked my associate to find for me."

Jonnie smiled but shook her head. "We have to check everything. We wouldn't want our guests to send themselves little goody bags filled with death."

Nice way with words. I silently took the box and opened it, taking care not to break a nail. Inside the outer wrap was, indeed, a shoebox. When I lifted the cover, I saw, nestled in pink, glitter tissue paper, Unja's camcorder—the same high-definition Sony Handycam he'd had strapped to his forehead all night long at the Oscar preshow. "See?"

"I'm afraid I do. I have to take it. No cameras allowed."

"What?"

"For the privacy of all our guests. It was clearly marked as a prohibited item on the intake document you signed. I'm sure you understand, Max. If our most famous patients were ever to feel victimized . . ." Jonnie held out her hand.

What could I do? Though it killed me to hand it over, that's exactly what I did. Damn it. Damn, damn, damn.

"I'm sure you can tell that's a valuable camera," I said. "And how do I know it will be kept in a safe place?"

"Oh, don't worry about that. It's kept in Dr. Deiter's office. You have no idea how many people think they can bring their laptops to rehab. We have dozens of them."

"No Internet?" I was stunned. No digital camera. No cell phone. No Google. No drugs. No wine. Why, it was almost like my mother's house in 1972. "So you keep our valuables?"

"Don't worry, all your belongings will be waiting for you when you leave us to go out into the real world next month."

What could I do? "Fine, good," I said, forcing my voice to sound reasonably compliant.

Jonnie beamed at me. "Time for small group now." Then she put my possessions down on the bed and held out her arms.

I looked at her. A hug? No, no, please. Tell me I was not standing in a rehab clinic in the middle of freaking Pasadena being hugged by a woman in a long, yellow dress.

"Don't take this the wrong way, Jonnie. You're a very nice girl. Really. I'm just not a hugger."

She put her arms down and tilted her head a little to the side. "Maybe not now, Max. But give us time. You will be!"

God. Save me.

From outside in the hallway I heard new sounds of activity. Jonnie led me out, and several women were closing their doors along the hall.

"Ready, girls?" Jonnie said to the group, raising her voice. "Let's show Max what Butterfly Wing can really do." She pulled out a pitch pipe and blew a note.

Oh, dear me. More songs.

In the sort of singsong cadence that is used in marine recruiting videos, when the troop of buff young men go running in the muck in their combat boots, handsome faces smiling, and chanting a rhythmic one-two-let's-go sort of rhyme, I now heard half a dozen women join forces and sing:

We're the girls of Butterfly Hall
We don't need no booze at all,
Gin and vodka, beer and wine,
Stick it where the sun don't shine!

Could I make this stuff up?

As the ladies burst into applause at their own efforts, Jonnie opened the outside door, and the group filed out. She told me, "We sing our hall song at the start of every small-group meeting. But I thought you'd love to hear it right away."

"Thanks. Lovely."

In the main house, I walked along with the flow of women until we entered a plush meeting room, furnished in upholstered pieces in burnt-sienna leather and soft, moss green velvet. The carpet on the tiles was a lustrous Oriental featuring the same mellow tones. Here I was, then, in this tastefully decorated chamber—the fraud of Butterfly Hall about to meet my fellow inmates. As the group took seats, I waited until they settled. Clearly they had their favorite spots. I had learned from Jonnie on the stroll to the main house that the small groups in Wonders comprised just six recovering addicts from each floor, who were led by their own personal counselor. I counted on the fact that each of the women in this group had known Halsey well. I could only hope not all of them had the stickler scruples of Jonnie about confidentiality. I'd have to play it carefully. I needed to make friends.

As everyone took her seat, I found an open spot on a leather sofa next to a girl who looked as if she'd been a beauty queen or the president of her college sorority. "Hi," I said, and she whispered back, "Get ready for hell."

Ah, nice welcome.

Around the circle of faces, I saw women of various ages, from the twentysomething blonde sitting beside me to a woman about my age across the way. All of them looked at me: fresh blood in small group. Some had open, friendly looks—fans perhaps? Some were harder to read. And one deeply tanned young woman kept shaking her head as if she couldn't get over how funny it all was. Open scorn, that's what I saw in her eyes.

"Let's get started," said Jonnie, standing before us and smoothing her yellow dress. "I would like to welcome our newest arrival here, Max. It's her first day, and she didn't need to go to detox."

There was a smattering of applause, and I felt rather proud.

Jonnie said, "We sometimes have famous people at Wonders but confidentiality is of the utmost. We're all working out our problems here, so we should treat everyone as equals."

"Like Halsey?" blurted the scornful woman to my right.

"Cherish," Jonnie said. "We will speak about Halsey at another, more appropriate time. Now, let's each introduce ourselves. Name and occupation, okay? Katie, would you begin?"

The pep-squad leader wearing the red-and-white gingham headband sitting on the sofa beside me bounced up. "Hi. I'm Katie. I'm a crack cocaine addict. I teach kindergarten."

In unison, everyone in the group said, "Hi, Katie."

Next, the woman who looked to be about my age—or so I imagine, since she hadn't had anything lifted or tucked that I could tell—stood up. A trim woman, she had short hair and a dull quality behind her brown eyes. "Hi, everyone. I'm Stella. I'm an alcoholic and narcotics abuser."

"Hi, Stella," chanted the group.

"I'm a pharmacist. Oh, and I'd just like to say I am a huge fan of Ms. Taylor's. That's all." She sat down.

Katie whispered to me, "Stella just joined our group this week. She's been in detox three weeks straight. Some people say it's a record. Any longer than two weeks in detox around here and they either send you to the hospital or bury you."

I looked at my fan Stella with newfound concern.

The next woman around the circle stood up. A tall woman in her early thirties with pink hair, she was wearing blue leather pants and a halter top that revealed a gallery of tattoos. "Hi. My name is Magdalene, and I'm an alcoholic and also became addicted to my pain meds. Yeah."

"Hi, Magdalene."

"Hi back, you fierce women. Welcome to the group, Max. Oh, and I play keyboards with Wink 22."

Drew would be so impressed. She had bought every one of that band's CDs. She and Burke had even gone to a Wink 22 concert at the Nokia Center last year. Damn that Burke with his magical access to every big event in town. He was probably delivering pills and who-knew-what to all the druggies in town, so of course he could get passes backstage. It had all become so horribly clear.

Magdalene was barefoot and sat back down on an overstuffed chair, tucking one long leg under while the next woman stood. This one wore a thin, black cotton sweater over a white T-shirt with khakis, and her shoulder-length, highlighted hair was well cut.

"Hi, everyone," she said, smiling. "I'm Dusty. I'm an alcoholic."

"Hi, Dusty."

"I'm glad to meet you, Max. I'm probably the only person here who isn't famous."

Several of the women protested.

Dusty continued, "Okay. But I'm the only one without a job. I'm a housewife and mom. That's about it."

She sat down, and we all looked to the last woman in the room, the one to my right. She didn't budge. Wearing baggy board shorts and rubber flip-flops, she was hardly dressed up. Her long, black hair, however, looked well combed.

Jonnie, our leader, spoke up. "Won't you please stand and introduce yourself, Cherish?"

Slowly Cherish stood. "I'm Cherish, and I'm here because my tribe is gonna cut off my money if I don't stay in."

Jonnie said patiently, "Cherish. Please start again."

"I'm Cherish, and I'm addicted to crystal meth. Is that better?"

I joined the wary and not terribly amused chorus and said, "Hi, Cherish."

"So, like I was saying, I don't have to work. I get my checks from the casino every month. My allowance. But unless I stay inside this prison for six months this time, I am shit out of luck. My people, my own compassionate people, are looking for any excuse to cut me out of my share that I'm due, okay? That way there is more for them, okay? Is that honest enough for group?"

Jonnie said mildly, "Thank you for sharing that, Cherish. Although, to be truly honest, you might ask yourself if you have done anything to show you can take care of yourself. If not, if you have shown you are only interested in self-destructing, then, no matter what their motives may be, I wonder if they are being cruel or kind to require you to be in rehab? Perhaps you should consult your higher power?"

Cherish said, "Fuck that," and sat down.

"Okay, then," said Jonnie, trying to move it along and turned to me.

My turn. Terrific.

"Well, Max. You've heard how it's done. Would you please stand up and address our group?"

I stood, and all eyes were on me. Friendly eyes, and not so friendly. Not a problem, since I've been working cold houses since I was sixteen and did my first open-mike night at Carolines nightclub on Broadway. "Hi, group members. I'm Max."

"Hi, Max," they said in unison.

Jonnie prompted, "And I'm a . . ."

I tried a few out in my mind . . . Diet Pepsi addict? Sweet'n Low abuser? Chocoholic? What could I say?

I started again, "I'm Max and I'm . . . not quite ready to burden the group with my little problems." I looked over at Jonnie, hoping it was enough.

"Whenever you're ready," Jonnie said, not perturbed. "The longer it takes to face the truth, however, the longer your road to recovery."

Katie whispered, "They always getcha," and I took a deep breath.

I continued, "I'm happy to be here with you. I hope you'll accept me into your wonderful group. I'm grateful to be in recovery. And if anyone knows what I can do with forty minutes of killer material that starts, 'A man walks into a bar . . .'" I waited for the guffaws.

Silence. Cold, cold crowd.

Then Dusty, the alcoholic housewife from the Valley, began to chuckle. And so did Magdalene. And so did Katie.

I even saw the beginnings of a smile from superstraight Jonnie.

Dusty said, "You're just what we girls need here, Max. You've got to sit with us at dinner."

And just like that, I had the perfect source of info on Halsey all lined up.

Jonnie looked at the clock on the wall and called out, "Look at that. Our time is up. Group hug, everybody."

Mercy.

19

Best Mixed Drink

Everything about being here is pretty horrible," said Katie, "except the food."

We were seated in a candlelit dining room located off the main Wonders courtyard. Three of us from small group were seated at a table for four: Katie, the perky kindergarten teacher; Magdalene, the rocker chick; and me. Dusty, the soccer mom, had an appointment with the clinic's leader, Dr. Deiter, and would join us soon. Stella the pharmacist had wandered off somewhere, a little vacant of eye, and Cherish didn't receive an invitation to join our table, which I took to be a long-standing snub. I watched Cherish from the corner of my eye, sitting at a small table alone, and I felt sorry that she had carved out a space for herself as the loner, angry American Indian lady.

Dipping a spoon into the Peruvian seviche, a bowl of tender mahimahi that had been marinated with lime, ginger, and aji amarillo chili, according to the waiter who set it down in front of us, I had to admit the food here was pretty spectacular for a place that wasn't in any Zagat guide.

I looked up and saw Katie and Magdalene staring at me. I stopped eating.

Katie said, "Max, we have to know. I'm sorry to bring up something that might be painful for you."

Oh, here it came. My addiction. Of course they would insist on knowing what I was in for. Damn. I hadn't minded the idea of lying to go undercover at Wonders, but the reality of now telling some outlandish story to these nice women who were suffering . . .

Magdalene broke into my thoughts. "It's Halsey. She left two days ago and hasn't come back. And now they let you move into her room."

I blinked. Halsey? These women didn't know about Halsey?

Magdalene ran a hand through her spiky pink hair and said, "Max, here's the thing. They don't let us watch the television. We can't listen to the news. We don't get the newspaper, and they confiscated our telephones."

Katie, lowering her voice in un-cheerleader-like gravity, asked, "What we want to know is, is Halsey really dead? That's what Cherish says, but we don't know."

In the only place, outside of *Sesame Street,* that hadn't been bombarded with the headlines of Halsey's passing, I got to deliver the sad news about their rehab friend: "Yes. I'm sorry to be the one to tell you. It's true."

Magdalene, who was usually so jovial and optimistic, lost her smile. "Shit, man. Cherish was telling the truth? Must be the first time, ever."

Katie looked stricken. "Halsey had been so healthy. What happened?"

I put down my spoon. "I'm not sure of the details. But she may have overdosed. Are you sure she wasn't still using?"

Magdalene nodded. "I just don't get it. She had already put in eighty-six days. Nobody has a slip with only four more days to go, do they?"

They told me about the 12-step program and how proud Halsey was that she would be getting a ninety-day chip. But I was beginning to wonder how Cherish, the least social one in the group, had come to know that Halsey had died. Wasn't that suspicious in itself, considering no one here could know that fact? I asked casually, "So Cherish knew all about Halsey?"

"Oh, yeah," said Katie, still preoccupied. "She told us, but we thought she made it up to upset us. Like she always makes stuff up."

Magdalene added, "But not this time. Weird."

I asked, "But how did Cherish know?"

Katie lowered her voice to a whisper. "She has a cell phone."

I looked shocked. "But they take our—"

Katie shook her head, still miserable with the news of Halsey. "Cherish knows all the tricks. You think this is her first time in rehab? Please. She's been in like five times already. So when they checked her in for this go-round, she was smart enough to hide a phone, and they never found it."

I was such an idiot. Why didn't I sneak in a phone?

Magdalene said, "You know we're allowed to make one or two calls on the house phone on Sundays, right? During calling hour. We have to split up the time between everyone on our floor. It's stupid. There are always fights. So Cherish makes extra money with her cell."

I looked up. "Black market?"

Katie nodded. "Yep. It's one hundred dollars for five minutes. Bitch."

Magdalene gave a rueful smile. "That's why none of us turn her in. We need her."

My, my, my. So Cherish had a phone and was in touch with the outside world. Well, that explained how she knew about Halsey. But this was intriguing. Had she also maybe sold phone time to Halsey when she was staying here? And did Cherish, perhaps, know who Halsey called? I'd have to find out.

Katie and Magdalene were subdued at the thought that Halsey had suffered a relapse so soon after she left Wonders.

Katie said softly, "I've only got another

week here, and I can't wait to get out. They're holding my kindergarten class for me, so I want to get back to all my kids." She shook her head, and her long, blond hair shimmered. "But now . . . if I get out and can't stay straight? I mean, what if I can't?"

Magdalene put her hand on Katie's shoulder. "Don't say that. Of course you can. Look how great you're doing."

"But it's easy in here," Katie said. "We don't have the temptations, and we're so sure we can get better. I mean, look what happened to Halsey. She was here longer than any of us, and now she's . . ." Katie pulled a few tissues from her pocket and dabbed at her face.

I took another tiny taste of the seviche. "You know, this isn't bad."

Just then, Dusty from the suburbs pulled out a chair and joined us. She hardly noticed the weird vibe at the table, so absorbed was she with her own fresh aura of gloom. "Shit," she said, pulling her chair up to the white tablecloth. "I can't believe it." The candlelight picked up the tracks of tears, which Dusty hadn't bothered to wipe.

Magdalene watched her closely and guessed, "Halsey?"

Dusty hardly heard the question, so intent was she on her own troubles. "I just got out of my private session with Dr. Deiter. He told me I wasn't ready." Her lower lip trembled.

I didn't follow. "Not ready for what, honey?"

Magdalene answered, "After two weeks at Wonders we get to meet with the good doc who runs the place. All the counselors meet about our progress, and then Dr. Deiter sits down and tells us how it's going. It's a no-bullshit session, I'll tell you. No one gets away unscathed."

Dusty said, "I have to stay here for ninety days. That's what he said."

I asked, "How long did you sign up for?"

"Thirty," she said, exhaling hard. "Thirty fucking days. And even that's so horrible I don't know if I can stand it. Thirty days is more time than I've ever been away from my kids in fifteen years. I thought, okay. I'll do this thing for them. I won't wimp out. I'll get healthy and come home in a month. But, Jesus, ninety days. I'll just . . ." The tears appeared.

Katie said, "It's okay, Dusty. It'll all be okay. Just tell them no. That's what I did. Dr. Deiter told me I had to stay longer, but my insurance doesn't pay anymore. I told him that. He pretty much left me alone after that."

So the guy who runs Wonders was storm-trooping up business? What the hell?

"You're lucky," Dusty told Katie. "Deiter knows we can pay. That asshole already called Brett and told him I have to stay here. Here I am, working so hard to get better and make my family proud of me, and Deiter tells them I'm still in terrible trouble."

Magdalene said, "He just means the odds are better for any of us the longer we stay in rehab. Not you in particular, Dusty. You're working real hard here. You'll do great on the outside."

I looked at Magdalene and asked, "How long are you here for?"

"Hell," she said, "I signed up for the full ninety the day I checked in. That's what they recommended. Hey, I figured I've been stoned since I was thirteen. I'm up for it."

Dusty continued, "Dr. Deiter said, 'It's

the gold standard. The longer you're in treatment, the greater your odds for success.'" Her hazel eyes had the puffy look of someone who isn't used to crying in public. "You finally admit you're sick, and then this guy comes along and says, no, you're really way sicker than you think you are. And Brett won't listen to me. Deiter already called him. He told him if I want to come home, I'm only hurting myself in the end. And Brett wants me to get well. I just hate this so much."

We all looked down in silence as the waiters came to our table, removed the seviche bowls, and delivered the main course. The head waiter announced, "Barbecued, boneless beef short ribs with creamy polenta, Bloomsdale spinach, corn salsa, and truffle essence."

Katie looked at my face and laughed. "Max, you are so cute. You look starved."

Dusty smiled too. "Hey, don't you worry about me. We all have these little breakdowns now and then. Doesn't that sound like fun? Aren't you glad you checked in?"

We all laughed at that. Dusty told me, "You'll get used to it. Go ahead. Eat. The food is the best thing going here."

So that's what we did. Between the ups and the downs of rehab, there was always the food. Magdalene and I went ahead and tried the beef. It was magical.

Katie smiled and handed Dusty some tissues. "No matter how many great chefs they bring in here to create the menu—"

Dusty nodded, wiping her face, explaining, "This is Susan Finnegan's recipe."

Katie continued, "—or nail appointments and personal trainers they get for you, this place is, no kidding, the scariest place I've ever been to in my life."

Dusty's lip trembled. "I don't know if I can even stand it one more day."

A stir of movement caught our attention, and we watched as a group counselor from a different part of our residential floor, a woman in her late sixties in a flowing, yellow muumuu, walked toward the table on the far wall where Cherish sat alone. They spoke for a minute, then the older woman hurried out of the dining room.

"That counselor is Linda," Magdalene told me.

"What was that all about?" Katie wondered.

We watched as Cherish stood up,

stretched, and caught us looking over at her.

"Please," said Dusty, looking down quickly at her untouched plate, "don't come over here, Cherish. I am not ready to put up with you right now."

But, as if called by the sort of high-frequency whistles only dogs can hear, that's exactly what Cherish did, and she headed straight for Dusty.

Cherish slouched next to Dusty's chair and said in a louder voice than was necessary, "Wow, you look like shit, honey. Did Dr. Deiter lay down the law?"

"It's none of your concern," Dusty said. "Thanks for asking, though."

Cherish snickered. "None of my concern? Babycakes, we're in small group together. You are my concern, and I am your concern. Aren't you all concerned about poor Cherish?"

Magdalene ran a hand through her pink spikes. "I'm so concerned about you, Cherish, I may have to write a song about you. How would it go . . . ? I know." Magdalene strummed an air guitar and sang, "'Back off.'" She stared Cherish down.

Cherish looked straight at me. "I don't

know, Max. Was that little slam supposed to be funny, do you think?"

Since I'd been addressed, I took the opportunity to change the subject. "What was going on over there, Cherish, when Linda came over? She looked so upset."

Cherish nodded. "Oh, that. Yeah. Linda was concerned about my buddy. My new buddy. You know how it works here, Max? We are all assigned our own little buddies. Like kindergarten, right, Katie?" Cherish snorted. "First I was assigned to look after Halsey Hamilton, the big movie star. I did a good job too. Halsey was doing just great until she went home. She took one look at me and thought, 'Oh, no! I can't end up like poor Cherish!' Now, of course, she's dead."

"Cherish," said Katie in a stern but kindly kindergarten-teacher voice. "Please."

"Sorry, sorry," said Cherish, not sorry at all. She had a gleam in her eye as she tried to get a rise out of each of the women at our table. "Did I hit a nerve?"

I asked, "So who is your new buddy, the one Linda was talking about?"

Cherish shook her head. "Damn if I don't get the worst luck ever. It's only been like two days, but my new buddy hasn't worked out too well."

Dusty looked up. "Stella? Didn't they assign you to be Stella's buddy?"

Stella was the spacey pharmacist I'd met back in small group. "Is Stella all right?"

Cherish mocked me, "'Is Stella all right?' Well, look how the new girl jumps right into the tank of sick sharks. Excellent."

I might have minded her tone more, but I actually liked that she called me a "girl."

Katie asked, "Where's Stella?"

Cherish swung her long, dark hair over one shoulder in a practiced move. "Oh, she's in detox again. Fell off the wagon big-time. Can you believe that? She already holds the world's freaking record in detox here, but three weeks wasn't enough for that gal."

"How can that be?" asked Magdalene. "Where could Stella get any drugs around here?"

I turned to Cherish, waiting for the answer. Perhaps there was a black market for pills, just as in secret phone calls. Could it be that Cherish was selling drugs right here? And if so, did she sell Halsey whatever she took that proved to be a deadly dose?

Cherish laughed. "Well, you will all be surprised to learn that I had nothing to do with it. That's right. My 'buddy' Stella found her own fun juice. While we were all here at dinner, Stella entered each of our rooms."

"What?" Katie sounded shocked.

"No keys, little one," said Cherish. "Anyone can walk in or out."

I noticed the diners at several of the tables around us had now begun to openly eavesdrop on Cherish as she crossed her arms and shifted her weight, slinging an insolent slender hip out as she stood by our table. Cherish realized she had built up quite an audience and raised her voice accordingly. "So Stella went into every single bathroom in every single room, and you know what she took?"

We just looked at her and waited.

"She took the Purell. Isn't that funny? She took all of the hand sanitizer in those plastic pump bottles."

Katie asked, "Why?"

"Because she wanted to mix it all up with orange juice and make herself sick on one very fucked-up screwdriver."

Dusty said, "Oh, good grief."

I asked, "Can you drink hand soap?"

Cherish answered, "If you really need a drink, Max. If you are really freaking parched. That Purell. It has like twice as much alcohol as in regular liquor. And it doesn't taste as bad as you'd think it would. I should know." She winked at me, then sauntered out of the dining room.

20

Best Name-Dropper

After dinner, we all hurried back to our rooms, where we had only an hour before we were supposed to attend a 12-step meeting. We had much to do, as we had been given a huge homework assignment. We were asked to produce a collage, made out of clippings from magazines, that represented our lives. No, I'm not kidding. I wish I were.

Each of us had taken a stack of old magazines and a pair of scissors back to our room. So what would I find in a 2002 issue of *House & Garden* that could sum up my life? Hmm. I flipped the pages. A thousand-thread-count duvet cover? A Henredon settee?

I put down my magazine and went to my door. Outside in the hallway was a small desk, and at the desk sat a woman who was politely called the staff-on-duty. Yeah, the warden.

I walked down the hall, noticed her name badge, which said INGRID, and said hi.

"Oh, hi, Max," she said, looking up. "Is there something I can do for you?"

"Can you come back to my room?" I asked, bright and sunny.

"I'm not supposed to leave my post here. Is there something wrong?"

"I'm . . . lonely." I wiped the bright smile off my face. "I miss my daughter. I thought maybe if you came into my room, we could talk, and . . ."

Ingrid nodded in sympathy. "Gee, I wish I could. But if you want to pull up a chair and sit with me right here . . . ?"

It would have to do. I went back to my room and came clomping back with a side chair. "You have a daughter too," I said, pointing to the picture in the plastic frame on the corner of her desk.

"Oh, no. My granddaughter," she corrected, smiling. "My Christina."

I looked utterly shocked. Really, I can be quite an actress when needed. "No! How can that be? You don't look old enough to have such a big grandchild. How old is Christina?"

"Seventeen." Ingrid beamed. "My pride and my joy. So I know the loneliness you speak about, Max. By the way, we haven't really met yet. I'm Ingrid, and I'm an alcoholic."

"Hi, Ingrid." I had clearly learned the required response.

She smiled. "My Christina, now she's a singer. She's my *sångfågel*. Like a lark."

"That's wonderful. What a joy! You must be very proud."

"Very proud," said Ingrid, smiling.

"I was just saying to my good friend, Paula Abdul, there are so many gifted young people these days. All they need is a chance."

Ingrid stopped smiling. Her body language changed entirely. "You know Paula Abdul?"

"Of course. We're like sisters. She's the older sister. And she and I were just saying to each other, after we had dinner at my house, that . . ." I watched Ingrid. She was hooked. "What is it?" I asked, faux-startled.

"I was just thinking what a miracle it would be if my Christina could ever meet Paula Abdul. And here it is, you come up to me tonight, and you actually know her."

"Of course I do. We're like Frick and Frack, Paula and I. How funny. Because I was just thinking, maybe your grand-daughter might want to try out for *American Idol* someday."

Ingrid grabbed my arm. "She does. She's old enough now. She wants to try out."

"Well, that's wonderful. I wish her good luck."

"If she could meet Ms. Abdul, I'm think-ing . . . ," Ingrid said.

"That would be perfect. I could intro-duce her to Paula, if you'd like?"

"Would you? Could you do that?" Ingrid was so excited that I actually had half a moment's regret. But it passed.

I stood up. "Come on down to my room. I have her phone number in my things. Of course, I can't make a call to Paula myself. You know. No phone. But come to my room, and we'll think of something to help Christina."

Ingrid stood up, but I could tell she was having a hard time leaving her post.

"Come on," I beckoned. "It will only take a minute."

She followed me to the door of room 122. Inside, I said, "Sit down there on the extra bed, Ingrid. Take a little break for a minute. I'll find Paula's phone number."

Ingrid sat. "This is so kind of you, Max. You haven't even heard my Christina sing yet. She's like ABBA. Not all the voices, just the good ones."

I said, "We do these things for friends, don't we?"

Ingrid smiled back at me.

I had my handbag out and was pretending to look for the number, but then I pulled out a piece of paper and sat down on the other bed. "Oh, no. Oh, dear."

"What?" asked Ingrid, concerned. "What's wrong?"

"Nothing. Nothing. It's just . . ." I looked at the paper. "It's a note I found in my purse from Halsey Hamilton."

Ingrid put her hands up to her mouth. "Oh, Halsey."

"It's okay, Ingrid. I know all about what happened to Halsey. I was actually interviewing her on the red carpet when she collapsed."

"I know," said Ingrid, suddenly subdued. "I was watching on TV. I always watch you and your daughter on the red carpet. I won't watch anyone else."

I loved this woman.

"But just after she came up to you on the carpet, your show was over. I never got to see what happened to that sweet soul. And I could tell something was wrong the minute she stepped on the hem of your gown, Max. I could see Halsey was in some sort of terrible trouble."

Who couldn't? Damn Will Beckerman, damn him to hell for cutting the live feed of my interview. All across America, my devoted fans were screaming at their screens, and it was all Will's fault for halting my interview.

Ingrid said, "And I think I heard on the news that your daughter and Halsey were friends." She shook her head. "Halsey and I spent a lot of time together, you know, here on the floor." She looked around, too considerate to tell me that we were now sitting in Halsey's former room. "Your daughter must be so upset."

"She's devastated. Absolutely devastated. And then there's all the fuss about Burke." I shook my head, but out of the corner of my eye, I watched to see if Burke's name brought forth any reaction from Ingrid.

"Not Burke Norris?" she asked, surprised.

Bingo. "Yes. He used to come here to visit Halsey. That was so nice of him. Did you meet him?"

"Twice," Ingrid said. "I don't work on the weekends so I don't know if he ever visited then. But I saw him with Halsey a couple of times. He's a very handsome man."

"Yes, he is," I said through clenched teeth.

"He was a nice friend for Halsey."

"Well," I said slyly, "they were more than just 'friends.'"

Ingrid looked up. "No. I don't think so. Halsey and Burke Norris? I never got that impression."

"Well," I said, recovering, "they had been together at one time. He as much as told me that the other night."

"Ah, maybe it was in the past," said Ingrid, nodding. "It was that other guy who caused all the problems here. That DJ or whatever he calls himself, Rojo."

I blinked. *Rojo Bernstein?* What other Rojo could she be referring to? My head spun. Rojo Bernstein was a martial arts instructor who had crossed over to rap stardom. He owned a new club in L.A. called Royt, the Yiddish word for "red," which was currently so hot you couldn't even get into *the line* to get into the club without knowing someone famous like Ashton Kutcher or Madonna's kabbalah rabbi.

I had to make sure I understood correctly. "Was Halsey taking kendo lessons from Rojo? Is that why he was here?"

"Oh, no. He was just here to cause trouble. Halsey thought it was hysterical. She'd help him sneak in. You know what kids are like. And when she didn't show up for her twelve-steps, they'd send me to come looking for her."

"Ah," I said, fully getting the picture. And

thought of the doors to the rooms. "No locks."

"And no sex is allowed at Wonders. No sex. We tell this to each client, and they sign a promise. So this wasn't fair, you see? Halsey needed to spend her time focusing on her recovery, not bouncing around on the bed . . ."

I followed Ingrid's eyes to the bed I was sitting on. "Doing the deed?" I asked, just to make sure I was getting the story straight.

"I can't talk about it," said Ingrid, suddenly realizing how many beans she had just spilled.

"So Halsey was involved with Rojo. Well, they kept that one hidden. Who knows, maybe he would have been good for her."

"Are you kidding me?" asked Ingrid, shocked. "They were always fighting."

"But I thought . . ." Hmm, Halsey was fighting with Rojo. "Weren't you saying they were always, you know, boinking?"

"They would fight, then they would . . ." Ingrid waved a hand, searching for the right word.

"Boink?"

She smiled and settled on ". . . make

up. But he would say very mean things. And they hurt her feelings."

"Like what did he say?"

"Like one time I came to her door, but I didn't want to barge in. I could hear raised voices inside. She knew she shouldn't have visitors, but I just knocked on the door to allow her some privacy. Inside, I heard Halsey crying. She was begging him to keep it all a secret. Their relationship. She didn't want her parents to find out about them yet. She pleaded, but he said he was sick of being her toy. He asked her, 'What am I? Only good enough to . . .'"

I looked at Ingrid, waiting. "Boink?"

"Yes. But he was very angry, very loud. He said he was giving the story to the *National Enquirer*. And Halsey told him she would just deny it. No one would believe him. And he said she would never get the chance to do that. That he'd . . ."

I was sitting on the edge of the bed now. "Do what? Kill her?" Had I had the wrong guy in my sights? Was Rojo Bernstein the crazy man who went too far?

"I can't say any more, Max. I realize you were a friend of Halsey, but this is her private business."

"But, Ingrid, this story may have something to do with her death."

"No, no. I saw her collapse, Max. On TV. Halsey was using again. They said so on the news this morning. You learn here in rehab that it's always easier to blame someone else. But this time Halsey had to assume responsibility."

Oh, great. More Wonders-speak. "But are you sure, Ingrid? Really sure?"

"After that fight, I heard them make up. Rojo said he loved Halsey, and the whole fight was over. When I entered the room, they were hugging and apologizing. No, it was just their way. Oh, mercy. Look at the time. We all need to be at the meeting. You just go down the hall and out past the pool. Follow the crowd."

I thought about my old theory now that karate king/DJ/lover Rojo Bernstein had entered the picture. Now what? If Halsey was no longer involved with Burke, what then? Was it possible he actually had nothing to do with her death? After all my conniving and undercover cleverness, had I inadvertently succeeded in clearing the man I detested?

21

Best Calling Plan

Out in the hall, I bumped into rocker rehab chick, Magdalene, now wearing a
skintight jumpsuit, the vivid-orange silk almost vibrating in contrast to her neon pink
hair. And I had been worried about what I
should pack for rehab. "You coming to the
meeting, Max?"

"And miss the entire group singing
'Kumbaya'?" I asked, shocked at the very
notion.

She laughed. "I'll walk you there. Say,
have you, by any chance, seen an extra
pair of scissors around?"

All of us were supposed to be working

on our personal collages and had a big deadline to get them in by tomorrow.

"No. Now that you mention it, I couldn't find the pair I took back to my room."

"Funny. None of the girls in Butterfly could find our scissors tonight. I didn't care. Hell, I'm in here for ninety. I got time. But it really pissed off Dusty. She's working hard, you know, trying to do everything they ask her to do. She was worried she'd turn her collage in late. So I lent her the little cuticle scissors from my manicure set, so she doesn't fall behind."

"That's very kind of you, Magdalene," I said, as we walked to the main house.

"Your first night at Wonders. I hope you find what you're looking for here," she said, wishing me well, no doubt, on my mythical recovery, while I was frankly hoping only to uncover any secrets I could about Halsey. I bit my lip as she continued, "It's cool you faced your demons. A person like you. Someone I really admire. I mean, you started your career back when there were very few women in power in Hollywood. You rock, Max. I'm glad you came."

But the truth was, I should be going. I

had no reason to remain at Wonders any longer. At dinner, the ladies from Butterfly Wing had told me everything they knew about Halsey during her stay here. It wasn't much. None of them had seen Halsey with a man; no one had seen anyone from her family come to visit; and in her small-group sessions, I gathered she talked about nothing more personal than her dream of winning the Oscar and her fear of losing a role in a future *Batman* sequel, and her troubles with Johnnie Walker and pills.

In fact, the gals from Butterfly Wing had less idea of why Halsey might have started abusing drugs again than I did. Looking into the faces of Dusty and Katie and Magdalene at the end of dinner, I had to give up on any more questions. Each was so deeply shaken that one of their own had fallen so far so quickly that, when they thought about Halsey, all they could see were themselves.

At the main house, Magdalene and I merged with a gathering group of the inmates, both men and women.

"The boys from Dragonfly," Magdalene said, nudging me. "This is a fun night."

I looked her over, reassessing her ultra-tight outfit. "You here shopping?"

Magdalene laughed. "We get a speaker from Narc Anon on Tuesday nights, and they are real hard-core. You haven't heard about 'hitting bottom' until you hear these guys tell it. They've got the stories."

Tempting as that sounded, I had made my mind up. "It's been a real pleasure to meet you, Magdalene. I'm sorry it wasn't under . . . more social circumstances, but even so, I really wish you well."

The tall rock musician looked down at me. "Are you bailing on us, Max?"

"Not so much bailing, as . . . well . . . leaving sooner than expected."

"Rehab's not that hard. You'll see. At first, the whole thirty days seems so long, but, after a while, you get to like the routines. The staff is wonderful. And once you clean up, your body feels brand-new. Clear."

"I'm sure you're right. Maybe some other time." I didn't break down and sing a chorus of the Butterfly Wing anthem, but I did want to show a little sisterhood, even if we'd only shared a few hours together in stir. Women behind bars really do develop a bond. So I reached up and gave her a little hug. "And please say good-bye to the girls from Butterfly Wing if I don't see them again."

"Aw, Max," she said in a soft voice. "I guess you gotta do what you gotta do. And I'm not even going to rag on you about the problems that brought you here. But you're throwing away a shitload of money."

I looked up. "What?"

"The thirty-five grand you paid when you got here? You can walk out anytime, but, baby, they don't give the moola back."

"They keep it?"

"Oh, yeah."

I gulped. "All thirty-five?"

"You gotta read the fine print on those contracts."

Oh, dear Gucci. When I handed over my Visa card, I hadn't been concerned. And how long would my little investigation take? One day? Two? Just as at the Four Seasons, I figured if you changed the length of your stay, you'd be charged, at most, for one extra night. "But I haven't even been here eight hours," I said, unable to keep a little whining tone from creeping into my voice.

"They play hardball," Magdalene said. "They make you pay for the full month up front so you really commit to the program. No backing out."

What had I done?

Magdalene said, "Look, since you're already out thirty-five grand, don't you think you should hang in there? What do you say? Give it a week."

A week. Well . . .

What the hell was I thinking? I couldn't. Burke had been arrested, and Drew was freaking out about it all alone. Sir Ian, I would bet money on it, was at this very minute on his way across the ocean and an entire continent to come rescue me from my phantom addiction. Malulu was, I was sure, doing her best to hold down the fort, but I had network deals to make and interviews to grant. And who would throw the tennis ball to Killer just the way he liked it? Hell, I had to attend Halsey's funeral, and that over-the-top event was scheduled for tomorrow.

I had come here for information on Halsey, and, even though I hadn't been able to tie her death to Burke, I had learned a lot. I had learned that getting through everyday life takes strength and courage, one day at a time; that, no matter how thirsty you might be, you should keep a healthy distance from the Purell; and that a kung fu star named Rojo Bernstein had been a lot closer to Halsey Hamilton than anybody on earth knew except for Ingrid and me. And he'd been heard making threats.

It was time to get my personal belongings back and get the hell out of Dodge. Of course, I would lose a chunk of money. It hadn't been the best investment. For roughly the price of a new Volvo, I had been frisked, given a nice dinner, and had eked out a few items of gossip. Not a bargain.

Most of Wonders' patients and staff had already filed into the main meeting room, but I remained outside the door with Magdalene. "I just need to get my things," I said.

"Well, good luck to you on that," she said. "They won't check anyone out of here at night. Huck and Dr. Deiter will probably be at the meeting. And I've got to warn you, if you're thinking of telling Dr. Deiter you plan to leave treatment, you'll wind up coming out of that conversation all signed up for the ninety-day gold package." She chuckled. "He is that good."

"Point noted." If I couldn't get my things back the civilized way, I'd find some other way. Where was I getting with all this undercover snooping? I needed to see the videotape Unja had made. I needed to check Halsey's cell phone for whomever she called the day before she died. I would have taken care of all this a long time ago if the prison guards hadn't seized my stuff.

Magdalene gave my hand a squeeze and slipped away into the meeting room, following a guy who looked like a male model, as I, in turn, backed my way out, mumbling something to the staffer at the door about looking for the restroom. I passed quickly through the empty corridor and thought I saw someone duck down toward the offices.

Stepping across the Mexican pavers, I looked out the front windows past mature palm trees and thick century plants into the cool, darkened Pasadena night.

"Boo!"

I spun around and found myself face-to-face with Cherish, the most difficult Native American in existence. "Very funny."

"Skipping out on your first twelve-step meeting, Max? That is not the road to recovery, sweetheart."

I looked at the young woman who tried so hard to be tough. "I'm not looking for salvation tonight, Cherish." I pulled out my change purse and opened it up. My hand held up two $50 bills. "What I'm looking for is a cell phone."

After a minute's negotiation, I bargained her up to ten minutes of phone time, and she took me to her room. Her cell phone was behind the heater register, and she guarded the door while I called Drew, Ian, Malulu, my manager, Steve, and Dr. Bob, leaving messages for all: I was ready to come home. Where the hell was everybody at eight twenty on a Tuesday night? Out joyriding in the Hummer?

"No one's home," I said. "Let me call Malulu again."

"Ten minutes are up," sang Cherish, enjoying my frustration.

"They teach you to tell time the same

place they taught you to steal scissors?" I asked, pushing buttons on her phone quickly. There on her nightstand. Six pairs of scissors. The Butterfly Wing bandit caught red-handed.

"No law against borrowing scissors," said Cherish with a slow smile. "You got one minute. Don't blow it."

I dialed the main number of the Hotel Bel-Air, asked to talk to the operator, then said, "Dorie, it's Max Taylor."

"Time's up!" crowed Cherish, reaching for her cell.

I picked up one of the scissors and held her off. "Dorie, I can't find Malulu. Do you happen to know if she might be eating in the dining room tonight?"

"Sorry, Ms. Taylor," said the hotel operator. "I think I saw her walking little Killer a while ago. Do you want me to go out and find her?"

My time was up. Damn it. "No, no, never mind. I left her a message at the room. Thanks, Dorie." I'd just have to get my BlackBerry back and call her again later.

"You are a cheater, Max," said Cherish. "You stole a whole minute from me. That's not very nice."

"You know, Cherish, that gives you and me something in common, doesn't it?"

"Maybe it does," she said, looking me over.

"How would you like to make some real money?" I opened my change purse and pulled out my remaining cash. Cherish, from what I'd heard over dinner, had been all but banished by her tribe, a group who had suddenly become wealthy ten years earlier when they built the first casino on their reservation. I counted out ten $100 bills.

"More phone calls?" she asked, eyeing the bills.

All the tribe members received a monthly allowance, their share of the gaming prof- its, but Cherish hadn't spent her portion wisely. She drank. She did drugs. She got pregnant. She had abortions. There were marriages to men who kept her high and stole her money. A boyfriend burned her with cigarettes when she was passed out unconscious one time. The tribe had voted. Tough love. Either Cherish stayed in rehab for a full six months, or she would lose her share. They had cut her off without a cent until she made her way out of hell.

"Here's one thousand dollars," I said, spreading the bills across the duvet cover. "You can't spend it on booze or drugs, or, I swear, I'll come back here and literally nag you to death. And you don't want a Jewish woman to nag you, Cherish. It's like hard time only with the audio turned up."

She smiled the first real smile I'd seen. Her face became pretty just like that. "So what do you want me to do?"

"Can you break into Dr. Deiter's office with no one the wiser?"

Cherish picked up the banknotes off the bed and tucked them inside her blouse. "Hell, Max. I had no idea you were gonna turn out to be so much fun."

"You'll do it?"

"I'da done that little scam with you for free."

Figures.

She added, "But we better go to the meeting right this minute, or they'll send the warden out looking for us. Meet me back at my room at four thirty in the morning. Trust me, you can do almost anything you want around this place at four thirty. Halsey and I used to get into all kinds of trouble, let me tell you."

22

Best Break-in

At exactly 4:28 a.m., I cracked open my door and peeked out. Positioned at the end of the hall, in front of the door to the patio, was the staff desk where Ingrid had been stationed earlier in the day. The guard ladies took twelve-hour shifts, and from nine at night until nine in the morning, Belle, a retired attorney and former cokehead, was on duty.

At this exact moment, Belle was snoring, her head of short, curly hair resting on her folded arms on the desk. Perfect.

I opened my door more fully and wheeled

one of my suitcases into the hall. Very slowly. Very quietly.

Over the next minute, I silently dragged each of my cases out of my room. Then, one by one, I moved them up the hall, away from the sleeping tigress and in front of Cherish's door. I didn't bother tapping. The doors aren't locked. I simply turned the knob, quietly, and slipped inside.

The desk lamp was on, and Cherish was sitting at the desk flipping through an old copy of *Vogue*.

"So," I whispered. "Glad I didn't wake you."

"I don't sleep so good anyways." She stood up and stretched, then took the magazine over to her closet. When she slid the door open, at least a hundred magazines were tossed on her closet floor, rising up about two feet.

"I don't believe this," I said. "You steal the scissors. And now you steal all the magazines? What is it? Do you have some gonzo competitive drive to make the best damn personal collage in the wing?"

Cherish shrugged. "I do it to get under their skin. Why not? Somebody needs to teach them all to lighten the fuck up. They are all so earnest; it makes me want to puke. Grown women, weeping over an arts-and-crafts project. Grow up."

"Not out to win Team Player of the Year Award. Got ya."

Cherish and I had each dressed in black, befitting our early-morning errand. We both looked chicly severe and Audrey Hepburn thin. She put a finger in front of her mouth and whispered, "Just do what I tell you to do, and we'll be all right. Stay quiet. Everyone goes to sleep on the night shift. By three o'clock, I can waltz around the place, the kitchen, the maintenance rooms. Do you have any idea what sort of chemicals they keep in the laundry supply room?"

"Oh, Cherish. You don't. Tell me you don't ingest any sort of cleaning products."

She smiled a wicked smile. "No, I don't. But I could. Security here is a joke."

"Okay, so we're going to Deiter's office?"

"Just follow me."

Cherish opened her room's door a crack. "Holy shit! Did you leave all these bags out in the hall? Like that's not too freaking noticeable?" She opened the door, checked in the direction of sleeping Belle, then dragged my luggage inside her room, trying not to make any noise. "Could you like *be* any more stupid?"

"Hey," I whispered harshly, "I need to leave right away. No one is going to keep me here against my will."

"Well, lady, do what you want. But I'm staying, see? I need to stick it out here, or I'm really screwed. So watch it."

"Okay."

"Okay."

I asked, "So what do we do if someone on the staff should happen to wake up and see us walking around the grounds at this time of the morning?"

"Don't worry. I've got a plan just in case."

We left my bags piled near her bed, then, checking again to make sure the coast was clear, we both tiptoed out of the room and up the hall, heading straight for Belle.

Sneakers may well be named sneakers, but they are less suitable for sneaking than the name implies. My stunning croc Stuart Weitzman sport shoes have rubber soles that squeak when I walk across tile. Squeaking during the day when one is briskly walking down a hall is one thing. Squeaking during the middle of the night when one is stealthily making one's escape from the Butterfly Wing is quite another.

Shhh. Cherish didn't actually make that sound, but that was the sound her mouth was forming, and she jabbed her forefinger in front of her lips. She wasn't in a particularly good mood from the pained expression on her face every time my Weitzmans let out a squeak.

We made it past Belle, who was quite dead to the world, her head still on her arms, which were folded on top of a light yellow sweater she had bunched up on the desk.

Cherish soundlessly flipped a little switch on the desk, then moved to the outside door that led to the patio by the pool. I tiptoed slowly, stopping each time the soles of my shoes squeaked, and finally made it outside.

There were miles of Mexican tiles to go, and Cherish whipped around and pointed to my shoes, mouthing, *Off.*

I took them off, and although the air outdoors was chilly in California in February, I padded barefoot on the pavers down the path. The flowerbeds near the pool were lit with small downcast garden lights, while the pool itself glowed pure aqua from underwater lights.

Past the pool house, we entered the main building and, so far, had not encountered any locked doors. Excellent.

Inside the door and quickly down the main hall, we arrived in front of a closed door that bore a bronze plaque with the name DR. EDWARD DEITER. Here we were. I slipped my sneakers back on and breathed a big sigh of relief.

But it was one sigh one second too soon.

"Hello," came the man's voice. "Can I help you two?"

I looked behind me. A man in jeans and a yellow wind jacket stood a few feet away. His name tag said KEITH.

Cherish reached her hand out and grabbed the back of my neck, then pulled me up tight toward her and planted her lips on my mouth. The kiss did not stop.

So this was her big plan. Oh, joy.

"Okay, sorry, ladies. I'm heading out of here. Don't want to intrude." Keith turned nonchalantly, then, using his staff key, exited out the front door, leaving us alone.

That was it? I guess any kind of private behavior was tolerated at Wonders, as long as it didn't include exotic substances.

I broke free from Cherish's grasp.

"You okay?" she asked, holding back a grin.

"Yes. Sure." I couldn't help it: I put my hand immediately up to my mouth and wiped. Cherish started to laugh. I said, "It was a nice kiss, don't get me wrong. It's just that I have a boyfriend. A jealous boyfriend. He's British."

"Put yourself inside the mind of the enemy. What are we doing skulking around in a deserted building in the dark? We're looking for a little romance. See? Just give the man an answer he can understand, and you're home free. They don't really care what you do as long as you aren't snorting Drano or something."

Cherish pulled a key from her pocket, and before I could register just how amazing it was that she had such a key, she'd slipped it into the lock and opened Dr. Deiter's door.

Inside, I turned on a small desk lamp

and hoped we'd be out of there before anyone noticed the light or heard any activity in the office.

I turned to Cherish. "That key?"

"I lifted it off of Jonnie the first day I checked in. That was one hundred and forty-seven days ago, Max. Not that I'm counting."

Leave it to a girl who had been in and out of rehab for the better part of her life to know how to scam her way around the system.

I walked up to a locked file cabinet. "I bet this is where he keeps our personal belongings. Damn. You don't happen to have the key to the files, do you?"

Cherish reached into the back pocket of her Juicy Couture Jeans and pulled out her key ring again.

"You do have the key?"

"Well, we'll see." She flipped through several small keys on her ring. "This looks like about the right size. I got this one off of the minibar at the Wynn Hotel in Vegas. You know they're all the same, don't you?"

"They are? All the minibar keys?"

"Mostly, yeah. They come from the same parts manufacturer. These guys use the exact same key for jukeboxes, office furniture, you name it. I had a boyfriend once who knew all about it."

I could only imagine.

She put the key up to the file-cabinet lock, then slipped it in. "Oh, yeah."

I'd clearly paid the right reprobate a thousand bucks. Bingo again.

In the top drawer were cardboard boxes with the names of patients written in Sharpie on the outside. The top drawer held names beginning with *A–F.* I closed that drawer and went straight to the bottom one, and before long I'd found the box marked MAX TAYLOR.

Cherish said, "Hey, you found it."

Inside the box were all my things. My BlackBerry was there. Halsey's expensive jewel-encrusted Prada phone was there. All my Madeline Bean mysteries and, of course, Unja's Sony Handycam. I'd take the entire box with me. I was done. I could leave.

Cherish was now seated at Deiter's desk, having fiddled her key in the lock on his personal file drawer.

I checked my phone reception and was in BlackBerry heaven, dialing Malulu, feel-

ing the joy of getting my little gizmo back—
and wondered if any of us were truly
addiction-free. As I waited for Malulu to
wake up and answer the phone, I watched
Cherish pull some files out of Deiter's desk.
"Say, do you think that's such a good
idea?"

She smirked. "Sure. Hey, I found my
personal file."

While I talked to Malulu, instructing her
to please come and pick me up this very
minute, Cherish tossed her file on the desk
and was going through other files in the
drawer. When I had disconnected my call,
she told me, "Being in here, you know what
I miss the most?"

The drugs? The booze? I waited to hear
what it would be.

"It's Austin. My little boy. He's five."

So Cherish had a little boy. That put her
in a totally new light. "That's a great age."

"Is it?" she asked. "I guess I wouldn't
know. I've been in here so long I missed
his birthday. They say when I get out of
here, they'll let me see him, though."

Oh my goodness. Had she lost her
son?

She looked over at me and said, her

voice filled with disgust, "Don't you feel sorry for me, you hear?"

"But . . ." I couldn't help the way I felt. "I do, Cherish. I just do."

She sat in the desk chair and pulled her long, black hair back from her face. "You want me to be nice to all those stupid women on our floor, don't you? You want Cherish to be sweet. But what the hell have I got to be all nice about? They all look down their noses at me, like I ain't as good as them. Well, maybe I ain't. But let them rot before I'm gonna help 'em any. They cry, and they moan. But they got families to go home to. They got jobs and boy-friends and everything goes back to normal for them. They've got lives waiting. They stay here for four weeks. Or maybe two months. Shit, Max. I've been here almost five months already this time. Five months. I've seen the ladies come and go. But I'm still here. And they ain't anything to me."

"I can tell you've had it rougher than most of them. But don't you see? You all have more in common with each other. Under the surface. Problems are universal, Cher-ish. That's what the group session is supposed to be about. To see how you are all alike."

"Yeah? Well, you're not like us, are you, Max?"

"I beg your pardon?"

She smiled a knowing smile. "You don't belong at Wonders. So what the hell are you doing here?"

"Me? Well, I had a little problem . . ."

She laughed. "Oh, really? Well, not with any addiction. I've been living in rehab for like centuries now, Max. I know what an addict looks like. I know what an addict smells like. You have been bullshitting everyone from the moment you got here."

"Oh, I . . ." Cherish had left her own file open on the desk, and on top was a letter on Wonders stationery addressed to her tribe, dated last week. I looked at it and stopped in mid-sentence. "Wait," I said, interrupting myself and reading further down the letter. "This is horrible."

"What's that?" she asked, looking down.

The letter was addressed to the tribal leaders and said, in essence, that Cherish was not making progress in her treatment and was not a good candidate for release after six months. She still showed signs of antisocial behavior, with a list of specific details.

"Shit!" Cherish said, sitting up in the chair and bristling. "Shit. They're gonna ruin everything. They even wrote how I been stealing all the magazines, for Christ's sake."

With growing alarm, we both read on. In conclusion, the letter from Dr. Deiter strongly urged the tribe to recommit Cherish Goodwater. With another six months of rehab at Wonders, the doctor hoped to see her have a chance at a true recovery.

Her eyes flew around the darkened office. "What'll I do? I'll go crazy inside this place. I'll go nuts. And Austin. I won't ever see my baby while he's still five years old."

"Easy," I said. "Let's think." The problems inside Wonders were not like the ones I was used to in the world of make-believe. Here people lost their freedom, lost their children, even lost their lives. "I'm going to tell you the truth now, Cherish. Can you take the chip off your shoulder for a minute and listen to me?"

Shocked at her sorry prospects, she nodded.

"Good. It's time for straight talk. You aren't better. You just aren't. All your hate and anger. You have to learn a better way to deal with it. Got me?"

She nodded.

"You laugh at the other women in the group. You insult them. But they are just as scared and angry as you are. No one gets a free pass from pain. No one. So lighten up on them, okay? And let the counselors help you. You have this incredible chance. So get well. Get well for Austin, your lovely boy. Use the money I gave you and buy him a birthday gift. A child is worth everything, Cherish. What wouldn't a mother do for her child?"

She looked at me but didn't reply. Did I get through to her? Who knows?

She said, "We can't stay here any longer. The morning kitchen workers get here at six."

"I'll close up in here," I said, looking at the boxes and papers we'd left lying around. "You go back to your room. I'll come back and pick up my bags."

Cherish didn't argue. At the door she turned and said, "You know, Max, I never liked your show on the red carpet."

"You are not the first to tell me that, my dear, so don't get excited."

"But, I mean, in person . . . you're okay."

After she left, I stuffed a few papers back into her file and moved it to one side of Deiter's desk. I heard Cherish come back, and I turned around, saying, "And if you don't like me on the red carpet, I can only—"

But it wasn't Cherish Goodwater standing in the doorway. It was a man I could only guess was the owner of the clinic and the office that I had just basically ransacked, Dr. Edward Deiter.

23

Best Bust

Grab her," said the compact, tanned doctor in the doorway.

A second man, dressed in a pale yellow Wonders wind jacket and name badge, rushed in, and before I knew it, he had me from behind, his viciously strong arms pressing tightly against my chest. On any other night, it might have been fun. But not now.

I croaked out, "Stop! Stop this. Don't you dare—"

"Maxine Taylor. I'm Dr. Deiter. You are in my office," said the man at the door. "You may be used to people in your life doing everything you ask them to do but that life has ended." He shut the door quietly.

I gulped. I mean, okay, I had broken into the guy's office and gone through his files. That couldn't look great. But I had a very good reason. "I was simply getting my belongings. My own. Look. You've got eyes. That box? It's got my name on it." As my arms were pinned to my sides in the giant's strong grip, I gestured with my chin toward the cardboard box on his desk.

"Peter, hold on to her," Dr. Deiter said in a cold voice, flipping on the office light switch. The Pasadena sky was still inky black as the office suddenly brightened by about a thousand extra watts. In the glare, I got my first good look at the man who ran Wonders, a guy whose thick, silver hair was cut bristly short and framed a narrow, intelligent face. Round, wire-rimmed glasses gave Dr. Deiter that professorial look I tend to go for in a man, that is, when I'm not being forcibly restrained by one of his henchmen. I like kinky, in theory. But in reality, it just leaves bruises.

As a trained fashionista, I couldn't help but observe that, over his Polo jeans, the doc wore a pale, suede Ralph Lauren jacket, and I could just see the Rolex at the cuff. Taste and money.

Despite the awkwardness of being held by a huge gorilla, I smiled at the man in charge. "Dr. Deiter. How nice to meet you finally." I used my lowest and sultriest voice, tapping into the last dregs of Max Taylor charm, and let me tell you, I was scraping the bottom of the barrel. It is for just such a reason I always wear really good earrings. Gives that extra zing of glamour that will boost a girl through any sort of jam. I had, after all, just been caught red-handed inside the doctor's locked private chambers. I pulled an arm free from the hulking Peter's grasp, gently touched one of my large Van Cleef & Arpels ebony-and-diamond button clips that screamed both wealth and breeding, and quickly figured my odds. Would he have a celebrity arrested?

The doc quickly locked the office door with a key and walked across the room. He spied the mess on his desk and touched Cherish's open file. I was so busted.

"Just getting your own things?" he asked. Then he nodded to the gorilla in the yellow jacket. "Search her. See what she's taken."

Oh, no. No. The man holding me shifted

his grip to pat me down. I slapped at him, suddenly worried. "Stop that," I squawked. "Don't you dare." I batted at the large moron when he let go his grasp. "Wait just a damn minute."

"Our patient is getting agitated," said Dr. Deiter. "We had better sedate her."

My eyes flapped open even wider. From out of his briefcase, Dr. Deiter had pulled a syringe. In one efficient motion, he tore open its new plastic wrapper, then produced a small vial filled with clear liquid from a locked case behind the desk.

"Look," I said, starting to panic. "There has been a mistake. I am not really, in fact, supposed to be in rehab at all. If you want to know the truth, I have no addictions. None. I just needed a day or two to figure out a few things. I was simply getting my own belongings and leaving."

One eyebrow lifted behind Deiter's wire-rims, producing a small crease in his tanned forehead. "I'm sure you've heard the psychological term *denial,* right?"

"Yes, of course. But I'm not in denial. It's true."

Deiter looked up at me, the syringe almost filled with the medicine from the vial.

"You have tangled with the wrong rehab clinic, Max. We know just how to deal with angry, abusive stars. We knock addicts down, and then, when you are really hitting bottom, we help you up. It's for your own good. Now just stay still."

This wasn't happening. The big guy's arms felt like three-hundred-pound iron bars. I couldn't budge when he held me tightly, as he was now doing.

"This is ridiculous," I said, trying to keep the fear out of my voice. "Look, your man here is hurting me."

Deiter flicked the liquid in the syringe and looked at me, his tranquil face not betraying a hint of emotion. "How did you get in here?"

"The door was unlocked."

He shook his head, dismissing my lie. "Why have you been looking at the private records of my patients?"

"It was . . . an accident?"

He held up a hand. "I have read the reports of your counselors. No other client has ever gone through check-in at Wonders, let alone small group, without confessing to what specific substance they are addicted. Even the doctor who wrote

up your diagnosis, even your interventionist, didn't mention your drug of choice. And
now you think you can just leave? After
you break into my office and read our patients' private files? I think we have an awful lot of work to do here, Max. And thirty
days, well, that's just not enough time to
get to the bottom of all your pain."

Whoa! What? Was he threatening to
keep me here? I kept my eye on the
syringe in his hand, and suddenly I was so
full of rage. "Right this minute, my 'pain' is
you. What's your big plan? Drug me, then
get me to sign on for a ninety-day term at
Wonders? It's the 'gold standard,' isn't that
how you sell it? You're a creep! You take
all these poor suffering people and sit
them down and tell them they're still fail-
ures. Oh, yeah, and please write another
check for seventy grand. Nice. Now let me
go!" I desperately tried to shake the big
guy off me. But despite my mighty heav-
ing and struggling, he barely budged.

"Any more resistance," said Dr. Deiter
coolly, "and we will have to sedate you,
Max." He was holding the syringe with the
long needle pointing up. "You will be kept
in our detox center for a week, strongly

secured to your cot, fed by IV, peeing into a catheter, until we see fit to allow you to leave. And the beauty of this particular drug here is that the patient has very little memory of what happened to her. I doubt you'll even be able to recall this conversation. If necessary, you can stay in that pleasant semi-sleep for days. Weeks. Do you understand?"

I nodded. With such power, a man like Deiter could do anything he wanted to the patients here. Who would be any wiser? I stopped fighting.

"Good," he said to me. Then to the gorilla: "You can let her go now, Peter. The door is locked. If she tries anything more of a physical nature, you know what to do."

Deiter motioned to the chair near his desk. "You'll behave?"

I took a seat in the chair. "You always threaten your patients?"

"I didn't threaten you. I just tried to calm you down. We love our patients here at Wonders." He said it without a trace of irony.

I always say, make the best of the cards you've been dealt. I forced a weak smile, hoping in the scuffle my lipstick hadn't been smeared. I was finally talking to the man who knew Halsey's medical condition. "Deiter," I said. "Please. I'm here because I've got to find out what really happened to Halsey Hamilton." I had to ask. Why else had I risked my life and freedom if not to find out everything I could about her time at Wonders?

Dr. Deiter stopped dead still. His eyes, behind the wire-rimmed frames, glistened. "You were with Halsey the night she died, yes?"

"Of course. We were on the air."

"Did you poison her?" Deiter asked, his breath shallow.

"What? Me? I beg your pardon!"

"Halsey was a very special patient," the doctor said, his voice low. "She would never have taken a drink or used drugs so soon after leaving us. She was very aware of the dangers. We'd had a week of private sessions."

I sat still and thought it through. All this time I thought Burke had been partying with Halsey before the Academy Awards. He'd probably poured her a few shots. Or maybe offered her some pills. Or, in another version, he'd left them behind, and in her nervous state before the Oscars, and having had a fight with her father, perhaps Halsey had taken a few pills out of spite and then spiraled out of control, taking more than she could handle. But maybe what Dr. Deiter and the women at Wonders were saying was true.

Halsey never knowingly took any dangerous substances. And if that was so, it meant she had deliberately been poisoned. This wasn't a case of accidental overdose, helped along by drug-pushing pals. It was, if I was to believe the MD who now was threatening me with a syringe filled with sedatives, a case of murder.

And since the doctors at Cedars had found no needle marks on Halsey's body, how had a fatal dose of drugs been administered to a healthy and drug-avoiding young woman?

I was forced to rethink just who might have done such a thing. Not the boy-most-likely-to, Burke Norris. He may have been stupid enough to get wrapped up in drug smuggling and a life of nonstop partying, but he didn't have the focus or even the prowess to be a cold-blooded killer. Even I, who thought all the bad things in the world about him, would never believe him capable of such cunning.

It wouldn't have been Dr. Deiter, either, although he had the cool determination and clearly had access to all the drugs in the pantry. Deiter's gig was "recovery," and what with his professional acumen and his talent for coercing patients into staying for ever-longer sentences, he was making a fortune in the wellness business. The last thing he'd want is for his highest-profile celebrity client to publicly crash and burn.

I looked up to see Deiter assessing me. "I just figured something out," I said. "Halsey must have been poisoned. I need to talk to the police."

"Nice try."

"Look here," I said, fed up. "Don't you get it? I'm Max Taylor, not some frustrated second wife from Brentwood. I am investigating Halsey's death. Her murder, in fact. So you'll just have to—"

Dr. Deiter interrupted sharply. "Have to? I'm not the one who has to do anything. Do you know where you are? We are the cold splash of reality, Max. You may be America's darling, a famous and talented star, when you are out in your world of overindulgence, but, to us here in this recovery war zone, you are no better than the crack whore off the street."

Nice image.

"The thing is," I said, now that we were talking fairly quietly, "a young girl who stayed here was just murdered. I'm sure of it now."

"And that's why you broke into my private office and looked through my private papers?" His voice was raised. "Looking for what? And what exactly did you find?"

"Well, now that you ask," I said, raising my voice. The best defense is a good offense, right? "What right do you have forcing your patients to—"

Peter, the behemoth who was standing by, must have caught a secret signal from Deiter because he suddenly swooped down on me again, grabbed me with his two great arms, and lifted me right out of the chair I'd been sitting in.

I screamed. But, with no one working in the early-morning hours in this quiet wing of the main building, no one would hear the faint sound. And even if someone did, would anyone come running? I was locked inside the office of the director of the clinic.

I began to panic again. I started swearing. And yelling insults.

"You cheat!" I yelled. "You low-life quack! You've got some scheme going here—bilking your clients and extorting them to stay here longer. You're no doctor! You couldn't even tell I have absolutely *no addiction.*"

Dr. Deiter said to Peter, "Hold her steady. She's obviously on something, and she's delusional."

I screamed louder as I saw Deiter approach me from around the desk, holding the syringe.

"No! Don't. Please." I kicked out. With Peter holding me from behind in a big bear-hug grip, I was able to swing both legs up off the ground. Peter didn't even sway. He was probably lifting weights heavier than me before breakfast.

I started yelling, "Rape! Fire! Murder!"

Deiter kept his distance from my swinging feet and told Peter, "Bend her down over the desk. Pull up one of her sleeves. Hurry."

Before I knew what was happening, I was slammed down on the desk, my face pushed into the scattered paperwork that spilled from Cherish's open file.

I screamed, "I am going to sue you for every penny. I will own this stupid clinic. And I'll tear it down. I'll . . ." With my threats for distraction, I wiggled my pinned hand and grabbed the long slender object crushed beneath me on the desk.

Peter leaned the weight of his massive body down on my back, smashing my chest into the desk. As he let go of me with one hand to find my wrist and push my sleeve up my arm, I twisted the free arm away from his grip and slashed out with what turned out to be Deiter's sterling silver letter opener.

A cry came from Peter's lips as his warm blood spurted out over my hand. He let go of my body to grab his wounded wrist, and I yanked myself away from the desk.

"Grab her!" Dr. Deiter ordered, alarmed.

Bleeding from the wrist, Peter nonetheless took a few steps, gripped my arms, and jerked me back to the desk, then bent me back down onto the surface and pinned me there. The bloodstains on my beautiful knit sweater would never come out.

I kept up my screaming, even louder now. "I'll have your license. Your clinic will be dead in Hollywood. I'll tell all your horrible secrets to Oprah!"

From my pinned position, I saw Dr. Deiter's tanned fingers, holding the needle aloft, coming closer.

"Hold her steady," ordered the doctor, and Peter complied.

Deiter pulled my sleeve up. The needle pricked my skin. I howled.

Then voices filled the room.

A scuffle ensued.

A lamp flew off the side table near the sofa.

A large woman in a lavender pantsuit took a fierce Limalama pose and faced the room with a threatening South Seas roar.

In an instant, Dr. Bob was at my side. "Stop that!" he shouted. "I'm Doctor Robert Hopeman, Ms. Taylor's personal physician. I forbid it." His voice contained a note I'd never heard before—sharp, in command, outraged. "Let her go now!"

The big, bleeding lug who had been holding me down backed off, releasing me.

I managed to stand up straight and face the new arrivals. "So *now* you get here?

Ten minutes earlier was out of the question?"

I suddenly felt gloriously relaxed.

"If you've hurt her . . ." Dr. Bob's voice shook as he looked at my arm.

"She's fine," said Cherish, walking into the disheveled office, pocketing her key, not impressed with my situation. "Look, the doc hasn't even pushed the plunger all the way."

It was true. My best friend, Dr. Bob, gently removed the needle from my arm. But the chamber of the syringe luckily appeared to be more than half full.

Dr. Bob explained to me in a soft, reassuring voice, "Oh, Max. We had no idea! We got your voice-mail messages that you wanted to come home, and Malulu called me asking what to do. I told her . . ." Dr. Bob bowed his head. "Well, I said she should get some rest and pick you up first thing in the morning." Malulu was clearly not going to forgive Dr. Bob anytime soon. "I told Drew and everyone else not to worry. But we were wrong!

"But then, an urgent text woke me up at three o'clock. I've got sensitive patients. I always keep my cell next to the bed.

Imagine my horror to get a text from some stranger saying you needed to escape from Wonders immediately! I drove right over to the hotel and woke up Malulu."

Cherish grinned. "Yeah, Max . . . all those people you phoned on my cell last night? I sent a group text SOS to all of them before we started our little adventure, just in case."

I was stunned. "You did?"

Cherish smiled. "The girl-on-girl kiss was my backup plan, Max, but you paid good money. I figured I'd throw in a *backup* backup plan, just in case."

"How are you feeling, Max?" Dr. Bob asked, his voice heavy with concern.

"Not bad," I said. "Sort of numb. This could be a great time to get a little lipo-suction." I looked, and Malulu returned to her crouched Limalama martial arts stance, weaving and bobbing and waiting for Peter and Dr. Deiter to make one false move. From her furious concern at letting me down, I could tell she was ready to whup anyone who so much as breathed funny. Dr. Bob was checking my vital signs, looking into my eyes, and taking my pulse. Cherish was slouching near the overturned lamp, smirking.

Dr. Deiter spoke up in a terribly irritated tone, "I don't know what movie you all think you are in, but you are in an amazing amount of trouble."

Dr. Bob spoke first. "*We're* in trouble? I beg to differ! For what godly reason did you inject Maxine Taylor against her will in the middle of the night? Of course, we'll be calling the police and filing charges." As he spoke, Malulu opened her cell phone and began to dial.

Deiter suddenly gave up the irritated voice, and said, "Calm down and think about whether you truly want to bring the police into this matter. I'm sure discretion is just as important to Max as it is to our clinic."

He had a point. Malulu stopped in mid-dial.

Deiter continued, "Your patient, Dr. Hopeman, was agitated and violent. She attacked my assistant with a weapon, as you yourself can see. In fact, despite what you think may have occurred, every single action I took was medically justified."

Suddenly with a woozy start, I realized how all this might appear if spun the wrong way.

Cherish looked at me with respect. "You cut the big dude?"

Deiter said, "Ms. Taylor signed our standard consent-to-treatment agreement when she entered Wonders. We have the authority to use any medical methods we deem appropriate to help her—"

"Okay, okay, okay," I said, stopping his maddeningly logical spiel. "Let's move on. For the record, I am not an addict."

"Really?" Deiter said, settling himself into the ultraexpensive ergonomic chair behind his desk. "Your doctor made a diagnosis and signed our form."

Dr. Bob cleared his throat and took up the story. "Max has been here undercover. Her intention has been to investigate the death of Halsey Hamilton, a close family friend."

"And so you falsified that document?"

I stepped in. "Not falsified so much as creatively interpreted. After all, no substance was specifically named." I smiled, filled with a happy glow. "Perhaps we had all better relax and get reasonable."

Deiter looked around the room, from Malulu swaying in her ready stance, to my most reputable friend, Dr. Bob, standing next to me, to the grinning Cherish, amused as always, to his assistant with his wrist now wrapped in his Wonders jacket.

"So," Deiter said, finally looking straight at me. "You really are not an addict?"

"No, no, no. Unless you call my admitted reliance on Sweet'n Low, a hunger for large, filled Hermès shopping bags, or my need to help the people I care about . . . *addictions*?"

Deiter had the decency to give me a tight smile. "Those are all fairly benign."

"So," I said. "It appears what we have here is a standoff. I say, you let me go, and I'll let you go."

"What?"

"Look. I don't know that I like the way you operate, with the lockdowns and the head trips, and the dicey way you get patients to recommit themselves for longer treatment. And I suppose, on second thought, that my investigation here at Wonders was a little . . . overenthusiastic. But the point is, I think you really did help Halsey. And a lot of the others I met here. Your clinic seems to work. So here's what I propose. You officially release me, give me my walking papers, and refund all of my money."

"Excuse me?" He sat up straighter.

"And I'll forget all about the nasty scene with the needle."

Hey, I might be marvelously relaxed, but I wasn't about to let thirty-five grand go traipsing away.

Deiter said, "I hardly think you are in any position to make such a demand. All your money refunded? Impossible. You signed a contract."

I smiled. "After the horrible press you are already getting over Halsey's death, can you really afford having a big celebrity out there bad-mouthing Wonders?"

He looked at us all one more time. "Get out of here."

"And the money?"

"You'll get your refund."

Yes. It's not every day a woman breaks herself out of rehab. And considering the stated purpose of the Wonders clinic, I suspected I was the only inmate that ever left the place higher than when she had arrived.

24

Best Funeral

At three o'clock in the afternoon that same Wednesday, Drew and I were dropped off outside the Kodak Theatre by Malulu, who was going off to valet-park. Only three days earlier, this had been the site of our Glam-TV red carpet preshow and, I should also probably mention, the Academy Awards. Just as the last time we had been here, the bleachers were set up and filled with fans, only this time they were dressed mostly in black, except for those who had bought the HALSEY HAMILTON REST IN PEACE commemorative T-shirts from the stand on the corner.

I wouldn't be surprised to learn Jimmy Hamilton had a piece of the action.

I was wearing a simple black Chanel suit with black Lou-boutin shoes whose red bottoms added just a glimpse of glamour and picked up the red in my M•A•C lipstick. Drew had on an understated, gray Armani suit. His clothes are always so simply cut, they work for a party or a funeral—a great way to amortize the cost.

"Oh, dear," Drew said.

"Unbelievable!" I agreed. We both had spotted the white velvet ropes draped between Plexiglas stands that surrounded the very spot on the red carpet where Halsey had collapsed during our interview. A shrine.

"Should we go in?" Drew whispered to me as we stood on the red carpet once again.

"Just give me a minute," I said. Over on the far curb, Matt Lauer was covering the event for NBC, and I noticed ABC had sent George Stephanopoulos. Even Devon Jones, from *ET,* wearing a red dress that showed off her cleavage, for crying out loud, was covering the funeral. "I want to absorb this scene of vulgarity a few moments longer. So I'll get all the details right when planning my own funeral."

Drew shot me a look, not entirely sure if I was kidding. I was. I'd never invite Devon Jones.

Gigantic banners showed blowups from all of Halsey's movies. She'd made fifteen in her nine years in Hollywood. Quite a legacy for such a young lady who had started working in movies at the age of ten. Rickey Minor and the Band were playing at the entrance, and *American Idol* winner David Cook was singing "Stairway to Heaven." I noticed the arriving guests were subdued as they marched past the press corps and into the Kodak, barely stopping to pose for more than two or three of the paparazzi. This is a town that knows how to respect tragedy.

We'd heard that Bono had written a special song for the ceremony. And Halsey's good friend Miley Cyrus was rumored to be performing it and another song later on.

Drew whispered, "Did you hear they asked Nigel Lythgoe to produce?"

I looked at her, surprised. "The funeral?"

See what happens? You go to Pasadena

for one lousy day, and you are instantly out of the loop.

"And Oprah's people are furious," Drew said. "She wanted to get an exclusive. Do an entire week on funerals."

I tsk-tsked. Still, I saw that Oprah's cameras were there amidst the throng. Gotta love Halsey's dad for selling the rights to each camera location.

We walked ahead as the stop-and-go line of mourners slowly moved forward. A little ahead of us, I saw the Jonas Brothers chatting with Little Richard.

My head began to spin—call it celebrity whiplash or the last remnants of my early-morning sedative cocktail. Only nine hours earlier (had it been only nine hours?) I'd been in a whole other world.

Back at Wonders in Pasadena, after our delicate agreement with Deiter, Dr. Bob had had to leave us almost immediately; he was due back home and had to dash. Dear Dr. Bob.

Malulu went to fetch my suitcases, and, on my way out of Wonders, I found a private moment to speak to Cherish, just as the clinic was waking up.

"I wanted to thank you, Cherish. You may

be a pain in the ass, but you're a good girl. You rode to the rescue."

She smiled and flicked back her thick, black hair.

"Like the cavalry," I added.

Cherish looked suddenly nauseous.

I smiled at her. "What a night, huh?"

"Life's a bitch," she said. "But I guess every once in a while a fish wiggles free from the hook. Take care you don't end up like one of us, Max."

"Look, Cherish. Deiter might be a little power-mad, true, but maybe that's what it takes to wrestle you hardheaded types to the floor. Just because you hate authority, my dear, doesn't mean rehab itself is a joke. Why don't you get smart? You've got a little boy to think about."

"Yeah, maybe so."

"You've still got time to straighten your-self out. Don't throw away your chance. Make the collage. Sing the freaking songs. Get better."

"Max, if you try to hug me, I'll kill you."

I laughed. As if.

I hoped she could hear me, though. A child is the one thing worth all the suffering. Take it from a mother.

Cherish went off with what I hoped was a more thoughtful expression than I'd yet seen on her strong-featured face, while Malulu came back with my luggage. As we walked out the front door of Wonders, I found my darling Killer waiting patiently in the back of the Hummer. What could be better? Finally finally free.

On the ride back to the Hotel Bel-Air, I pulled my thoughts together as the sedative wore off. It was my first chance to really examine my stash of clues since they'd been taken from me the day before. I began by scrolling through the entries on Halsey's Prada phone. On the day in question, I noticed Burke Norris had called. And so had Rojo Bernstein. She had taken both calls. But in the Missed Calls list, at least a dozen calls from her father's phone were unanswered. In addition, there was a 310 number that didn't have a name attached: 310-555-2520.

The area code was for L.A.'s Westside, and I had tried calling it right then on our ride back to the hotel, but a generic, male answering-machine voice was on the other end. I didn't leave a message.

As for Sent Texts, I noticed Halsey had

sent only one that day: to Drew. The heads-up that she would be coming to the Os-cars after all.

While Malulu drove westward across L.A., rattling cheerfully on about how much Killer had missed me, and as Killer himself curled into a ball of fluff and settled into my lap for a nap, I finally had a chance to re-view Unja's private red carpet footage. Would it reveal some great secret?

I fiddled with the buttons, cursing up a storm and, by cleverly hitting the tiny but-ton marked PLAYBACK, eventually figured out how to watch the tape.

First I rewound it to the spot where Halsey made her wobbly entrance. On the videocam's small screen, the tape played on, and Halsey's scantily clad body and slurred comments were pretty much ex-actly as I remembered.

I pressed STOP, and with a little more swearing, I managed to back up the tape so I could watch the show all the way through, from my first on-air guests, the amazingly handsome Aaron Eckhart and dear Michael Caine, who, in a certain light, resembles my own Sir Ian. It was, I had to admit, a wonderful interview, filled with their good spirits and high hopes over the huge number of nominations for *Dark Knight.*

The replay showed nothing new in regard to Halsey. Then, I watched Halsey's interview one more time. Unja's tape had caught it all, every second that was broadcast by Glam-TV and the sad minutes after that idiot Will Beckerman pulled the plug. There was Cindy dragging Halsey, the poor thing, forward. Her drunken stagger. Our descent to the red carpet. And her breathy final words.

When I had asked her point-blank why she had been drinking, she said, "I would never take a drink. Never. I swear." I was sure, now, that she had been telling me the truth. At the time, I figured she hadn't meant to slip, but someone must have tempted her. On the tape I watched her say, "Don't blame Burkie." It had seemed a clear indictment of Burke Norris, but was it? Now I wasn't so sure.

I watched the tape play on, then got the most damning jolt, just as I remembered it. Halsey said, "Tell Drew . . . I don't blame her."

Nothing added up. I sighed. Eventually, we pulled up to the Hotel Bel-Air. With

Malulu carting the bags and me tugging Killer gently by his leash, we finally returned home. Only when I got back to my Herb Garden Suite, after I'd changed out of my prowling clothes and into the tailored black Chanel suit, and stepped out of the croc sport shoes and into my Louboutin pumps, did things become clear.

Malulu asked, "Have you finished looking at Unja's video, Mrs. L?"

"It's all so sad," I said. "That poor kid."

"So if you don't mind, could I take a look?"

I stared at Malulu. This was the first time she had ever expressed curiosity. "You want to see Halsey's final minutes?"

"Oh, no. No, no, no. I was hoping I could see if I am on the video. You know, when we first got to the theater before your big show."

Until that very second, I hadn't thought to start the tape all the way back at the very beginning before we went on-air, so Malulu helped me plug the small camcorder into the Garden Suite's large, plasma-screen monitor, and this time I started Unja's videotape from the top.

He had begun taping when we first

arrived, about an hour before the Glam-TV special began airing. At the beginning, you could see a lot of the broadcasters setting up on their marks and hear snatches of conversation of the backup crew. Unja was zooming in and out, grabbing shots of Jillian Reynolds, a local on-camera host who was doing a rival broadcast, the Sullivan brothers from MTV, and anyone else he could find that he recognized.

Malulu said, "There is no shot of me, Mrs."

"Just wait a second, Malulu. I think—"

"Oh, Mrs. L!" Malulu gasped as she saw what had just happened on the large screen. Devon Jones, the entertainment reporter who might, so they say, be losing her gig over at *ET,* and her crew were setting up their equipment right next to us. When my back was turned, Devon stuck her tongue out at me. Oh, ho! She must have had no idea that Unja had her in his shot. I laughed it off. Rivals. But Malulu was not amused.

The phone rang, and I picked up the call myself. It was my dear friend and attorney, Sol Epstein, with the latest news

about Burke and his arrest. I listened in-
tently to his update, thankful that Burke
Norris seemed to be cooperating with the
federal authorities.

My brain buzzing, I let the videotape play
on as I walked across the living room to my
bedroom, where I kept my jewel case. For
the afternoon's funeral, I thought I'd perhaps wear one of the pieces my late husband had given me. I had collected some
fine Fabergé jewelry, and now I selected
a large, gold, antique, crescent-shaped
brooch, made circa 1890, about two and a
half inches in length and covered with sixty-
five old-mine diamonds. Well, sometimes
one has to show one's respect, and I
hoped Halsey, who had always loved spar-
kly things, would approve.

I was just walking back to the living
room, pinning the brooch to the lapel of my
jacket, praying it wouldn't leave holes in the
Chanel, when I heard a familiar voice coming from the videotaped recording. Looking
up, I saw that Unja had focused the camera
across the red carpet where, much farther
down the row, he'd spied Shia LaBeouf.
But the voice that was picked up so distinctly

on Unja's microphone belonged to Jimmy Hamilton, in the foreground.

I sat down, riveted to what I was hearing. Jimmy's image was slightly out of focus, and he was talking to someone off-camera. He said, "No. She won't answer. I swear she's so stubborn sometimes, I think she isn't fit to live."

Oh, my heavens. Was he talking about Halsey? Well, who else could it be?

Jimmy continued talking, unaware that all he said was being recorded by my hair-stylist, Unja, only a few feet away, star-struck by the sudden LaBeouf sighting farther down the walkway. Jimmy said, "I told her, if she wasn't gonna do it the way we all planned it, then she better just stay home. Know what I mean? Who was forc-ing her to come? And those tears she puts on, let me tell you—they are just water-works she turns on and turns off. So I made sure she wouldn't come here and embar-rass her mother and me."

In what way did he think Halsey would embarrass him? Had she been drinking at home, and he didn't want the press to see her?

A man's voice that I didn't recognize

came from off-camera: "So what did you do?"

Unja's camera, focused as it was on a distant Shia LaBeouf as he walked down the carpet, drifted away from Jimmy's image altogether, but I could still hear his voice loud and clear on the tape: "I took her gown, right? She was walking around the damned house in her bra and panties all afternoon. So I took the gown and threw it in the oven and turned it up to five hundred. This is after the stylist has already left, and there isn't another thing for her to wear in the whole place, right?"

"She must have been mad," said the second guy.

Jimmy's voice sounded petulant. "Hell, yeah. But now I just got word that she's gone and left the house anyway. In that limo. Damn her. She can't show up here, that's for damned sure, or I'm out a hundred and fifty grand."

I was mesmerized. Neither man was on-camera at the moment, and I silently prayed that Unja would unzoom on Shia and at least give me one quick view of the two men talking.

That's when the other guy answered,

"Let me fix this up for you, Jimmy. Don't you worry. I'll make sure your little girl doesn't ruin all your plans."

What, what, what? I couldn't believe it. I cried out, "Malulu, did you hear that? Did you hear that man? He is talking about Halsey. Oh, my stars."

Malulu just grunted, unsure what I was raving about, but looking sympathetic.

I was further frustrated when Unja finally adjusted the focus on the viewfinder and the camera shot centered back to me and my crew. Me! I was in despair. On the side where Jimmy Hamilton had been standing just minutes before, there was no one of note. Damn it.

"Dat's me!" chirped a suddenly happy Malulu. "Look. Dat's me and Killer. Do you think that color orange makes me look heavy, Mrs.?"

Had Halsey's dad actually been involved in her death? I tried to calm down. It was clear he stole her dress. That's why she arrived without a stitch of couture on her night of nights. He admitted it. Bragged about it. That man and his sinister deals. What was he so worried about, anyway? Why shouldn't his daughter come to the Oscars?

Was the mystery man I heard on Unja's videotape responsible for drugging her? I replayed that section of the tape over again before leaving for Halsey's funeral and listened carefully. If I heard that voice again, I'd know it.

A few hours later now, I was standing in front of the Kodak Theatre in line with Drew and the other invited funeral guests. I made small talk and waved at friends, but I was on alert for any man who might be that one guy. And I freely eavesdropped on every conversation I passed by, listening for that man's voice.

While I had my daughter to myself for a minute, I decided the time was right to tell her what I knew. "Drewie, we've got to talk about Burke."

She looked so beautiful and so vulnerable just then. She didn't give me her usual joking put-off; instead, she said, "Tell me, Mom. What did you find out when you were at Wonders? Is it . . . Did Burke have anything to do with Halsey's death? I don't want to believe it. I don't think it's possible. But then, sometimes at night, I think that maybe he did. Isn't that awful?"

We had heard early reports the day

before that Burke had been arrested for murder, but that turned out to be exaggerated. Burke had been arrested the day before, true, but only on charges of transporting controlled substances into the country illegally, charges that went back several years. It was a federal case, but my genius attorney, Sol, had somehow been able to persuade the feds to set bail. For now, the LAPD was saying that Halsey's death was an apparent accidental overdose. No one believed it was suicide, as no one could imagine she would commit suicide in such a way and at such a time, and her family was heavily lobbying the coroner to close the files. Since the LAPD had no witnesses or other evidence to show Halsey might have been forced to take the lethal dose, they had to cool their heels for now. But I was certain the police were quietly looking into Burke as a possible suspect in Halsey's death. After all, he knew her well and had a connection to drugs. Drew turned to me and said, "I can't listen to Burke's side anymore. I need you to tell me the truth."

I blinked. Could this be? This was the moment I'd built up to, the moment I'd been planning for, the moment where I would gently tell my daughter the brutally sad fact that her ex-fiancé was a murderer. Only here the moment was, and based on the facts, I couldn't.

But there was plenty I could say.

"You know all those times he took you to the resorts in Mexico? He wasn't just there for the margaritas and guacamole, sweetie. He was buying pharmaceutical drugs in bulk and then smuggling them across the border."

She blinked at me but didn't interrupt.

"And if that isn't bad enough, darling, he was using your car and bringing you with him. If the customs agents or border guards had ever searched your vehicle, you'd be rotting in a prison right now, and not that half day of photo ops they gave to Nicole."

"He was using me?" she asked, her eyes searching mine. "To smuggle drugs? Oh my God, Mom, is that really true?"

She hadn't known. I could tell by the sudden look of pain in her big brown eyes. My baby hadn't known about the drugs.

"I could kill him," she said quietly.

"Take a number and stand in line," I agreed.

"How could I have trusted him?"

"Because you're an idiot?" I smiled at the sun breaking through my daughter's two years of clouds.

She looked at me. "Oh, God. I hate this."

"Having your heart broken?" I asked, worried.

"When you're right."

Of course. I smiled. "But you and Burke are history. Over. Finished. He's out of your life."

"Right. Right." She smiled a little and squeezed my hand. And under her breath she said, "I'm over him."

I squeezed back and enjoyed an unprecedented moment of mother and daughter in total agreement. "Men are scum, darling."

Then, without warning, I heard a voice that I had never expected to hear right then and there. A deep bass with a darling accent. "Maxine, I say. Wait up."

Aha! It was my own favorite British invader. I turned to see Sir Ian, dressed in a perfectly understated charcoal Savile Row suit, making charming excuses as he edged past some of the crowd in line behind us and came to my side.

I looked him up and down. "You're . . . here." I knew he couldn't stay away. I show him one lousy fake weakness, and he dashes across countries to take care of me. How many times had I invited him to attend celebrity dinners or join me to visit friends? For that, he was too busy. But just have me do a guest spot on Howard Stern and say I felt like I needed a little rest, and Sir Ian is rushing to the rescue.

"You look quite good," he said, giving me the once-over. "Really, just splendid."

"As opposed to the way I normally look?" I really hate a fuss. But I was pleased.

Behind his back, Drew mouthed the words, *Men. Scum.*

Just then, I heard my name called again. We all turned, and this time Dr. Bob and his gorgeous wife, Sheree, made their apologies as they jostled their way ever so politely closer up the line.

Dr. Bob shook hands with Sir Ian, and Sheree gave Drew a hug as we passed the bandstand outside the Kodak and showed our tickets to the usher at the door. As we entered the foyer, Sheree craned her neck. Although it was hard to be sure exactly what Sheree was saying most of the time because her lips were so plumped, she may have said, "Boy, take a look at all the flowers!"

We looked. It was as if half the floats in the Rose Parade had taken a wrong turn on Colorado Boulevard and found themselves suddenly here.

"Is that a pirate?" asked Drew. There was an entire jungle raft, made up of geraniums, and a dozen rain-forest animals made of gerbera daisies and pampas grass.

Sheree, never the subtlest among us, took a peek at the card hanging from the massive depiction of Snow White and the Seven Dwarfs made from orchids, mustard seed, and moss. "'I will love you forever and ever, Rojo Bernstein.' Oh! Isn't he that cute guy with the karate studio?"

I said, "There's a story there, let me tell you." All my friends gathered round and heard about Rojo and rehab.

Dr. Bob said, "Rojo Bernstein. Point him out to me. I don't think I know what the man looks like." Perhaps a guy who gets kicked in the face for a living sounded like a potential customer.

I had no idea what he looked like, but

Drew did, and she searched the crowded foyer but couldn't see him.

As we turned to enter what we thought was going to be the theatre, we encountered a curtained-off section that had been constructed as a large viewing room. Set up on a small platform, awash in the glow of a spotlight, under a crystal dome like the one Snow White had been sealed in, was the body of Halsey Hamilton, laid out in eerie splendor.

It was a shock. Drew cried out. Ian put his hand on her shoulder. Sheree said she felt suddenly faint, and Dr. Bob grabbed her by the elbow and steered her away toward the seats in the auditorium beyond, mumbling that Sheree had that very morning undergone a tiny cosmetic "procedure" and was perhaps still feeling the effects of the anesthesia.

I was more disturbed than all of them combined. I gasped and looked more closely. It was true. They were going to bury that sweet girl in a $30 knockoff from T.J.Maxx!

25

Best Suspect

As I stood there, stunned, looking at Halsey, a woman's voice commented, "Pathetic, isn't it?"

Amid the steady stream of funeral guests entering the viewing area, Devon Jones met my eyes.

"Hello, Devon."

She smiled. "Everything you see here—the Kodak, the entertainment, security, even the minister doing the eulogy—donated. When Jimmy couldn't get any hot designer to give him a dress for free, he decided to spite the entire fashion world and bury her in that *shmatte*."

My eyes narrowed. It always pissed me off when someone started using Yiddish expressions around me, as if that made us kin. "Halsey was a beautiful girl, no matter what she's wearing."

Devon moved closer and whispered, "But doesn't it kill you to see her spending eternity in *that*?"

I hated to admit it, but it did.

"Say, Max, I know you were busy with that rehab stunt, but have you been avoiding me?"

I knew what she wanted and had absolutely no interest in doing a segment about Halsey for Devon's show. I said, "Me?"

She put a hand on her skinny hip. "Maybe your staff is incompetent. Did you ever get any of my messages?"

"This is hardly the place," I said, standing right in front of the glass-entombed body, for God's sake, "to do business."

A middle-aged couple passed by the glass casket, the woman holding a Kleenex up to her nose.

Devon shrugged and gave a little smile. "See you later, then." She walked out toward the foyer.

I stood there, taking my own moment with Halsey.

How had this happened? I silently asked her. *Who put you here, honey?* If it wasn't Burke Norris, and I was now sure it wasn't, who else could have taken such a promising life? I looked at her again. *How hard you worked to get your life back. And now the whole world thinks of you as a fallen drug addict. That's not fair. I'll see this through, Halsey. You deserve a little honor.*

People were entering the viewing room, then passing along into the Kodak auditorium, where the funeral service was to start in fifteen minutes. As I spent another silent moment with Halsey, a group approached, and one of the women, a girl in a lime green miniskirt who obviously came from the celebrate-life school of bereavement, asked, "Can you handle this, Rojo?"

The hell with rude. I couldn't help it— my eyes darted to the young man she was addressing. He was tall and lean and obviously well built and had more piercings than he had tattoos, and he had plenty of tattoos.

Another friend, a short, young guy in a tight black suit, murmured, "It's okay, Jess. Rojo is medicated, babe."

So this was Halsey's latest love, Rojo Bernstein.

Then Rojo said, "I'm in the darkest pit of despair. I'm numb from grief."

That voice. I actually spun around and stared at the man, dumbstruck. *That voice.* How could this be? This was the voice I'd heard on Unja's tape, the one talking to Jimmy Hamilton about fixing things so Halsey wouldn't arrive at the Oscars. The voice had belonged to Rojo Bernstein, Halsey's secret boyfriend? *How could that be?*

"Oh," said the girl named Jess, alert to my open staring. "Hi. You're Max Taylor, right?"

Rojo looked at me but didn't really see me—his eyes were like an ocean. I snapped him out of his fog. "Rojo, we haven't met," I said, taking a step toward him. "But you and I, mister, have got to talk."

"We do?" he said. "Right now?"

The people in his group started moving off, the other guy muttering, "It's Max Taylor, dude. Show some respect."

Who said the younger generation had lost their manners?

I took Rojo by the cuff and led him farther away from the casket, where we could talk in private. "Look, guy, I know we haven't met before, but I was close to Halsey and so were you."

"I loved her, man." As I listened to him, I was even surer that this was the voice I'd heard on Unja's tape.

"I know you did," I said, soothing him, then added, "Please don't call me *man*."

"Sorry."

"This is very important, Rojo. Do you know how Halsey died?"

Rojo, looking stoned himself, said, "Drugs? Like an overdose?"

"She was murdered. Someone wanted her out of the way. Do you know who that someone was?"

"What? That's not right, man. I don't know what you're saying."

"Rojo." I stared straight into his blue eyes. Maybe I'd have to talk in his language to get through to him. I gave him the rapper hand gesture, making an upside-down number three with the three fingers pointing down, and patting my right shoulder. "Keeping it real, bro. Feel me?"

"For real," he said in shock. "How would I know about any of that shit? I loved her, man. She and I had a connection."

I was getting nowhere. "Did her father approve of your relationship?" I asked, trying to make sense of what I'd heard on the tape and what he was telling me now. Ingrid, the staffer in rehab, said that Halsey and Rojo had fought about it. That she didn't want her dad to even know that they were a couple. I waited to see if he would tell me the truth.

"It was complicated," he said, twisting the fabric of his black cummerbund. Or wait? Had my eyes deceived me or was Rojo Bernstein wearing his karate belt as a fashion accessory? "We couldn't tell Jimmy yet. It was delicate, man . . ." I gave him a little tilt of the head on that last word, and he corrected it. ". . . Max. Her dad, Jimmy, was a business partner. He was investing some big coin in my studio."

"Movie studio?" I was surprised.

"No. My karate studio. Well, studios. Rojo Bernstein's Kick-Ass. The last two s's are like dollar signs. I designed the logo myself. We're franchising all over the map. It's a sweet deal. We'll have two hundred store-fronts open by 2012."

"So, let me get this straight: you were going into business with Halsey's father, and yet the biggest control freak in America didn't know about your affair with his daughter?"

"Yeah, right. It was fucked, Max."

"But what happened on the night of the Oscars? I heard you, Rojo. On a tape my hairdresser made. You and Jimmy were talking on the red carpet about keeping Halsey away."

"Oh, that." He shook his head. "That's just Jimmy. He has to run everything. He was ticked off because he'd made some deal and got paid a lot of money and Halsey wouldn't go along with it. Some big media deal. Anyway, I told him I'd take care of Halsey because then he'd leave it alone."

"So you never intended to stop her?" Could that be true? What had I heard, exactly? Just some guy telling the blowhard Jimmy Hamilton he would make sure Halsey didn't show up. Not really a threat.

Rojo took a deep breath, then let it out in a shaky stream under pressure, the sort of thing a guy does to maybe keep the tears from flowing. "Look, Max," he said, his voice tight. "I wouldn't have stopped Halsey from . . ." He looked again at the beautiful body in the casket. "I'd never stop her from doing anything she ever wanted. I was just in love with that little girl, okay?"

Rojo mumbled some sort of kung fu/DJ rap blessing over Halsey's body and moved off into the auditorium, and I had to rethink. If Jimmy thought that Rojo was "handling" Halsey, and Rojo had never intended to stop her, then who gave Halsey the overdose of pills that ended her life?

My moments of deep reflection were constantly interrupted by the ebb and flow of mourners shuffling into the chamber and then out again on their way to find a seat in the auditorium. Many of them were people I knew or had worked with in the past, and we gave discreet waves as they passed by. But now, I looked up and made eye contact with Will Beckerman, Glam-TV's most incompetent director. He was dressed, for once, in a nice suit and tie, and that wasn't the only thing different about Will on this day. His face was red and wet from tears. Tears?

"Hello, Will," I said. "I've been trying to reach you."

"Hi, Max," he said, wiping his face. "Yeah, you wanted to rip me a new one for cutting out on your last interview. I meant to call you back, but then I heard you were going to rehab . . ."

"I went; I'm home. So what the hell happened that night? We had gold, Will. And you threw it away."

"Max," he said, cringing. "Shhh. I mean, she's right here."

I looked around, then I realized Will was shushing me in front of Halsey. I suddenly put two and two and two together: the tears. The insane decision to stop recording Halsey as she collapsed. And now, the shushing. Had Will Beckerman been in love with Halsey Hamilton too?

"You and Halsey?"

"I wish," said Will, a fresh torrent of tears washing over his face. "I mean we went out. Twice. But she never . . . I mean we never . . . but I loved her. That much is true."

"Oh, Will." Why did these young men

fall in love with the least appropriate women they could possibly pick? "She was . . ."

Will nodded, wiping his face with a large hand. "Not in my league? Or in my universe? I know."

"I'm so sorry." So that was it. Will had, against every instinct he had honed at USC film school, in some insane twenty-first-century gesture of chivalry, decided to spare his lady love the public humiliation to which another fall from grace would expose her. In other words, he pulled the plug on the most important red carpet interview in history to spare Halsey Hamilton such a disgrace. I didn't know whether to hug him or slap him.

I shook my head. "You couldn't have given me two more minutes?"

"Sorry, Max. I cracked. I couldn't believe we even got her, you know? I'd been in negotiations with Jimmy Hamilton for a week to get that exclusive interview with Halsey at the Oscars."

"Wait." I put up a hand and had to take that bit of news in. "You knew in advance that she'd be there?"

He nodded. "Do you know how much

her dad was asking? A hundred and fifty grand. For like five minutes. And that was for the preshow, before we'd even know if she won the Oscar. Glam couldn't afford it. They passed."

I shook my head at all the wheeling and plotting. Jimmy Hamilton and his big plans.

A cell phone rumbling on vibrate interrupted our talk. Will apologized and pulled out an iPhone with Halsey's press photo as its preset image. Oh, Will. And then I saw the number on the display: 310-555-2520.

Will looked down. "That's okay. I can take this one later."

I grabbed his hand and stared at the number. "Will. Whose number is that?"

"Nobody big." He shrugged. "Devon Jones. She's been calling me to set up a meeting. She's pitching some specials for Glam. Guess the rumors are true. She won't be with *Entertainment Tonight* for much longer."

I turned and rushed away in the direction I'd seen her heading ten minutes earlier, out toward the foyer.

"Max," Will called to me, startled, "I think the funeral is just starting."

"Take notes," I yelled back. "Is Devon still

outside? Call her back. Tell her I need to talk to her."

The foyer of the Kodak Theatre was almost empty now, with a few late stragglers arriving as I pushed open the big glass door and walked past them to get outside. A handful of camera crews and network announcers were wrapping up live, remote funeral-day reports to America. Across the plaza, dressed in her hooker red, I saw Devon Jones standing with her crew, her blond hair almost white in the afternoon California sunlight.

"Hi, Max," she said as I approached her. "Too bad you waited so long to get back to me. That footage of Halsey and her collapse? That's yesterday's news by now. Not sure I could even get my show to pay fifty bucks for it now, no matter what she was saying to you when she went down. Now, had you made the deal right after the Oscars, when I called you several times? That would have been the time to strike, yes?" She smiled a dazzlingly insincere smile.

"I'm not interested in selling my videotape," I said, my voice quiet. "I've got a huge network deal for that."

If possible, she got even colder. "Well, this isn't the best timing for a social chat, either. We've got to move our setup to the cemetery." After the funeral and memorial concert at the theatre, a helicopter was set to move Halsey's body to the Hollywood Forever Cemetery, where Wolfgang Puck had kindly donated an amazing dinner to be served there alfresco among the headstones. The guests would be eating, in a way, with Rudolph Valentino and Estelle Getty. A lavish celebration would follow. Only those stations with really deep pockets could afford Jimmy Hamilton's fees to shoot it.

"Lucky girl," I said. "Your show is one of the very few to get inside with cameras. I hear *Extra* refused to pay Jimmy's mandatory bribe."

"I know," said Devon, showing all her superwhite teeth in a big Hollywood smile. "Our numbers will go through the roof with this coverage."

I looked at her. "And do you think maybe this ratings bonanza you are reaping off of Halsey's dead bones will let you hang on to your pathetic job for one more season, Devon?"

She looked at me, startled. "What did you say?"

"Hey, I have an idea. Just us girls. Just for fun."

"What?" She looked peeved.

"Where's your producer, Shirl?"

"She's already gone to the cemetery. Why?"

I turned to Devon's crew. "Hey, fellas, kick up the lights for Devon, could you?" I waved at the camera guy. "You still have a tape reel loaded? Can you shoot us now?"

The floodlights were switched on, and the cameraman, now standing behind the camera, called out the warning words, "In three . . . two . . . one . . . ," and the camera's signal light suddenly glowed red.

"What are you doing?" Devon squeaked. "I said I didn't need you anymore." Then realizing all of this was indeed being taped, she smiled her trademark smile and tried to sting me with the gibe "You're old news, Maxine Taylor."

Ignoring that, I smiled into her camera too. "I'd be happy to add any insights I have about the tragic death of Halsey, Devon. Perhaps the people at home would finally like to hear what Halsey really said just before she died."

Of course my spiel into the camera was just being recorded on videotape. None of the things we were saying were being broadcast live. This impromptu interview would just be added to all the other material they'd taped today to be rushed back to an editing bay, to be cut by her producer, Shirl, into their final show. But who in our business would turn down a free sound bite such as the one I was dangling on the line?

"Okay," said Devon. "Let's go, then." An assistant gave her a hand mike, and she smoothed down her red dress, finger-fluffed her blond hair, and turned on a most heartfelt smile, speaking directly into her camera. "We all know that Halsey Hamilton lost her battle with addiction and succumbed to a tragic accidental overdose on the night of the Oscars. And the last person to speak with Halsey got to see the wreck she had become right at the end. Let's ask Max Taylor: what did Halsey have to say in her final seconds on earth, when the last breath was about to leave her fragile body, when she might have preferred to be with her family or loved ones or anyone of significance to her, but was instead forced to spend those last heart-breaking moments alone with you?" Then Devon turned and smiled that phony smile and held the microphone out to me.

I looked into the camera. "It's an odd thing, Devon. When I saw how shaky Halsey appeared to be, I was shocked." I knew I could rattle on and say anything I liked. Later, in editing, they would cut away all the meat of context and insight and just use the shortest, sweetest bite that held the zinger. I would make sure my zinger met with her producer's approval.

I continued, "But it was no accident that Halsey was overdosing."

"What?" said Devon, her hand flying up to her mouth.

"Halsey was murdered. And I think you know very well who did it."

26

Best CliMax

Devon, her eyes frantic, turned to her cameraman and shouted, "Cut. Cut it, Phil. Stop taping."

I pointed at him and raised my voice. "Don't you dare, Phil. Keep rolling. You've never seen an exclusive interview like the one you're getting now." I'd lost one amazing story to a guy stopping tape, I'd be a fool if I would let—

The red light suddenly flicked off. Damn it. Why, why, why?

Devon tore off her clip mike. "Let's go."

I raised my voice. "You knew you weren't

good enough. You lined up the interview of a lifetime, but what skills did you have? Your chemistry with Halsey? Your great reporting talent? Your own emotional depth?" I laughed a throaty laugh. "Clearly not."

Devon spun back at me and spoke up so her assistant and Phil could hear. "I have no idea what this woman is talking about. Pack it all up. We're through."

"Not yet." I grabbed her arm, but she pulled away in a little fury of resistance.

"You're crazy, Max. Certifiable." Breaking free, she turned her back on me and started off across the now empty grandstands and nearly deserted plaza heading toward the back entrance of the Kodak.

Phil and the assistant began packing up, pretending not to notice the scene playing out. Their paycheck depended on their getting along with Devon. How many of her tantrums had they had to endure over time?

But I would be damned if I let her pull that crap on me. "What would make your scoop even better?" I said, almost catching up with her. "Wouldn't you be a lucky girl if Halsey had a little relapse right on-camera during your interview? Is that what you thought?" I reached out and caught her wrist and, this time, held it tight.

"Max, please." Her voice had become suddenly low and reasonable. "Let go."

Right there, at the very spot where the Oscar telecast had been broadcast a few days earlier, I was struck by the enormity of this crime. Not only had a young talented girl been murdered, but her reputation had been murdered as well. From now on, Halsey Hamilton would be the name of the girl who destroyed herself with drugs. I thought of all the people who knew Halsey, from the millions of girls who adored her to the cynical world of showbiz that had depended on her. Before a dozen lawyers and a fleet of public relations reps and a thousand reporters and tabloids spun every ounce of reality out of Halsey's story, I aimed to get the truth out of Devon. My nails dug deeper into her bare arm, making marks in her sprayed-on tan. Good.

She was trapped. If she pulled any harder, we'd be in a full-on brawl, just the sort of scene she wanted to avoid in front of the few remaining journalists wrapping up. She noticed my Hermès bag—so large,

I might just be able to knock her out with it if I had to—and stopped squirming. "What the hell do you want from me?" she said.

"You murdered Halsey."

"Look." Her eyes were darting, aware that one or two people were looking in our direction. "It's not what you think. I'll tell you everything. I will. But not here. Let's go inside." She indicated a door on the exterior of the theatre building a few feet away. I nodded, and, leading her by her arm, I walked her over to the door, where we awkwardly made it inside. We were backstage at the Kodak, the funeral service in progress, and a stagehand walking past seemed to recognize us at once. Max Taylor and Devon Jones. Why wouldn't we be backstage at Halsey's funeral?

"You ladies need any help?" he asked tentatively.

Devon gave her bright smile. "No, no. We're fine." She turned to me and whispered, "I've got a lot to tell you, Max. A lot. But let's do this in privacy, right?"

A backstage speaker allowed us to hear the in-progress service, which was taking place on the massive stage off to the right. Britney Spears was reading from scripture.

It would be hard to carry on a conversation so close to the stage, so I nodded and pushed her along toward the back of the darkened area off stage left and through a door that led into a long, wide hallway. It ran behind the stage for sixty feet. But my hand was getting tired. Any minute Devon might realize she was actually strong enough to pull free.

From the hallway speaker, we heard Britney begin to sing "Amazing Grace." I indicated a doorway near us and whispered, "In there." Still holding her by the forearm, I pushed her inside ahead of me.

Three sinks, a large mirror, three stalls, all with their doors half-open. The ladies' room was empty.

I kept my voice steady. "What did you do to her, Devon? Send her a bottle of something . . . Perrier? Diet Coke? You drugged it, didn't you? And sent it to her house or . . ." I remembered the trash we found in the Hummer. "It was the Voss water," I said, suddenly certain. "And you sent it to her in the limo."

"Stop. Okay," Devon said, shaking free of my grip and rubbing the welt on her forearm. "Jesus! Look what you did."

"Talk to me, Devon. Explain it to me so I understand. Otherwise, I'll run outside and make such a noise the entire funeral will hear me. You won't get far."

Devon's eyes looked past me over to the door and then back. "Don't do that. Come on. Calm down."

"You want calm? Then tell me what happened. You sent the drugged water to Halsey's limo. Did you put a cute little bow on it?"

"I always send gifts to my stars. They expect it. I sent her a gift package with some chocolate-covered strawberries and a wheel of Brie, and a big bottle of her favorite water. That was respectful, right? For a girl who just got out of rehab?"

I stared at her. Was she mocking the girl she had killed?

Devon smiled. "Oh, you are *so* superior. But come on. That girl was a train wreck, Max. She was already dead. If it hadn't happened at the Oscars, it would have been some other time soon."

"I see." I closed my eyes for a second, sickened at her staggering justification. "If she was going to die anyway, why not on your show?"

What had Devon put in that water bottle? It couldn't have been vodka—Halsey would have tasted it. But perhaps, if a capsule had been opened and the contents didn't have a bitter taste . . . maybe the muscle relaxants Halsey used to take in her wilder days? I looked at Devon. "Was it Soma? For heaven's sake, how many pills did you put in that bottle of water?"

"I wrenched my back after two miserable days, up on a rooftop, covering the birth of J. Lo's twins. But I had to keep working, didn't I? Back then, my doctor prescribed Soma. And lucky me, I had eighteen pills left." Devon turned from me and looked at herself in the huge wall mirror above the sinks. She smiled at her reflection and touched the side of her mouth, patting a tiny speck of lipstick. "*You* know what it's like, Max. The pressure to top your best. The chances we all take. You know. So don't go all holy on me. You'd have done what I did. Don't lie. You'd do it tomorrow if you thought you could hold on to your gig at Glam."

"You and I," I said firmly, "are two completely different people. One of us is human."

"Look, she's the one who broke our deal. Why didn't she talk to *me* on the red carpet?" She shrugged at herself in the mirror.

"Halsey was a nineteen-year-old kid," I said. "Who knows why? She had been working like a dog for the past nine years. Teenagers rebel." And growing up under the grip of a manager/parent who forgets the second part of the job description can't have been easy.

My heart felt sick. After Halsey's fight with Jimmy, she must have gotten into the limo to the Oscars, found the bottle of Voss, and, upset and alone, just drank it down. Hey, it was only bottled water. By the time she arrived on the red carpet, she was seriously ill. She never even knew what was happening to her.

Devon shook her hair, the blond tufts keeping their bounce as only good on-camera hair can, but then she frowned into the mirror and watched as the lines on each side of her mouth cracked her thickly applied makeup. She turned to me and snapped, "Give me your foundation."

She was concerned with her makeup? To keep her talking, I stuck a hand into my large, black, crocodile Birkin, rummaging around for the makeup bag. "So Halsey must have finished the entire bottle of water. And she died."

Devon held her hand out and took the tube of makeup I finally offered. "My bad luck wasn't that she died," she said, bitterness cracking her voice, "it was that she died on *your* show."

I met her eyes in the mirror. I was looking at a monster.

"Don't you see the irony here?" she confided, applying more makeup to her face as she spoke. "I paid a hundred and fifty thousand dollars to Halsey's dad out of my own pocket. You didn't know that part, did you? An investment. A way to guarantee I got a new contract."

I stared at her.

"Hell," she said. "You'd do the same thing. We're all hanging on to our jobs by our fingernails, right?"

In the mirror, her face was now flawless, her cracks patched. In her garish party dress, Devon looked like a pretty doll, a caricature, a cartoon.

Look, in life there are no free rides. Everything we gain has its price. In my

career, no one ever gave me a break because they thought I was cute, or maybe
they liked my legs. Please. Nobody liked
my legs, damn them. I worked for everything I got. I had my comedy clubs, my
specials, my fashion segments. If the
Glam-TV gig evaporated, I had a hundred
things I could do—write a play, do a talk
show, host a telethon. I had earned my
spot as a performer and writer. Not like
Devon. She really only had one thing—
young and perky. And that one thing was
fast slipping away.

"You'll go to prison, Devon. Or worse."

"You think you're so smart," Devon said,
still smiling. "You think you tricked me into
revealing all my secrets, don't you? *My big
confession*. But no one will believe you.
You are in much worse trouble than I am.
And you don't even know it."

"You're planning to kill me too? How?
Because I swear, I'm not drinking anything."

"Very funny, Max. Your trademark
humor. Well, ha fucking ha."

I edged closer to the door, ready to
make my move.

"I'm not going to kill you, you moron.

I've got something even worse in mind. I'm going to kill your career. Yes, even better. The lead story on *Entertainment Tonight:* Max Taylor and her stupid daughter, Drew, and their wicked plot to poison Halsey Hamilton."

"You're crazy."

"Well, ask yourself, Max—who stood to gain the most from Halsey's death? Who was it that got that last, fatal interview? It was you."

"Ridiculous."

"And your slutty daughter, Drew, and Halsey had a rivalry, a bitter rivalry. Even more motive."

What was she talking about? Halsey and Drew were friends. "You're sick."

"Am I? Well, maybe you don't know as much as you think you do. Once upon a time, Halsey was in love with Burke Norris. Back when she was seventeen. Did you know that?"

I didn't. Could that be true?

"Not common knowledge. After all, she was underage, and he was twenty-seven. Only their closest friends knew about them. A friend who needed money, I'm afraid, came to me with the story. I was just about to break it back then, exclusive, but then Halsey's dad, Jimmy, came to me and paid me even more money to bury it. Isn't that how we all make a little extra money?"

"Not me," I said, disgusted. So she was also a blackmailer. Perfect.

Devon said, "Back in the day, Burke was getting his little girlfriend, Halsey, high on all sorts of pills. A mature man and an underage girl with an image to protect for her next Disney release?"

"I don't believe you."

"No, you wouldn't." Devon shook her head at me. "But ask Burke. He sold me his life story." She smiled. "Exclusive, kiddo. The whole tawdry mess. Including how your daughter, Drew, came along while Burke was still with Halsey and swept him off his feet."

"Shut up. This has nothing to do with my . . . leave her out of it."

"When I break the news tonight that you and Drew murdered Halsey at the Academy Awards, imagine my numbers, Max! Through the roof! Burke and Drew had just broken off their engagement. Why? Because he was getting back together with

Halsey. He was seen visiting Halsey again in rehab. It all adds up. Drew despised Halsey and wanted her dead. And you were just desperate enough to help her poison Halsey. Quite a story. America will love it."

"But it's impossible."

Devon looked at me in amusement. "You didn't know? Well, why would a daughter tell her mother she had just stolen a man from one of her little girlfriends? It would make that daughter seem like a . . . what is the term I want? . . . a tramp? A despicable lowlife? A two-timing bitch?"

I had suspected there was more to Burke's past with Halsey. But I had the story switched. They had dated before he took up with Drew.

Devon loved it. "When Burke left Halsey, she went wild. Burke said it was messy. Suicide notes, even an attempt that got hushed up because she was a kid. Halsey never forgave Drew after that. She just partied harder. If that's possible. And you know the rest."

"We'll sue."

"And what about the fact that your daughter was running drugs across the border with her fiancé? Soma, wasn't it?

That's the tip I got from my friend in the DEA. Now the story really gets good. You used those drugs to kill Halsey and get the biggest story of your career. The way I'll spin it, even your boyfriend, Sir Galahad, will believe me. I'll destroy your reputation forever and send your daughter to prison."

I was stunned into silence. Would people really believe Devon's lies? I knew how scandal worked. If she went on the air with those allegations, even if she protected herself from litigation in a cloud of insinuations and hints, our good names would be smeared. How many would believe our version? It would be a long and ugly road.

"So," Devon said, shrugging her thin shoulders, "It will be your word against mine. Sure, I killed Halsey Hamilton. But you don't have one shred of evidence that links me to her murder. Who's going to believe you?"

I walked to the ladies' room door, opened my Birkin bag, and pulled out a palm-size object. Unja's small Sony camcorder sat in my hand. When I got the cosmetics Devon wanted, I had pushed the right button. Thank God. To my relief, it still had plenty of space on the tape and it had patiently recorded every word.

"I misjudged you," I told Devon. "I used to think that soon you'd be out of the public eye for good. But no such luck. This tape. Your trial. Your sentencing." I pushed open the restroom door. "Your walk to the electric chair."

I rushed into the darkened hallway that ran behind the Kodak Theatre stage, escaping Devon's madness. Around me backstage were several ten-foot-tall, golden Oscar statues, stored back here after the awards show but not yet loaded into trucks, apparently. They stood silent guard around me as the disembodied voice of Simon Cowell could be heard coming from in front of the cyclorama, the thin curtain that separated this backstage area from the stage.

"Ladies and gentlemen, I present Prince."

All along the taut, gauzy curtain, the lighting changed, each cluster of primary-colored lamps fading and brightening. Right beside me the orange backdrop changed to a pale purple. It was eerie to be standing just ten feet behind the band, unseen behind the cyc. Then, just as the musicians played their first, loud electric chord, I was flying forward, the cement floor rushing up at me.

In an instant, I had to choose: it was either me, my fabulous bag, or the precious camcorder that would take the brunt of my fall. I clutched the Sony and hit the floor hard. With Prince wailing his heart out, no one could hear the noise.

The sharp toe of Devon's knockoff Manolos struck my shoulder, and I had no choice but to put my hands up to protect my head and face. Pain shot through my arm and side as she kicked again and again. In an instant, the camcorder had shaken loose and was pried from my hands, but as Devon reached down, I tried to swing at her with my bag. Pissed, Devon couldn't resist giving me one more ferocious kick.

I blocked the brunt of it by putting my beloved Birkin in front of my chest, and as she drew back her foot, I grabbed her ankle, and she almost went down on top of me.

A full gospel choir must have entered the stage from the wings because we could hear a hundred breathtakingly beautiful voices swell on the chorus of "Purple Rain."

By the time I got to my feet, shaken and bruised, Devon had taken off toward a rear exit. I followed right after her, screaming her name, but against the amplified swell of the chorus nearby, it was as if I hadn't uttered a sound.

I got close just as Devon realized the door she was pulling on, not an exit after all but to a storeroom, was locked, and I almost caught up to her as she ran into an open elevator, one used for moving large stage pieces.

I looked right and left, hoping to spot a stagehand or assistant director, but no one worked back here during the performance. They were in the wings most likely, running the show.

My heart was racing. All I could think was she was getting away. And she was going to smear my name and Drew's. The best proof I had that Devon had poisoned Halsey was on that camcorder inside that elevator car. Damn it. The large metal doors on the backstage lift began to close.

What could I do? I kicked off my Louboutin shoes, set down my Birkin, and threw myself inside.

Devon, shocked at my sudden entrance, started to laugh. "You poor idiot," she said between laughs. She held the camcorder high and away from me by its strap.

The freight elevator began to slowly lurch upward, its chain-link sides padded with huge, beige blankets. The elevator's control panel displayed buttons for five levels. The stage was level three, and we were rising.

"What are you doing?" she screamed above the loud music. "You think I'm going to hand this over to you?"

"Be smart!" I yelled. Right. It would be the first time in her life.

She said something and made a bitter face, but I couldn't hear her. I looked at her thin frame, her toned arms. She might not weigh much, but she looked as if she worked out. Well, so did I. I only had to get the camcorder away from her and back down to safety. It was all on that tape.

The elevator passed the fourth level and kept climbing until it jogged to a stop, and we could go no higher. Here, about thirty feet above stage level, the rear cyclorama curtain was fixed to a pipe spanning the sixty-foot-wide stage. The large elevator doors opened onto a metal catwalk, a flimsy suspended walkway without sides. It was primarily meant for the lighting and stage crew when they set up a show, and I felt dizzy looking down to the purple-lit stage so far below. Only a narrow pipe railing ran the length of the catwalk, supported about every eight feet by thin, metal uprights. The entire thing could have been constructed by a kid with an old Erector set.

Devon backed out of the elevator. Holding out her hand, she dangled the camcorder over the edge of the railing high above the stage. "Want it?" I had to read her lips over the swelling notes from Prince's band.

Now, strictly speaking, I am not a wimp. Hospitals don't scare me; I can face surgery without batting an eye. I regularly drive on Los Angeles freeways. I even go into the ocean—the hell with sharks. But I do not care for extreme heights. At all. I looked down. The top of Prince's well-coiffed head was quite far away. From this extraordinary angle, I noticed the cut of his suit jacket. Custom-made.

But never mind. I took a tentative step out onto the catwalk, keeping my eyes on Devon's wrist, from which hung Unja's precious camcorder.

"I can see you like heights," she screamed at me, and in that split second my eyes, against my will, swept downward over the railing, and the sensation of phantom falling rose in my stomach. She lunged at me, swiping at me with her free hand. I screamed, falling back away from her and slamming into the pipe railing, but who could hear me? She grabbed me by my hair and yanked hard.

Hell. Not the hair. I need every damn strand. I fell to my knees on the metal flooring and felt them burn with pain.

She yelled, "Glad you're along for the ride, Max. You deserve this. You owe me."

Five hundred mourners were sitting in the auditorium below. It was maddening. No one could hear us. Too many decibels. No one could see us. The catwalk was masked, of course, by the proscenium arch of the grand theatre.

My eyes were transfixed on the video-cam dangling from Devon's wrist, and I tried to gauge how hard I could hit her without also causing that camera to fall.

She looked at me as if I were the enemy—not just now, but always. "I did all the dirty work, but who got the story of the decade?"

Me. The career paranoia and desperation were now aimed at me.

Sitting high up on the catwalk, I slowly wrapped my arm around the support pipe. From there, it was easy to see my advantage. I was balanced and stable, while Devon was tottering on one broken heel. I could almost reach the dangling camcorder, but the strap was wrapped around her wrist.

Devon looked over the railing. "The song is almost over, Max. Damn it. I love Prince." She focused back on me, sitting on the catwalk near her feet. "So let's get this finished." She unwrapped the strap and held the camcorder out toward the rail to which an array of Fresnel lights had been fixed, all pointing downward. A roar of applause came from below, the kind of subdued and respectful applause that a memorial service would warrant, but it went on for a long time. Just as it died down, and just before she could completely untangle the camcorder strap from her wrist so she could let the evidence against her drop, there was finally silence.

And in that sudden silence, we both heard a most ferocious yip.

Devon's head snapped back toward the elevator shaft, and in the opening door, there stood Killer. All Yorkie rage. Alongside him was an agitated Malulu Vai.

In that instant, I pulled my knees up to my chest and kicked them out as hard as I could, hitting Devon's shins and knees. The push had made her swing her arms inward. A lucky swing. When the camcorder flew from her hand, it fell onto the metal walkway between us. Killer was there before any of us, standing over the camera and baring quite a few sharp and pointy teeth.

Devon screamed in frustration. I unwrapped my arms from the metal pipe and reached for the camera. But Devon was furious, and just as I had the camcorder in my hands, she realized that I was no longer secured to the post and lunged for me.

In less than a flash, I clutched the camera for dear life and rolled onto my side to avoid the attack.

And just as the first note of the next piece was struck, Devon Jones in her bright red dress sailed right past us on the catwalk. She plunged over the railing, soaring ten feet out in front of the cyclorama, and down thirty feet onto the floor of the stage below.

She must have been so startled, she forgot to scream, but her perfectly made-up lips flew open, and I could see her wide eyes staring up at me all the way down until the moment her body landed right in front of the drum rig, center stage.

Whether the guests in the auditorium had half-expected Prince would present quite a show, I can't say. But aside from a few aahs and oohs, no immediate concern was expressed at the sight of the red-dressed body slamming to the stage floor.

Until, that is, Prince's brilliant rock drummer missed a beat.

A woman falling to her death right in front of your eyes will do that to you.

27

Best Heart-to-Heart

I arrived at the cemetery, late, to the roar of wild applause.

No, not for me.

Halsey's friend and favorite teen-rock superstar, Miley Cyrus, was just finishing her Hannah Montana hit song "The Best of Both Worlds." How ironically appropriate, I thought. She and her backup dancers were performing on a temporary stage beside a field of headstones. Not your grandmother's burial.

Only two hours earlier, the coroner's truck had left the Kodak with Devon's body. And just one hour earlier, her flailing body had slammed into the stage, landing in a position so twisted it defied nature. No matter what one felt about Devon, the sight was profoundly disturbing. Dr. Bob later told me that from the way she was splayed out, he'd guess fractured back, fractured neck, fractured arms and legs. From the dark blood pooled under Devon's sunny blond hair, we all suspected she'd fractured her skull as well. The story spread, which I hoped was true, that Devon's death had been instantaneous. I could still see her image in my mind's eye: that cartoon face, as it flew past me, suddenly a blank slate of panic.

The auditorium had quickly been cleared of attendees, their reactions ranging from horrified to numb and uncomprehending. Devon's terrible plunge cut the planned three-hour memorial extravaganza for Halsey down quite a bit, and that caused a standoff between Jimmy Hamilton and the EMTs. But at some point the big promoter had to throw his hands up and let the LAPD take over.

The guests were asked to wait outside, with nothing to do but mill around while

Devon's body was cleared and the forensics team investigated. In a town that thrives on gossip, someone soon started the rumor that Devon Jones had been Halsey's secret lover and had leapt to her death to "be with" Halsey again. Someone else figured that Devon had been stalking Prince and had become despondent when an interview never materialized. If those tales were interesting, just wait until they heard the real story.

Of course, after Devon fell off the catwalk, I hurried down to the stage, and told the stage manager what had occurred. In what seemed like only a few minutes, Malulu, Killer, and I were standing in the wings, talking to two detectives from the LAPD, and I turned over Unja's digital video camera, which contained, I prayed, Devon's taped confession.

It was all there. Thank goodness the sound quality was decent. Devon's clearly recognizable voice admitted to killing Halsey and then tried to intimidate me with threats. The detectives listened to it a few times, and after hearing Malulu substantiate my account of what happened up on the catwalk, they agreed Devon's death would be classified accidental until further investigations could be conducted.

The cops released the crowd but asked Malulu and I to stick around and make an official statement. We saw everyone leave the theatre plaza and depart for the nearby Hollywood Forever Cemetery, where the pageantry would continue. As we sat in the back of a detective's unmarked Chrysler, writing out our accounts of the events in longhand on two legal pads, I explained again why Devon had poisoned a teen-aged megastar to hike up her ratings. The noise of a helicopter's rotors distracted us for a moment, and I looked up to see Halsey's body lifted in the air and flown away. In the end, the detectives had us sign our statements and told us we could leave, that they'd get in touch with us later.

At the cemetery, Malulu dropped me off and went off to find parking. I walked quickly past a few small temples and a mauso-leum, tugging straight the ripped sleeve of my black Chanel jacket. I stopped for a moment, removed the diamond brooch from the lapel, and used it to reattach the almost completely torn pocket. With my torn hem hanging slightly asymmetrically, I might just get by with making a radically chic deconstructionist statement.

In the pinkish pre-twilight glow, the cemetery's stone obelisk cast a long shadow, and, seeking out Drew and Sir Ian, I scanned the crowd of mourners milling around the buffet tables on the lawn. A hand touched my sleeve.

I turned and looked up into the angular, beard-shadowed face of Burke Norris, lately arrested on charges of illegal distribution of prescription drugs and, apparently, just now released on bail.

"Hi, Max," he said softly. "I wanted to stop and say thanks."

"Thanks?"

"You know," he said, meeting my eyes with his cloudy, hazel gaze. "For taking up my case. For hiring me your lawyer, who is the bomb. And . . . well . . . for believing in me, I guess. You believed in me when you had every reason not to."

"Oh." I couldn't say *you're welcome,* could I? Especially since none of what he thought was true. I had suspected him of murder. I really had. And why? Doesn't everyone deserve our presumption of innocence? Oh, those founding fathers. They got it right, damn them. Just because a man could break your daughter's heart doesn't mean he's bad. Just bad for *her*.

He reached for my hand, as if he were going to shake it, then held on to it gently and looked down at me. "Maybe we never got along as well as we could have. Maybe you wished Drew was dating someone else. But I always thought Drew was the luckiest person I knew. I was kinda envious."

In that moment, I almost liked him.

He continued, "Guess I wished I had a grandmother like you."

All my hate returned.

He said, "I might not have made such a mess of my life if I'd had someone who was watching out for me."

It killed me, but I felt a little weak in the knees. He was so good-looking, and so sincere, and so . . .

"Max, I'll do better. I have a lot to make up for, but, anyway . . . don't worry about Drew. She never knew anything about that business in Mexico. Nothing. I've worked out a deal with the DA, and her name will never be mentioned."

Drew in the clear? My heart began to sing. And not one of those stupid rap tunes, something more like a Broadway show-stopper.

"Are you going to prison?"

"Naw. We've worked out a deal with the feds. I'm providing some information they want on how certain controlled substances can be brought over from Mexico. So it's all good."

For whom? My heart sank. I don't mean to be cruel, but where the hell was justice? They weren't going to lock him up? What about consequences and paying for mistakes? It was infuriating, "Burke, I want to tell you, and I mean this from my heart, you are a total shit."

He smiled. "Yeah. I hear that a lot."

"Okay," I said, figuring that justice being what it was, I couldn't hold my breath until this guy was behind bars. His kind wiggles free. Karma would catch this rat in another trap. "The diamonds. The ones you gave to Drew to pay for a lawyer. They came from Halsey, didn't they? From her Academy Award bra?"

He ducked his head again, in his boyish way. "Pretty much, yeah."

"And she gave them to you on the afternoon of the awards? I know you called her that day and went over to her house."

"See, here's the thing, Max. Halsey and I had been like a couple. Long story. Anyway, back when Halsey and I were together, she got kind of ticked off when we broke up."

I nodded. "You broke up with Halsey to date Drew, is that correct?"

"Right. Sort of blew Halsey away, which it shouldn't have. I mean, I had a history as a player, right? And she did too. But I guess she hadn't had anyone leave her that way, and it was rough at first. So anyway, she wanted to let me know she was, like, pissed, and she took my car and ran it into a tree. Basically totaled my Lamborghini. Yeah. So that was like a two-hundred-grand loss right there."

"Ouch."

"I know, right? Anyway, since Drew and I split up this last time, I've been cleaning up my act, right? Only, without my former cash stream, you know, it's been pretty tough. So, anyway, I had been back in touch with Halsey, and she was doing great in rehab." He paused, then his eyes went suddenly glassy, struck as we all can be at unexpected times, with the shock of loss. "You should have seen her, Max. She was so happy and centered."

I felt a momentary rush of tears too, but with effort kept them down. "I'm glad she was getting her life in order," I whispered. "Good for her."

"I know," said Burke, no tears shed, the moment passing. "And now that she was sober, she was totally sorry about killing my car. Anyway, I called her. You know, to see how she was doing. And she said come on over to the house, and she'd give me something to make up for the Lamborghini."

I patted at the corner of my eye. "The diamonds."

"Right. Like her dad kept all her money locked up in investments or whatever and was giving her a real hard time about paying me back. And this bra was a gift, right? So he didn't even realize they were real diamonds yet, she said. Turns out her stylist took the diamonds off the bra that afternoon, so Halsey could wear the bra under her gown, and Halsey just handed them over. Like we're even. Like it was one of the twelve steps she was working on, she said."

"I see. So they really are yours."

"No." He pulled a little velvet bag out of his jacket pocket. The diamonds. "Drew said she got them from the hotel safe this morning. She gave them back to me at Halsey's service. But I want you to keep them." He handed me the bag. "To pay you back for the lawyer's retainer fee and everything."

I felt the weight of so many small stones inside the bag. "Well, you're going to need money. Sol was able to negotiate you out of an international-drug-running rap. It'll cost you a hell of a lot more than that retainer. On the other hand . . ." I thought of the pain and suffering he'd caused us. "Perhaps I'll just keep them."

"Okay, Max. Like I said, thanks."

"And one more thing, what I heard, you were selling your story to Devon Jones."

"That? Nothing important. A week ago, maybe two. I was looking for ways to raise cash. Legitimate ways. So when *Entertainment Tonight* was doing a piece on the hottest clubs in town and beyond, I signed on for one. Why not? They gave me five thou. Nothing too drastic."

I knew how this worked. Devon had lucked into that little featurette, a filler piece, and the video interview it provided her with. With Burke's past connection to Halsey, that innocuous footage of Burke talking about clubs and vacations of the young, rich, and famous could be rejiggered and maybe spun into gold. It didn't matter what he had really said or what questions he had answered, a creative editor could make it sound as if he were responding to new questions about the death of Halsey.

"Did she ask about Drew?" I asked, checking my theory.

"I think so. Yeah. I mean, of course, she knew we had been engaged. She asked about all the friends in our group, really. Halsey too. Where we all liked to play, hang out, things like that."

"And Mexico?"

"Drew and me hanging out in Cabo, sure," he said, his face suddenly starting to cloud. "Why?"

After hearing gossip on the Hollywood circuit for years about Burke and Halsey and the trouble these kids had with booze and muscle relaxants, Devon must have done some decent guessing about where they got their recreational drugs. Mix in Halsey's overdose on Soma, a death that she herself had orchestrated, and there you have it, ladies and gentlemen, a little thing we laughingly call "the news."

"Devon Jones was a liar and much worse," I said. "Why would you tell anyone *on-camera* about your trips to Mexico? You have to think first, Burke."

He looked more upset. "I only talked about the discos and beaches."

"Look, there are a lot of things you're going to learn about dealing with Hollywood sharks. But let me give you a lesson right now. The only crazy bitch I ever want to hear you've sold a story to again . . . is me."

He crossed his heart over the polo-player logo on his jacket. "It's a deal."

He drifted away, and I kept my eye out for my own tight, little circle of friends. So far, no sight at all of Dr. Bob and Sheree, or of Sir Ian, or Drew. Perhaps they hadn't waited around for the dinner? Nah. They must be here.

I walked past the memorial wall that separated the cemetery from the Paramount Studios lot to the north, a long, blank wall upon which was projected scenes from all of Halsey's movies. Now, a close-up of Halsey, tantalizingly alive, her long, dark hair whipped back in the wind. Such beauty. I couldn't hear the sound, but I recognized her Oscar-nominated performance from *The Bones of War.*

"Mother? Is that you?"

I turned to see Drew. "Darling."

"What on earth happened to you?" She looked at me closely, upset.

"The suit was an old Chanel, anyway. The shoes are another story . . ."

"Not your clothes, Mother," Drew said, exasperated. "You."

"Me? Nothing. Nothing at all. I had a little business that came up and—"

But before I could drop the big bomb, Drew, quite remarkably, was the one to explode. "You! You are *always late.* Aren't you? I waited. But I knew what was happening."

I shook my head, stunned. "What are you talking about, honey? I was—"

But she never let me explain. Instead,

my girl, who never cries, began weeping. "You're so busy with your clothes and your appearance, you even let me go to the funeral. All alone. You came late."

And I suddenly realized Drew was not talking about this funeral. Nor was she crying entirely about Halsey. I was stricken. "Your father?"

"My father was a wonderful man," she said, her voice harsh and gravelly. "He deserved more from you. He . . ." Her sobs had taken her over.

"Oh my God, Drew," I said, shocked at her pain. "I *did* go to your father's funeral."

"Liar!" She kept crying. "I was there, Mother. There were only three of us. Just Auntie Julie and Uncle Richard and me. You came late. You didn't even stand with us."

"Shhh," I said, pulling her close to me. She didn't resist, so I held her tight. "Drew. Shhh. I was there just behind a tree. I was wearing my Cavalli camouflage dress." It had been ten years, but it was like yesterday. "You know how much publicity follows me everywhere. It's a fact of life, of course."

Even ten years ago, when the paparazzi

weren't half as bad, and when most stars received less attention than someone like Halsey Hamilton, the story of my ex-husband's death had rocked the tabloids. We had divorced two years earlier, but his suicide was big, ugly news, and I was followed wherever I went. "Honey, Uncle Richard didn't want me there. He begged me not to show up. They were afraid that the press would make your father's funeral a circus. So I snuck in. I was the green bush next to that massive oak."

"What?" asked Drew, looking up at me. "I never heard that."

"You were young, sweetie. You'd just lost your wonderful father. Who wanted to burden you with all the stress? Uncle Richard wanted me to stay away. It was his brother who died. He had a right to ask it. Richard wanted me nowhere near that service. And neither did Aunt Julie. So I hid. Of course I was there."

"But I stood there, all alone," Drew said, her tears still falling.

"I made a deal with the rabbi," I said, smoothing her hair as I talked. "He let me come to the mortuary very early, before anyone in the press arrived outside. I came and I sat with your father that day. And we talked, honey."

"Oh, Mom."

"And I told him I was sorry, sweetie. Not that he wasn't totally responsible for our divorce. But I wanted him to know I wished we had made it work out. For you." I opened my bag, pulled out a tissue, and handed it to Drew. "I'm sorry, Drew. For everything I couldn't make right."

As she patted under her eyes to save her makeup, I thought I saw the beginning of a smile. "But you are such a control freak, Mom, that you do. You make it right all the time."

I think there was a compliment in there, somewhere, and I hugged her again.

Drew said, "I'm glad I'm standing here crying, I really am. Believe me, I have plenty to cry about. I had a lot of things I never got to say to Halsey, Mom. It's a lesson. We have to say we're sorry when we have the chance."

I looked up. "Drew, I never told you the thing Halsey said to me, when she was so sick and . . . dying. Remember I was upset, and she had been rambling?"

Drew looked at me. "Sure. What did she say?"

"She said I should tell you she didn't blame you. I thought she was confused, honey. Why should Halsey blame you? But now, I just realized . . ."

"Burke," Drew said. Then she smiled at me, wiping more tears as they fell. "She finally forgave me for Burke." Then she turned her head. "Glam-TV, approaching on your left."

I turned and watched Nicholas Milo, the movie-star handsome young president of Glam, approach us.

"Max and Drew," he said, "I'm glad I found you together."

"Hi, Nick," Drew said.

He gave us each a kiss on the cheek. "You okay, Max?" he asked, noticing my non-outfit.

"Deconstruction, Nick. It's what they'll all be wearing to funerals for years to come."

He nodded, perhaps making mental notes to tell his girlfriend to rip a seam. "Look, you were terrific this year. Just terrific. Our overnights were amazing, and we owe it to you two."

A job well done. We both beamed.

"This isn't the time or place to start a big negotiation, but I wanted to give you a heads-up. I've been in contact with Steve. We want you two to do the Emmys this fall. Think about it."

Think? I was dizzy with joy. "If we're available," I said with a friendly twinkle.

Nick left us, and we hugged. Drew said, "The Emmys! We booked the Emmys."

"If we don't get a better offer from a network." When the full story emerged about Halsey and Devon, who knew?

"Look out," Drew warned, and I pulled back to see the gang had arrived. Malulu had hooked up with Sir Ian and Dr. Bob and Sheree. In their gaggle were also the missing Unja, along with my makeup girl, Allie, and Cindy Chow.

To Malulu, I asked, concerned, "Where's Killer?" Several signs at the cemetery warned NO PETS ALLOWED.

She put a thick finger in front of her lips and looked nervous. Malulu hated to break a rule, any rule. And she had clearly stuffed dear Killer into the new Fendi tote she was carrying.

Unja said, "Sorry, Max. I was a very bad

boy." He giggled. "But I had the time of my life. Hollywood. I love it here." He snapped his fingers and made a sweeping circle gesture with his arm that, unfortunately, encompassed a field of headstones.

"It's okay," I said. While my starstruck hairdresser's camcorder hadn't recorded any incriminating evidence in Halsey's murder, it sure came in handy when Devon was bragging about it.

"All forgiven?" Cindy Chow asked hopefully. "We still your number one team?"

Drew said, "Tell them, Mother."

I asked, "What are you all doing in September?"

"The Emmys?" squealed Allie.

"The Emmys?" echoed Unja, his eyes aglow.

"Me too?" asked Cindy, her voice low and serious.

"All of you, yes," I said.

Just then, the wind picked up, and Dr. Bob's wife, Sheree, had two blond hair extensions blow off her perfectly tumbled mane and flap away. She barely noticed and said, "You all have so much fun."

Ian put his protective arm over my shoulders and drew me away from the group.

"My dear, we have hardly had two minutes to speak. It's all well and good for you to run around for days on end, but I'm sure we could both do with a bit of time to settle down, actually, and get a grip. Yes?"

"It's been a hell of a day."

"Agreed. And I'm quite sure," he continued, blue eyes twinkling, "that properly motivated, I could think of *something* to make you happy, certainly."

I did have something in mind, but not what he was thinking of. I pulled the little velvet bag out of my tote. It can be such a comfort to have a diamond trader about.

He took the bag, curious, and poured the diamonds out into his palm. "Little beauties?"

Our friends oohed and aahed. I think Sheree even managed to blink.

Sir Ian said, "Shall we sell the little beauties or get them set?"

Drew and I said in unison, "Set them."

"Very well," said Ian, professionally putting them back into the pouch and placing the pouch in an inner jacket pocket. "And that reminds me, Max. I have a little something I brought for you." He pulled a small black velvet case from his outer pocket. "You have been through quite a lot these last few days. The death of that young girl. The . . . substance issues. Whatnot. And, well, watching you deal with it all, so brave . . . facing your demons and all that . . . Well, I guess it reminded me of just what sort of woman you are, my dear."

"Why, Ian!" I hardly knew what to say. The group looked on as I opened the case.

A perfect emerald, which is to say an enormous one, was held in a platinum mount. Just the sort of extravagant ring one might wear with a new outfit. I felt a bout of shopping coming on. "It's magnificent," I said.

He said, "Nothing too showy. Just a token of support as you step upon the difficult road to recovery, that's all."

Throughout history, women have received baubles based upon much greater misunderstandings. Naturally, I was too polite to correct this particular misunderstanding in public. I don't know what got into me—the adrenaline that had kicked in a few days ago when Halsey collapsed and that had kicked into higher gear when Devon attacked me was still pumping. I kissed Ian right there in front of the gravestones, the hell with his British sense of reserve.

"How sweet that you came to help me," I said.

He smiled. "Now, now. Let's not get carried away."

Just then, a waitress walked by holding a tray filled with champagne flutes. I reached for one and murmured, "Thank God. I need this."

At which Ian raised an eyebrow and gently removed it from my hand just as it was raised to my parched lips. "My dear, so soon after leaving rehab? I think not."

At that moment Killer popped his head out of Malulu's tote bag and started to howl.

I knew exactly how he felt.

ACKNOWLEDGMENTS

From Joan Rivers

In Hollywood, the only thing larger than a red carpet arrival is Queen Latifah's thong . . . and I, of all people, should know, since I've been covering the extravagant, bigger-than-life affairs for more years than I can even remember. Let's just say that when I first started interviewing Tinseltown's elite on the red carpet, Michael Jackson liked girls! Paris Hilton was a hotel in France. Lindsay Lohan wore panties! Oh, where have all the years gone, besides to Tommy Lee Jones's face?

But seriously, what a great job it is to be interviewing the stars as they arrive at award shows, highlighting the jewels and the fashions, pointing out the celebrity dieters who went too far—and those who didn't, frankly, go far enough. People have said that my daughter, Melissa, and I have turned walking into a building into an internationally televised event.

But what happens backstage? You think the night of the Academy Awards is all congratulations and swag bags, all eyelifts and romance, all Botox and Jimmy Choos? Hah. Celebrities get tense. Tears are shed. Cell phones are tossed. Even I, a woman of notoriously sweet temper, have felt the pressure as I smiled at yet another glittering fashion train wreck.

Two hours with a mike in my hand takes its toll. At times, I won't lie, I honestly felt like killing several impossibly thin cue-card girls and the gal who invented Spanx—that sadist. But if working the red carpet could provoke even *me* to contemplate murder, imagine how Björk must have felt wearing that *shmatte* with the swan around her neck. If the girl had come to her senses and pecked her designer to death in front of 50 million people with that wretched beak, would anyone have had the heart to convict her? In Hollywood? Don't make me laugh.

But that certainly doesn't make it right. When comedy turns to tragedy, we all must care. An unnatural death cries out for closure: the killer must be caught. It's the essence of every great mystery novel and, even in Hollywood, a life and death matter. (Sort of.)

So what would happen if . . . into this awards-frenzied cesspool of glamour and anxiety we dropped a little murder? Say there was a sexy, crazy, outrageous death at Tinseltown's biggest event. And say that no one—certainly not the police—could figure out whodunit. To whom would our poor, frazzled world turn for justice? That's right. To me—Joan Rivers. Or in this case, my slightly younger, slightly blonder, extremely fictional literary counterpart, Maxine (Max) Taylor.

Max and her also extremely fictional daughter, Drew, can investigate and solve a celebrity murder at a red carpet event faster than you can say *after-party*.

Leave it to me—the Red Carpet Murder

Mysteries are a fictional spin on my life, and while they are truly works of fiction, they are based on my own experiences and observations. The world depicted in these books could not be any more authentic, raw, and filled with peril—and that's just the stuff of my online experiments with JDate.com.

Even though the idea to write these mysteries was right under my nose, it took acclaimed film producer and mastermind book packager, Larry Thompson, to bring it to my attention. Before he even finished pitching me the idea of the Red Carpet Murder Mysteries, I said, "Oh, yeah. I'm in. There are so many people in show biz that I would love to kill." I am so grateful to Larry not only for his ideas and creative talents but also for his passion and belief in me. He's drop-dead smart and a real keeper.

After Larry lit the match, he and his most efficient head of development, Robert G. Endara II, discovered the mystery-writing talents of my cowriter, bestselling novelist, and new friend, Jerrilyn Farmer. Her Madeline Bean mystery series has been at number one on the *L.A. Times* bestseller list multiple times, won a host of awards including two Lefties, given to the Funniest Mystery Novel of the Year, and spent weeks on Amazon's Hot 100 list. Jerrilyn is also a TV writer who has written comedy for Dana Carvey and Jon Lovitz and now teaches mystery writing at UCLA Extension Writers' Program. With the good taste and encouragement of Jerrilyn's son, Nick, and the help of her ace literary agent, Evan Marshall, our partnership clicked. The two of us are like the mystery/comedy dream team—I like to kill audiences and she likes to kill fictional characters that remind her oh so much of the people who bug her in real life. We've laughed together. We've walked down Madison Avenue together. We've hung out in L.A. together. We've puzzled over what makes people tick together. Thank you so much, Jerrilyn.

Next, the literary agency Dupree-Miller & Associates joined our team. They deserve a big kiss. Jan Miller, a star maker and superstar herself, with her ever-vigilant and enthusiastic paisan, Nena Madonia, went immediately to Simon & Schuster and threatened, "We have an offer you can't refuse."

And then it was real.

With much enthusiasm, I want to thank everyone at Pocket Books and Simon & Schuster who rolled out the red carpet for me. First, my love, love, love goes to my glorious and talented editor, Mitchell Ivers, who listened to Larry and me at lunch, got it, laughed, and has escorted us every step of the way down the publishing red carpet. Also at Pocket Books and Simon & Schuster, big hugs and no small thanks to Deputy Publisher Anthony Ziccardi, and Publisher Louise Burke, who at that love-fest lunch also laughed and said yes. I think they all ordered the salmon.

I hasten to say thanks to my constant traveling companion, personal manager, and cheerleader, Billy Sammeth; my theatrical agent, Joel Dean; my entertainment lawyer, Kenneth Browning; my business manager, Michael Karlin; my indefatigable personal assistant, Jocelyn Pickett; and my longtime publicist, Judy Katz. With that payroll, you know why I work my ass off.

On a serious note, I would like to thank the Academy (I've always wanted to say that), especially, my pussycats, Gil Cates, the quintessential producer of the Academy

Awards telecasts, and Sid Ganis, who is president of the Academy of Motion Picture Arts and Sciences, for granting us permission to use the Academy's registered trademarks Academy Awards® and Oscars® in our title and first book of our series. I am so appreciative. They love me . . . they really love me.

I also want to thank every star I have ever interviewed on the red carpet. Whether you won that night or lost, you are all winners to me.

And lastly, a huge thank-you to my one and only, darling daughter, Melissa, and her adorable son, Cooper, for allowing me to embark on yet another creative effort that robs us of our precious time together. To Melissa, who calls me by the most beautiful name in the world, Mom, and to my grandson, Cooper, who refers to me after each of my beauty enhancements as Nana New Face, I want to say, "Thank you for everything, and I love you very much. You both really do 'complete me.'"

So, enjoy *Murder at the Academy Awards*® and the sequels that will be coming soon. And since I won't be asking you my proverbial red carpet question, "Who are you wearing?" but instead, "Whodunit?" feel free to wear anything you wish while helping Max solve these mysteries, knowing that I will not comment to the media on your appearance or sense of fashion. In fact, simply having you read while lounging comfortably in flannel pajamas adorned with delicious chocolate ice-cream stains will make me appreciate and love you even more.

From Jerrilyn Farmer

This book was a joy to work on, and with deep gratitude I wish to thank the following for their help and encouragement:

My friendship with Lee Goldberg has seen us through some excellent times, sitting side by side at so many book signings in our mystery-writing community, but I will always owe him a debt of gratitude for introducing me to Larry Thompson, one of the most brilliant and enthusiastic book packagers and film producers I've had the pleasure to work with. In turn, I must thank Larry for bringing me into this lovely partnership and introducing me to a woman I so admire for her talent, graciousness, and legendary wit—Joan Rivers.

Thanks most warmly go to Joan, the shining star with her daughter, Melissa, of this and every red carpet, whose friendship means so much, for sharing her incredible life and point of view, and so generously throwing herself fully into this project.

I'm also beholden to our fabulous editor, Mitchell Ivers, whose devilish wit rose to every occasion, and my dear literary agent, Evan Marshall, who again saw me happily through another wonderful endeavor. I owe much to others as well.

I must thank Michelle Dewey and the impressive writing students I work with from the UCLA Extension Writers' Program. Thanks to the wonderful Robert G. Endara II and the incredible Jocelyn Pickett for helping facilitate the complex logistics of a merry troupe who worked together on this book on several continents, most notably our wonderful Joan, who seemed never to be in the same city for two nights in a row.

My sweetest thanks go to my dear family, who have always cheered me on as I embark on each new journey. In particular, my talented son, Nick, who urged me to find time for this project, amid a sea of plans and school forms that had passed their deadlines. With the help of my darling husband, Chris, and my wonderfully capable oldest son, Sam, our world made room for a project I truly loved taking on.

Not everyone gets the chance to wear the fur coat of a superstar and walk a mile in her Manolos. Thanks to the brilliant Joan Rivers, I got that chance. It was like a Fantasy Camp for Fashionistas. Thank you, again, Joan for welcoming me into your world.